MW01199394

BEYOND ADDICTION

to Kim:

Finn's got your back!

Kit Rocha

kit rocha

Beyond Addiction

Edited by Sasha Knight

ISBN-13: 978-1500847289
ISBN-10: 1500847283

This book is dedicated to our readers.

Sector Four may not exist, but its camaraderie lives in all your hearts.

zan

FIGHTING FOR YOUR life wasn't so bad, on occasion. It woke you up, stirred your blood. Reminded you that you were still alive, goddammit.

Christ knew Zan felt it, clear down to his bones. The joy of victory, and the satisfaction that came with helping to defend his home. It warmed him more than Trix leaning into his side—and that was saying something.

She sighed, her breath puffing out white in the cold air. "Thanks for walking with me, Zan."

"Any time, darling." He slid his hands into his pockets and looked around. No one lingered on the street corners, not even to gossip about the fight that had rocked the market. "Not that many people are out tonight. I'd say Dallas made his point about who still runs things."

"Not like he had a choice."

Dallas never did, not when his sector and his people

were threatened. He had to act quickly, decisively, because power in the sectors was like a fat wallet in your pocket—eventually someone would try to snatch it, and then you had to beat the bastard down. “Hell, no. It’s been coming for a while. That’s the price, right? You can be easygoing most of the time, but when it’s time to teach a lesson, you better make it stick.”

She was silent for half a block, wrapped up in her thoughts. Finally, she tilted her pretty face up to his. “Do you think Fleming will let it go, or come after Dallas?”

Only one way to answer, and Zan didn’t hesitate. “Doesn’t matter. Dallas won’t let it go. It’s going to be war, one way or another. Only question is who hits first. And who hits hardest.”

She stiffened, and her voice was laced with resignation. “I left Sector Five behind for a reason. I guess I’m not excited to have it all back in my face, is all.”

“I know.” He draped an arm around her shoulders and pulled her more tightly to his side. “We won’t let those drugged-out bastards fuck with you. You’re an O’Kane now. Don’t forget it.”

“Thanks, Zan. That means a lot.”

She seemed so fragile in the dim light. Breakable, and it roused his protective instincts. “Any time, girl. Now where are we—?”

The sound of a vehicle screeching around the corner raised the hairs on the back of his neck, and Zan reached for his gun. He’d barely touched it when shots erupted, and fire blazed through him.

The pain drove out everything else for a paralyzing heartbeat—the street, Trix, even his own goddamn name. Then it exploded in a red haze that blanketed the world. He hit the wall, his fingers still folded tight around the butt of his pistol.

He tried to pull it free, to fire back, but he was frozen, not with cold but with the scorching pain. He could only slide down the wall to the cracked concrete. Trix’s screams roared in his ears, but he was helpless to do anything about it.

Move, dammit. Move. His traitorous body ignored him, and he lay in the pool of blood that seeped from his body. It steamed in the chilly night, just like Trix's breath had, and a perverse urge to laugh gripped him.

Fighting for your life. It sucked, after all.

Dimly, he heard male voices, a van door slamming shut. It peeled away, and Trix was gone. No witnesses, only Zan and his blood, growing cold on the ground. Only failure.

I'm sorry. The thought flitted through his mind but vanished in a split second, swallowed up by blackness.

1

LOGAN BECKETT WAS one sincerely unsettling motherfucker.

Finn recognized the irony of the sentiment. Next to Beckett's tailored suit, polished shoes, and clean-shaven jaw, his own three-day stubble and bloodshot eyes weren't exactly a character recommendation. The battered leather boots didn't help. Neither did the tattoos. Mac Fleming made a big deal about how his sector was *civilized*, and Finn had always figured the tattoos reminded him of Dallas O'Kane.

Reminding Fleming of Dallas O'Kane wasn't exactly the way to get ahead in Sector Five.

Beckett knew that. He knew how to fake civilized like it was going out of style. Perfect clothes, perfect grooming, perfect loyalty. Hell, he even had a perfect wife—Mac Fleming's eldest daughter, the ultimate accessory for an ambitious man eager to take on a leadership role in the family business.

What he didn't have was a shred of humanity in his cunning gaze. Finn wasn't in a position to throw stones there—he'd done shit that had given him horrifying dreams, and a few things so bad the dreams were better company than the memories.

But goddamn, at least he *had* nightmares.

"You heard me," Beckett said smoothly. "As of now, nothing recreational hits the streets without additives."

Fuck, Finn hated the additives. The people who wanted oblivion were already wasting their money and lives, and they were doing it willingly. Drugs didn't have to be a messy business anymore, because science had taken addiction out of the equation.

Beckett was putting it back in. With interest.

Though arguing with the bastard was pointless, Finn still tried. Not because he thought it would help, he just liked irritating him. "Doesn't that make shit more expensive?"

The man sighed. "In the short term. But once all of our customers are equally dedicated, price increases will be well tolerated."

Equally addicted, you mean. "And if someone doesn't want to get that dedicated? Are we not selling the regular stuff at all anymore?"

"Of course we are. If the price is right." Beckett shuffled some of the papers on his desk and stifled a yawn. "I don't want any of the small-time dealers handling it, though. Those bastards can't be trusted."

Maybe not by him. Finn crossed his arms over his chest, forcing Beckett to stare at the lines of ink winding up his left. "They'll do what I tell them to do."

Beckett sat slowly back in the chair and studied him. "At one time, I would have agreed."

Not an unreasonable doubt—at one time, Finn hadn't been slowly undermining the whole damn sector. "You saying I can't keep my boys in line?"

Beckett smiled. "Yes, that's exactly what I'm saying."

A chill slithered up Finn's spine. Christ, that smile was creepy. It was off, like the man knew how to move all the right muscles but didn't have anything to back it up. The only emotion lurking behind those cool blue eyes was anticipation.

Something was really fucking wrong. Beckett might hate Finn, might sneer down his nose and drop barbs into every conversation, but he'd never crossed the line into outright disrespect. *Someone* had to do the man's dirty work.

Finn tensed, fighting the gut instinct to go for his gun. Shooting his way out of Five was a suicide mission—and a last resort. So he played the game, twisting his features into a scowl. "If you have a problem with how I run shit, maybe you should lay it on out."

That chilling smile grew as Beckett leaned forward. "All right—" A quick chirp from the small tablet on his desk interrupted the words, and he glanced over at it with a sigh. "Mac wants you in his office."

"Guess you'll have to give me that job critique later." Finn rolled out of his chair, his hand still itching for his gun. The spot between his shoulder blades itched just as much when he turned his back on Beckett, even though he'd stopped caring about taking a bullet in the spine a long time ago.

He'd stopped caring about damn near everything a long time ago.

Mac's office was the last place Finn wanted to be. The man had been unlivable since Dallas O'Kane had thwarted his attempt to set up a puppet as the new leader of Sector Four. He'd spent an entire afternoon raging, swearing he'd call the sector leaders together and accuse Dallas of violating his territory.

Which, to be fair, he had. O'Kane and his men had blown up a warehouse on the edge of Sector Five. Under any other circumstances, that might have brought retaliation from the other leaders. But Mac had been financing bootleggers who'd been doing a little violating of their own when it came to O'Kane's territory.

No high ground there.

Finn had barely taken three steps out of Beckett's office when Ryder fell in beside him, a deeper-than-usual frown creasing his dark face. "We've got trouble."

Great. Just fucking *great.* "Does it have anything to do with why Beckett's looking so damn pleased with himself tonight?"

"If he's happy, it won't be for long." Ryder cursed under his breath, vicious and low. "That asshole O'Kane kicked out of Four is gonna get us all killed."

"Who, Dom?" More evidence of Mac's slipping grasp on reason. Dominic wasn't even a useful asset, just some stupid, bitter brute whose explanations for why Dallas O'Kane booted him got more ridiculous every day. No useful intel, no brains. All the bastard ever did was spew bile about his former boss while Mac hung on his every word. "What the hell did he do now?"

"Not what he did—what Mac did *for* him." Ryder shook his head, his shoulders tight. "The motherfucker kidnapped one of 'em. Don't know what she is to Dom, or why he wants her, but she's got the ink."

Finn stopped so fast his boots squeaked on the hardwood floor. "Wait, back the hell up. Mac did what?"

Ryder spun around, his expression grave. "He snatched an O'Kane right out of Sector Four, and we're all fucked. We're in it now, whether we want to be or not."

Jesus fucking Christ.

Finn stared at his closest friend—his *only* friend—hoping for one crazy second that it was all a twisted joke. But Ryder stared back, grim and angry, and Finn flashed back to the last time he'd come face-to-face with Dallas when someone had endangered one of his women.

He'd almost gotten his head blown off.

"So that's it," Finn said. "This is how we go down. Riding Fleming's hate right into our graves."

Ryder arched one eyebrow and tilted his head down the hall in the direction of Fleming's office. "Talk him down. Tell him we'll fix it before things go too far."

How were they supposed to do that, drop the girl at the edge of the sector and hope she didn't blab? That was assuming any bird with O'Kane ink wouldn't turn around and go for their balls.

No, Finn had been laying this groundwork for far too damn long. Chipping away at Mac's base of power, delivering frustration instead of victory. He'd known it would all blow up in his face eventually.

Hell, he'd counted on having a front row seat. He hadn't bothered with an exit strategy because he hadn't wanted one. He deserved the fall that was coming.

Ryder didn't.

Finn grabbed his friend's arm and hauled him into the nearest empty room, slamming the door behind them with a bite of temper. This was why making friends was stupid. Caring about people complicated shit.

Finn had never planned on liking Ryder. The other man was nothing like him. He was smart. Ambitious. He'd rocketed up the ranks of Mac's organization through wits and stubbornness, somehow always finding that line Finn wove back and forth across, the one that made a man decent, even if he was ruthless.

He held up both hands now. "Whatever you're about to say—"

"Shut up." Finn braced his hand against the door, as if he could hold it shut if Ryder really wanted to get through. Not that Finn wasn't tough, but Ryder had always been in a different league. A better league. Everything about him screamed polish, from his fitted leather jacket to his tattoos—high-quality black and gray etched into his brown skin, the kind of artwork Finn couldn't have afforded when he got his first ink.

Ryder had never belonged in a hellhole like Five, so Finn was going to get him out. "There's no fixing this. O'Kane will burn us to the ground, but you're new enough to make it out first. So you need to take that girl over to Four and buy your way into O'Kane's good graces."

"I can't."

"Yes, you can. I'll distract the guards, and you—"

"I can't leave," Ryder repeated flatly.

Final fucking words, and they were out of time. Mac would send someone to fetch him if he didn't arrive like a good guard dog, and he couldn't *make* Ryder save himself.

Finn's best intentions had never been worth much.

Exhaling roughly, he jerked open the door. "Fine. Do you know which woman he grabbed?" *Please don't let it be Lex.*

"I don't know—some redhead."

Fuck. Damn near four years, and it still felt like getting kicked in the gut. Thank God redheads were rare—he'd known just a handful, and only one who really mattered. Maybe he'd never be able to think of red hair without imagining her the last time he'd seen her, sprawled lazily across his bed, floating on the rush, her long red hair a tousled halo around her pale face.

He hadn't given her the drugs that killed her that night, but he'd given her enough over the years to have no illusions about his involvement. Her death was on his shoulders, her blood on his hands.

He could almost feel it as he approached Mac's office. He was shocked not to see his fingers dripping red when he reached out to rap on the heavy oak door and waited for permission to enter.

Instead, the door slammed open to reveal Dom's glowering face. "Don't get any bright ideas," he sneered. "That bitch is mine." He shoved past Finn and stomped down the hall.

Finn tilted his head, and Ryder headed after Dom with a short nod.

Bracing himself, Finn swung into Mac's office—and stopped cold.

Tracy.

It couldn't be. He blinked and let his gaze sweep over the woman, trying to discount that first disorienting impression. She was tied to a chair, the plastic ties digging into skin marked by O'Kane ink. She was disheveled, her clothing askew, ripped in places, her red hair wild. Killer curves, a pointed chin, a split, bloody lip that someone needed to die for giving her—

Glassy, blue-green eyes. *Familiar* eyes.

Tracy was alive.

She stared back at him—frozen, scarcely breathing—and Mac stepped into the silence with a quiet hum of approval. "She looks good, doesn't she?"

Finn barely heard him. Barely saw him.

Fucking hell, *Tracy was alive.*

She sat there like a statue or a ghost or a fucking hallucination until Mac brushed her cheek. When she flinched away, he grabbed her by the hair and jerked her head back.

Finn's fingers flexed, and he could already feel Mac's throat beneath them. He'd crush the fucking life out of his boss and consider it his best day ever. "Get your hand off her."

"I don't think so." Mac bent low, putting his face close to hers. "She stole from me."

That got her attention. She turned her head so fast she almost bumped into Mac. "I did not, you lying asshole. You gave me those drugs."

It made a sick sort of sense. The leader of Sector Five didn't mess with common girls. Only the best for him—young, pretty, and drugged out of their minds. Eager to do anything and everything to stay that way. It was a soft, blissful life, a *short* one, which meant Mac was always on the prowl for a replacement.

He would have taken Tracy just to prove he could. "You told me she overdosed."

"I honestly figured she had." Mac studied her. "But you sold it all and ran, didn't you, love? Over to Sector Four."

So casual. Curious, but only vaguely, as if he didn't care about the answer one way or another but was simply going through the motions. Finn knew better. Mac had staged this melodramatic reveal for him, and this was just the opening act.

Finn had to get them both out of there before Dom came back for the big finale. "Yeah, she ran straight into Dallas O'Kane's arms. Is this really how you want to start a sector war?"

"War was inevitable, and it's already begun," Mac said absently. He was focused on Tracy, staring at her like he was trying to decode an unfamiliar language. "We all thought you were dead. Finn, too. You walked away and never looked back—that's stone cold, darling. Color me impressed."

Her jaw clenched, her gaze clashing with Finn's before she looked away, and it didn't matter that four years had passed. He knew what she'd been thinking the day she'd walked out of Sector Five, out of his life. Once Mac set his sights on a girl, her opportunities narrowed to two—survive as long as she could as a high-class junkie whore, or die trying to get out.

Tracy had picked the path that wouldn't take Finn down with her.

He rolled his shoulders, letting himself really feel the familiar weight of his shoulder holster. His gun was right there in easy reach. Two big steps and he could have it shoved under Mac Fleming's jaw. He owed her that much.

Christ, he owed her everything.

"You cost Dom his O'Kane ink," Mac continued, his

voice taking on a wicked, sharp edge as he pulled her hair harder, pulled until a whimper escaped her. "Have you seen his scars? He's eager to show them to you. Every...single...one."

Finn didn't choose to move, but then he never made choices when it came to Tracy. Every damn time she brushed his life, he stumbled forward without control or reason.

He didn't stumble now, just took those two steps and dug the barrel of his gun under Mac's chin. "Let her go. Now."

Mac's eyes went wide before narrowing as he barked out a laugh. "You stupid bastard."

Finn ground the gun deeper into the man's flesh, pressing up until Mac had to stretch onto his toes. "I'm not telling you again. You can let her go back to Sector Four and fuck what Dom wants, or I'll blow off the top of your head right now."

Mac stared back at him, his eyes burning with outrage. "Do it. Neither one of you would make it out of here al—"

Finn squeezed the trigger. One shot, and it splattered Mac Fleming's fucking brains all over his office.

It was loud, reverberating through the room as Finn watched his boss fall to the floor. Putting another round in his head as insurance would have been smart—just to be sure he was well and truly beyond saving, even with regen tech—but Mac's last words had been truth.

If Finn wanted to get them out of Sector Five alive, he didn't have bullets to waste.

Her nightmare had taken a turn for the better.

Trix stared down at the blood on her clothes, frozen in an interminable moment of confusion and torn between a laugh and a scream.

Mac Fleming was gone. Better than gone—*dead*—and the laugh won. Only it didn't come out sounding like a laugh at all, more like a frightened, strangled whimper.

Warm hands cupped her face, and a broad, calloused thumb swept over her cheek. "I got you, girl. Stay with me."

Finn's words echoed in her ears, as surreal as the sensation of his hands on her face. "This isn't real."

"I know how you feel. Look at me, Tracy."

Her vision swam as she lifted her gaze. Finn had always been a rock, the only solid, reliable thing in her old life. Surely if this was a dream or drug-induced hallucination, he'd look the same—serious, intense, the barest hint of one of his rare smiles lifting the corner of his mouth.

Instead, he looked worn. Not just older but haggard, his beard scruffier than she remembered. His eyes were bloodshot and red, as if he hadn't slept in months, and her mother's voice drifted up somewhere behind her. *Ten miles of bad road.*

"Fuck," he whispered roughly. "Close your eyes and breathe."

He bent to tug at the plastic tie securing her hands. The room went dark for a moment, and Trix opened her mouth to remark on the darkness before she realized she'd only closed her eyes.

She licked her lips and winced at the pain—and the taste of blood. "They gave me something—"

The door opened and slammed shut. "Holy fuck," a new voice growled.

Trix snapped her eyes open. The man who had come in was dark—dark clothes, skin, eyes, hair. He locked the door behind him and stepped forward, but all of his attention was focused on Fleming's body.

Finn pulled a knife and cut her hands free. "Ryder, meet Tracy."

That stopped the man in his tracks. "Tracy?"

"Yeah." Finn rubbed Trix's wrists before rising, the knife still gripped in a steady hand. "Shit's about to get real ugly."

Ryder's jaw clenched, and he dropped to quickly check the dead man's pockets. He came up with a small pistol, which he pressed into Finn's hands. "Come on. Hurry."

Finn didn't ask if she could stand. Instead, he hooked an arm under her legs and one behind her back, lifting her with familiar ease. "I'm going to get you out, girl. One way or another, you're going home. You hear me?"

Ryder headed for the back of the room and the narrow, cleverly concealed hallway leading to the exit from Mac's office. Trix had stumbled down it before, and she closed her eyes now to block out the memory.

"I can't help you much," Ryder bit off, his words clipped and urgent. "But I have some resources in place."

Finn's body tensed. His arms tightened, crushing her body to his chest. "What kind of resources?"

"The kind that just might save your life."

They burst through the back door, and a wave of cold air cleared Trix's head a little. "The border," she mumbled, gripping Finn's vest. "If we can make it back to Four—"

"You won't," Ryder said flatly. "Not on the streets. Any minute now, the whole goddamn sector's gonna be swarming with Fleming's men."

"Beckett's men," Finn corrected with a rumble. "He'll need to make a good show of it."

"He gives zero fucks," Ryder agreed, heading down the shadowed alley toward a back street cluttered with delivery trucks. "But there's no time for him to gloat. Especially when he could have your fool head on a platter, too. What the fuck were you *thinking*, man?"

A grunt. "Doesn't matter now. All that matters is getting her back to O'Kane."

"Yeah, good luck with that." Ryder took a left down a narrow gap between two buildings.

The space wasn't wide enough to be considered an alley, and Finn let Trix slide to her feet before urging her into the darkness. She tripped over a loose brick and pitched forward, landing hard against Ryder's back.

He turned and stared down at her, backlit by the faint moonlight filtering down between the buildings. He looked like an angel—not the kind with harps and halos, but an angel of war, fierce and terrifying.

"Hopkins picked her up," he growled. "He uses hallucinogens."

"Christ, that explains it." Finn caught her chin and tilted her face toward the light. "Shit. *Shit.* She can't be stumbling around the sector in this condition."

"She won't be." Ryder shoved a tall crate aside, revealing a dented door behind it. The lock was new, electronic, and advanced. Out of place in a shitty, narrow alley behind Mac Fleming's office.

Trix blinked at him. "Who are you?"

Instead of answering, he opened the door and snatched up a small black duffel before waving them in. "I didn't pack enough supplies for two people," he said, thrusting the bag at Finn. "Three days, tops. There's a map of the tunnels in the side pocket."

Finn caught Ryder's arm, and the two of them exchanged a look Trix couldn't decipher, some sort of silent communication that ended with Finn biting off a curse and seizing the bag. "You're crazier than I am, you know that?"

"Hey, somebody's gotta be." Ryder shrugged. "How else is all this shit gonna stop?"

"Don't get dead," Finn ordered, swinging the heavy duffel up on one shoulder. His other arm slid around Trix's waist. "Tell them I ran south. Beckett'll believe it."

The only thing south of Sector Five was desert, wide and open under the sky—and Finn's tiny cabin, the one he'd fixed up with his own hands.

She'd been there only a couple of times, riding the whole way on the back of his bike, not quite sheltered from the wind by his solid shoulders. She could feel it now, whispering over her skin and roaring in her ears.

She might as well have been back there, watching idly as he stoked the fire, gentle light playing across his bare skin. Her lips moved, and she found herself asking him the same question she had then. "Do you ever think about ending it all?"

"Not tonight, doll." His arm tightened as light flared in front of her eyes. A flashlight, bright enough to illuminate a narrow tunnel leading down into the ground. "Come on, Tracy. Just put one foot in front of the other, and you'll be back with the O'Kanes before you know it."

"Trix." She braced one hand on the pitted wall. "I changed my name because of you." So no one would put two and two together, so Fleming would never come after her and use her to hurt Finn.

"Trix," he echoed, his voice rough around her name. "Whatever I call you, doesn't change facts. We've got to move. Can you walk, or do I need to carry you?"

"I'm fine." Her spinning head threatened to turn her into a liar. She shook away some of the haze and focused on taking even, careful steps into the darkness.

Whatever waited there couldn't be more terrifying than what was behind them.

2

RYDER'S MAP WAS meticulously labeled in his precise hand, and it outlined multiple routes out of Sector Five. The one to Four was straightforward enough, but there was one big damn problem.

It led straight under the factory Dallas O'Kane had blown up earlier in the week.

Finn stared at the rubble from the cave-in while Tracy—*Trix*, and wasn't that a guilt-punch in the gut?—slumped against the wall, trying not to show how hard she was coming down. It took effort not to swing her up into his arms over her protests, but doing anything over her protests didn't seem like a smart move right now.

Stomping down panic, Finn shoved the useless map back into its side pocket and turned to her. "We need to find a place to rest for a few hours. Get some food into both of us. Can you make it back to that four-way intersection? A few of those doors had old-fashioned locks."

She nodded, then winced and pressed the heel of her hand to her temple. "What the hell did they give me?"

Christ only knew. Hopkins had a new favorite rush every week, and most of them jacked you up so high you saw pink dragons and polka dots. "Probably nothing too heavy, if you're walking straight and still know your name. Need a hand?"

"No." She took a shaky step away, then turned back down the tunnel. "Supply hubs. Noah said there were storage rooms under Five. For the factories."

Finn froze. Adrenaline had faded enough for his brain to kick in, and connecting the dots stirred rage. Noah Lennox had popped back into Finn's life and work with the same abruptness as he'd left it, mouthing big claims about how he was ready to help Mac take Dallas O'Kane down.

Finn hadn't bought it. He wasn't sure Mac ever had, either. Noah wasn't a great liar or an eager criminal. But he had a weak spot—a girl who'd ended up with the O'Kanes—and Mac had never questioned Noah's claim that Dallas tried to blackmail him with the girl's safety. It was exactly what Mac had been planning to do, after all.

Mac should have known better. Dallas O'Kane didn't bully men into working for him. He seduced them with big dreams, soft living, and the fantasy of brotherhood. In return, he enjoyed the kind of loyalty most petty kings only dreamed about.

So it wasn't a shock that Noah had been playing both sides, sharing information about Five with the O'Kanes. Finn wasn't exactly the poster boy for sector loyalty, either. But that bastard had sat across from him as recently as four days ago, knowing Tracy was alive, knowing how Finn had always felt about her...

Nothing. Not a word. Not a fucking *hint*. "So you and Lennox are tight now?"

"He's trying his best," she muttered. "We all are, Finn. Don't blame him."

"Don't blame him for what, Tra—?" He bit off her name. Her new one felt like battery acid on his tongue. Tracy, turning tricks. Turning into Trix. Because of him. "Trix."

"For not telling you I was in Four." She shuddered. "It's not his fault. I wasn't ready to face you. I'm still not."

Another knife in the gut, but he didn't let it show. "Fair enough, doll. As soon as you're snuggled up in Sector Four again, I'll be out of your face."

She whirled on him. "That isn't what I want."

He almost asked what she *did* want, but his lips wouldn't move. They'd hit the part of the tunnels lit by emergency lights, a soft glow from strips high on either wall that softened the shadows and washed away the worst impact of the drugs and her fear.

She looked fierce. Healthy. Getting away from him had given her a chance to bloom, to become an independent woman instead of some fading junkie. She'd gained weight and curves, the kind men lost their minds and their good sense over. The kind men started *wars* over, on the off chance she'd cast those big, beautiful eyes your way and smile.

Hell, he'd just started a war for her, and she could barely look at him.

"Let's find one of those storage rooms, and we can figure it out. Okay?" He held out his arm.

Reluctantly, she took it. "I'm doing this all wrong."

He didn't know how the hell to comfort her, so he fell back on old habits. Lazy and sarcastic, because even when he'd cared, he hadn't known how to do it well. "If there's a right way to get kidnapped, sweet cheeks, that's news to me."

She sucked in a breath, sharp and rough. "Zan."

It took Finn a few seconds to connect the name with

a face. A bouncer at O'Kane's bar, one of his soldiers who had been a member for a long time without rising into Dallas's inner circle. Important to recognize on sight, but not a player. Not in Finn's world. "What about him?"

She went pale. "He was walking with me. They—they shot him—" The words broke off, and her hand clenched on Finn's arm.

He bit back another curse and swung his other arm around her. "I'm sorry, honey," he whispered, pressing his lips to the top of her head. "I should have put that bastard down months ago. Years ago."

Trix took another shaky breath and broke free of his embrace. "You're not the only one."

No, but he was the one who'd had a thousand opportunities. So many times he could have put his gun to the man's head and pulled the trigger, but he hadn't. Not when it could have done some good. Logan Beckett had undoubtedly already stepped into Mac's shoes, an even bigger monster with an even smaller conscience.

Too little, too late. That was his go-to move. And he still wanted to pull Trix back into his arms, wrap himself around her, breathe in her scent until it felt like his own. He wanted to run his bloodstained hands over all those perfect curves and watch her chest rise with each breath, because every fucking part of this moment was so surreal, he was probably dreaming.

Mac Fleming was dead. Tracy was alive.

I missed you. He had no right to say that to her, not when she kept pulling back. She was radiant, and he was the dirt and muck of her past, still clinging to her boots. "Is your life good in Four?"

She reached the intersection and stopped, spinning around to peer down each corridor before answering simply, "It's home. I have a family there."

Family was more than he'd ever given her. So he steeled his heart and his nerves and focused on the one thing that mattered—getting her back to the people she loved.

The people who deserved her.

They tried four corridors and backtracked twice before Finn found a promising door without a fancy card-swipe control panel. His picks were tucked inside his boot, so he let Trix hold the bag as he knelt and studied the lock. "Bet Noah Lennox has fun down in these tunnels with that big brain of his. Hacks his way past all the fancy security, huh?"

"He spends most of his time with Emma." She hesitated. "Cibulski's little sister. You remember him, right?"

Finn glanced up, but Trix didn't look like she was digging. Maybe that was a blessing, that she still had that much faith in him. Someone else might have asked, but there would have been a second question beneath the first. An accusation.

Did you kill him?

He hadn't. Cibulski had sealed his fate when he'd taken the drugs he was supposed to be dealing, but Finn hadn't pulled the trigger on him. He'd just cleaned up the mess—his own way. "I never meant for the kid to find him. Noah was supposed to be on his way there."

"Oh." Her hand grazed his shoulder, a light touch that ended too quickly. "You were trying to warn him."

He turned his attention back to the lock, but his movements were simply muscle memory and instinct. His focus was still trapped in the fleeting whisper of her touch on his shoulder and the deeper heat kindled by her lingering trust. "Mac was going after the sister next, trying to get Noah in line. None of us needed that. Mac's too greedy. He'd have gotten us firebombed inside a year."

The lock yielded under his hands, the click of the tumblers almost drowning out her soft noise of assent. "And now he's dead."

"Now he's dead," Finn agreed. "And his crazy-ass son-in-law is up there, getting real comfortable in Mac's chair. It's Beckett's best day ever."

"You can't stop them all, Finn."

He tucked away the tools and rose without looking at her. "Stopping him's not on my radar. Nothing is right now except for getting you home."

She laid her hand on his arm and, this time, left it there. "Thank you."

He hadn't brought his jacket, so she was touching him, brushing the tattoos just beneath his shirt sleeve. Her fingers were pale and delicate against the vivid ink, bringing back memories he'd locked away out of self-defense. It felt obscene to slide his own rough hand over hers, but he couldn't stop himself.

And God, her skin was soft. Smooth. His calloused fingertips scraped over the back of her hand as he traced up to the raw spots around her wrist. "Ryder probably has a med kit in this thing."

She stared up at him. "What?"

"For your wrists." He brushed his thumb over hers, and the catch in her breath wasn't his imagination. Neither were the sparks. They'd always been there, buried under their respective layers of drugs and hopelessness. Nice, but dull. Muted.

Not anymore. That tiny hitch sparked all over him, carving out a wanting he couldn't afford to indulge. He needed to get his hands off her. He needed to back off, so he wouldn't end up hiding a boner behind the fucking duffel bag while she shivered through withdrawal and worried about her friend.

He needed to do *anything* except hold her gaze and stroke her wrist again.

Trix sucked in another breath. "Finn—"

A thundering sound shook the ground above them, a strange galloping noise that made no sense until the distant buzz of shouting voices joined in.

"Shit." He wrenched open the door and scanned inside with a flashlight, taking note of boxes, a dusty floor, and not much else. Barely bigger than a closet, with just enough room for them to stretch out side by side.

It was all they had.

He hustled her inside with a hand at the small of her back and checked the outside tunnel to make sure there was no sign of their passage before swinging the door shut as quietly as possible and engaging the lock.

Trix huddled against the wall, still except for her trembling. "Will they find us?" she whispered.

"No. Hell, no." He made his voice more confident than he felt. "They'll figure we made a run for it, not hunkered down right under their feet. Probably no one will even come into the tunnels."

"If they do..." She licked her lips and squared her shoulders. "You could go back. Tell them I shot Mac."

"Tell them—" The words really penetrated, and then he was moving again. Moving without thinking, crowding into her space to slam both hands against the wall on either side of her head. He loomed over her, intimidating, trapping her and not caring as he lowered his face until she had to look at him. "Don't you fucking think it, woman. Do you hear me?"

Her angry, fierce gaze clashed with his for one heart-stopping moment before she turned her head, averting her eyes. "Hypocrite."

He caught her chin and forced her gaze back, his heart slamming against his ribs in full-on terror. He had to head this off, had to make her believe, so he gave her the truth. The raw, messy truth. "I'm breathing because you're breathing. You hear me? I was on a slow trip out of this world before you showed up. You dying would only speed that shit up."

Trix stared up at him, her eyes wide, her chest heaving with shallow, quick breaths. "Okay," she said finally. "Okay, I get it."

He forced himself to release her chin before his fingers dug bruises into her delicate skin. But he'd already left marks—smears in the sticky, drying blood splattered across her face. He'd blown a man's head off not two feet from her, while she was tripping through daisy fields, rolling on Jesus knew what.

And she was still holding it together. He had to do the same. "I'm sorry." He gentled his voice. "It's not gonna come to that, okay? The only guy up there with any brains at all is Ryder. By morning, he'll have them crawling all over the area south of the sector."

She nodded, then sagged against the wall, sliding down it as her knees gave way. He helped her sit, and she combed her hands through her tangled hair. "It'll be all right," she muttered.

Finn murmured reassurances and dragged Ryder's bag closer. It was packed with the medical kit he expected, plus emergency rations, water, and a tiny radiant heater with a fully charged battery. He also found a loaded handgun and a tightly folded reflective blanket.

Ryder had been ready to run, which explained a lot of things. Why he hadn't taken Finn's offer. Why a man with his brains and skills was in a shithole like Five to begin with. Men with morals didn't rise high in Fleming's operation unless they had a reason to.

Clearly Ryder had a reason. Whatever it was, Finn hoped the man could keep his hide intact while Beckett seized power. Then again, considering Beckett's disdain for Finn and appreciation for culture and class, Ryder probably had Finn's job already.

That was good for Finn. He pulled out the blanket and handed it to Trix. "Wrap yourself up while I see about your wrists. It's going to get cold in here tonight."

She obeyed, though it took her several moments to work the blanket open, and her shaking was worse. A lot worse. "They don't hurt."

Shit. He dropped the kit and settled against the wall next to her. "Come here, doll." Not quite a command, and he didn't reach for her. Instead, he held his arms open, offering her the chance to come to him.

She closed her eyes, as if shutting out the sight of him. "Don't."

It hurt. But he had it coming, so he didn't let it show. He took the blanket and tucked it around her without touching her. Her jaw clenched, and she held herself stiffly, her back rigid and straight.

Oh yeah, he had a lifetime of this coming. He'd lost the right to touch her the first time he'd laid hands on her, all those years ago when he'd still suffered under the delusion that he was a half-decent guy. Wanting her had cured him of that. Losing her had driven the lesson home.

All he could do was get her back to Four, back to the loving arms of her real family. Preferably before she figured out Dallas O'Kane wouldn't greet *him* with hugs and kisses.

Chances were fifty-fifty he'd end tomorrow in a ditch with an O'Kane bullet rattling around in his skull. As long as she was safe, he'd consider it a fair trade.

She couldn't stop shaking.

At first, it terrified her. She had no idea what drugs her abductor had forced on her—and whether they were laced with the addictive additive Mac Fleming favored. It had been years since she'd suffered through the twists and pangs of withdrawal, but the memory was etched in her brain.

Agony. There was no other word for it, not just the pain but the *craving*. The bone-deep knowledge that she'd die without the drugs, the moments where she would have done anything to end the torment. Watching Jade scream and cry through the same thing so recently had brought those memories rushing to the surface, sharp and stinging.

Gradually, Trix realized this was different. Not once had she thought to ask Finn if he was carrying, and that fact helped to settle her. At one point, she'd have done more than ask him for drugs—she'd have climbed into his lap, cajoled, whispered filthy promises in his ear.

At one point, she might have shot him in the fucking head and gone through his pockets afterward.

The thought almost brought her off the wall to put more space between them. But he was cold, too—he hid his shivering well, but he couldn't stop his lips from turning blue—so she eased closer and shifted the blanket. "Here."

"I'm okay," he replied quietly, but he didn't move away. He caught the edge of the blanket and held it against his chest, his focus never wavering from the door.

The urge to touch him damn near overwhelmed her, and it only grew stronger the closer she got. But she couldn't keep pulling away, so she settled for stroking his forearm. "I think they're gone."

"Probably." He tensed under her fingertips, his strong muscles flexing. "You should eat and drink something and get a little more rest."

Nothing he planned on doing himself, obviously. "I'd like to clean up."

After a moment of silence, he snagged the medical kit from the bag. "Will you let me bandage your wrists, too?"

Anything to give him a task, something to distract him from staring at the door with a gun in his hand. "Thank you."

He moved slowly. Precisely. He'd always had a lazy patience to his movements, but it seemed more serious now as he took inventory of the kit and pulled out gauze, med-gel, bandages, and a handful of antiseptic wipes. He laid out the supplies in a neat line before shifting to his knees, one hand hovering beneath her chin. "Can you tilt your head up a little?"

The hesitation made her chest ache, so she guided his hand to her jaw as she complied. "I'm not scared of you, Finn."

"Never thought you were, doll." He cupped her chin, warm and gentle, and began to carefully clean her cheek. "I'm sorry about this. I should have handled him better."

"You did what you had to do."

"No, I did what I *wanted* to do. The usual."

"You're too hard on yourself. You always have been."

"Have I?" He snorted as he tilted her head back and worked his way along her jaw. "It's been a while, Trix. Things change."

"Yes, they do." She closed her eyes and tried not to focus on the impossible gentleness of his rough fingers. "You haven't asked me why."

"Don't need to. You always were smart, even when you were high. You did the smart thing."

"Not the leaving. After I got clean, I meant to get in touch, let you know I was okay." Maybe even to ask if he would ever consider leaving, too. "I never could figure out what to say."

He sighed softly. "You don't have to explain. You didn't owe me anything, you got that? Other way around, really."

"It feels like I did." He'd been the one to keep her from spinning out of control, from winding up dead because she was too fucked up to keep herself alive.

"Uh-huh." He tilted her head in the other direction, his touch still gentle. It lingered this time, his thumb making small, soothing circles against the underside of her jaw as he cleaned her left cheek. "Well, thinking I'd gotten you killed got me clean, so whatever feelings you have, count us square."

Clean, maybe—but he seemed hopeless, not happy, such a far cry from her new life in Sector Four. Guilt suffused her. "After everything you did for me—"

"Stop," he grated out. "Just—you live in Four now, don't you? Land of the motherfucking heroes. You should know the difference between being good and not being as bad as you could have been."

Tears stung her eyes, and she blinked them away. "All right."

He muttered a curse and dropped his hands. "See? I'm still a shitty hero. But I'm trying this time."

She felt the loss of his touch so sharply. In the weeks and months after she'd kicked the drugs, that had been the thing she'd struggled with the most. The previous years of her life had been blurry, every sensation vague, and getting sober was like waking up to a whole new world.

She had relished it, thrown herself into a hedonistic pursuit of sensory decadence. Food, laughter, sex, dancing. Everything had been *real*, maybe for the first time ever...and her only regret was that Finn hadn't been there to share it.

It was easy to see now that he'd been wallowing in blame and self-loathing, instead.

Trix moved without thinking, taking the wet gauze from his hands and turning her attention to the blood smeared on his cheeks. "I missed you."

It was his turn to close his eyes. "Me too, Tracy. Trix."

His brows drew together, and she smoothed away the furrow with her thumb. Such a tiny bit of contact, but it zinged through her like a shock, and she realized it felt *right*, like a habit she'd completely forgotten.

She'd touched him like this before.

The feeling of familiarity only increased when he rested his hands on her hips. "You seem good."

"Good?" Across to his temple, down over his cheek to the rough beard covering his jaw.

"Happy. Healthy." His thumb swept over her hip in a slow arc, tracing the curve. "You were always too damn skinny. I used to worry."

I know. But the words failed her as heat washed up her spine. Oh, she remembered this. His hands, scorching even through layers of fabric.

It wasn't enough.

She stared at his mouth. It would be easy to blame her arousal on the adrenaline, on emotion and danger running hot and high, but the ache ran deeper than that. Harder.

"Trix."

He was watching her now, and she met his intent gaze with another jolt. It was stupid to sit here and not touch him, assuage that ache, especially when she'd lain awake so many nights wanting to do just that.

O'Kanes didn't deny their desires. They indulged them.

So she shifted, leaning closer, until her lips almost touched his. "What?"

"If you're up to it, we should keep moving."

The regret in his voice—and the reality of their situation—helped to ease the sting of his words. She leaned back and nodded. "Right."

"Hey." Roughened fingertips touched her cheek, and he smiled as he let his thumb ghost across her lower lip. "You just returned from the dead. I need to keep you that way. Alive."

"Is there a way around the collapsed section of tunnel?"

"Probably, but not one we can use. Most of the locks are electronic, and I can't do shit about those. We're going to have to risk going up."

There was a rumpled map sticking out of the open bag, one she vaguely remembered him cursing at as they made their way through the tunnels. She pulled it free and unfolded it on her lap.

A maze of tiny, intersecting lines confronted her. She blinked to clear her lingering double vision and tilted her head. The whole thing looked like a wheel, a blank central point surrounded by a larger circle marked off in radiating sections.

The sectors.

She traced a finger from Five due east to Four. There were fewer tunnels marked in that direction. Most of the map seemed dedicated to the opposite—multiple routes leading across the river through Sectors Six and Seven, all the way up to Eight. "It looks like your friend planned on going this way."

"Six," Finn said after a moment. His finger joined hers, sliding over the lines that delineated the sector. "I know people there. If we can't get across the border to Four, we can go that way."

But Four was so fucking close. All they had to do was cross the damn street, and she'd be there, *home*. Did they even know she was gone yet? More importantly, had they found Zan in time?

Trix pressed the heels of her hands to her eyes. "They have to know we might try to run for it."

"Yeah." He smoothed her hair. "If we get to Six, we can send word to O'Kane, one way or another. You'll be safe, and they'll figure out a way to get you home."

It wasn't enough. "We both have to make it through this, Finn. Promise me."

Finn caught her hands and tugged them from her face. When she looked up at him, he smiled. "I can't keep you safe from the grave, doll. I promise. I'm not looking for a way out of this life."

The way he said it made it sound like a new development. "It was the truth, wasn't it? You were waiting for a chance. Not just to take him down, but to kill him."

His smile didn't falter as he rubbed his thumbs over her palms. "I've been waiting to kill him since the day you died."

And Mac Fleming deserved it. Because of the drugs, because of the way he used and disposed of people, and because he'd created a culture of hopelessness in his sector, where even men who wanted to do the right thing couldn't. Where men like Finn bowed under the pressure until they broke.

In the end, there was only one thing to say. "Good."

dallas

FOR THE THIRD time in under a week, Dallas was in danger of losing one of his men.

Zan's blood was everywhere. A goddamn miracle, considering how much of it he'd left back in the alleyway where they'd found him—alive, somehow. Zan was a stubborn bastard clinging to life with both massive hands, and Dallas already knew from the look on Doc's face that it might not be enough.

And Dallas was fresh out of miracles.

Doc faced him, grim and ashen. "I'm getting really fucking tired of delivering bad news, O'Kane."

"So don't," Dallas growled. "Tell me you can fix this."

"Your man damn near bled out on the street...but he's conscious now. Asking for you."

And Dallas would have to face him, look him in the eyes, and know he'd failed him. Because he'd pissed off the wrong sociopath, the one with a stranglehold on the regen tech that could keep Zan alive. The only promise Dallas had left was revenge. "Did he see who shot him?"

Doc grabbed Dallas's arm, his grip surprisingly strong. "He wasn't alone."

The next second took forever. He lived a damn lifetime of panic between one beat of his heart and the next, his brain tripping down the list of his people, trying to remember which ones he'd seen in the past hour. Noelle, Mad, Lex—thank *God*, he'd seen Lex—

"Who?" he asked hoarsely, already turning for the door. Rachel and Cruz were curled safely around Ace. Six and Bren had been on their way out to Sector Three. But there were so many more names, so many people in danger now that war was coming for them.

Zan was whispering something beneath his breath as he fidgeted restlessly on the bed, his skin pale and sallow. His heart heavy, Dallas gripped the other man's hand and leaned down. "I'm here, Zan."

The whispers solidified into one terrifying syllable. "Trix..."

Fucking *hell*. "Trix was with you when you were shot?"

Zan shook his head and grimaced. "They took her. Fle-Fleming's—"

"Shh, okay. We'll get her back." Dallas pressed his free hand to Zan's forehead, wishing he could will strength into him. "I need you to hold on for me, you hear? We're gonna fix you up."

"I tried, Dallas."

"You did good, man. You did real good."

Blood trickled from the corner of his mouth. "Not enough."

Dallas squeezed Zan's hand, unwilling to let go and turn to face Doc. He already knew what words would be coming, the same Doc had murmured over Ace's almost-dead body.

I can make him comfortable had to be the five most

helpless words a leader could hear. All of his power, all of his wealth, all the *things* he'd wrested from the hands of other petty dictators, and it still came down to this. Easing his man—his *friend*—out of the world.

He'd choke the life out of Mac Fleming with his bare hands for this.

"Declan."

Lex's voice was usually a comfort, but now it was heavy with the same pain that twisted in his chest. When he turned, he saw that pain reflected in her eyes. Zan was theirs, a man who'd pledged his loyalty and trusted them with his life.

And he was dying. The hardest lesson of all was the one Dallas still struggled with—sometimes you had to see to the living. "Fleming has Trix."

"Not anymore, he doesn't. He's dead." Her hand tightened on the doorframe. "His successor is on a video call for you."

Maybe he wasn't out of miracles after all.

3

FINN COULDN'T DECIDE what painted a bleaker picture of Sector Six—the fact that they were crouched in an abandoned warehouse that should have been packed to the rafters with this year's harvest, or the unlit, unguarded street outside.

"We shouldn't have to go too far," Finn murmured, still watching the street through the dirty window. "I think I know where we are."

Trix kept her back flat against the wall and nodded. "I'm just glad to be out of the tunnels."

So was he. It had taken a full day to make their way this far, a day spent in the darkness, advancing and backtracking, wasting hours trying to find a path that didn't end abruptly in a solid door with an electronic lock. A day watching their rations diminish while he refused to consider the possibility that they might end up lost and wandering the underground labyrinth forever.

Finn pulled their last bottle of water from the bag and passed it to Trix. “Drink. Are you hungry?”

“Anxious. I don’t steal cars during desperate escapes all that often.”

“Don’t be.” He kept his voice easy and confident, trying to will a little of that into her. “All we have to worry about here is being scarier than the other criminals, and I could do that in my sleep.”

A tiny smile tilted up one corner of her generous mouth. “I know.”

That smile made everything better, so he didn’t mention the larger dangers. The leader of Sector Six loathed Mac Fleming and was supposedly allied with Dallas O’Kane, but Timothy Scott was also an idiot. Finn couldn’t trust their safety to the whims of an idiot, especially not a greedy one who might be swayed by a phone call from the new head of Sector Five.

Besides, you could still find honor among thieves, if you knew the right ones.

Trix handed the bottle back to him. He took a few careful sips and ignored the empty rumble of his stomach. “Looks safe to move,” he told her, stowing the bottle next to the meager remains of their rations. There’d be food soon enough—unless there wasn’t, in which case she’d need every advantage he could leave her. “You ready?”

“Finn.”

He fixed his expression before glancing at her.

She stared back, serious and pensive. “I’m not delicate,” she whispered. “Not anymore. I can do this.”

He reached for her hand, and his thumb brushed the bandages around her wrists. They covered more than her wounds—they covered her ink, the tattoos Dallas only gave to full members of his gang.

No, whatever the hell else she was, she wasn’t delicate. This confident creature at his side, with her healthy glow and her serious eyes, was nothing like the dreamy-eyed waif who'd first crawled beneath his skin. But the parts of her that had attracted him were still there—her wit and her smiles and her style. Three things she always clung to, no matter how shitty a hand life dealt her.

Squeezing her hand, he smiled for real this time. "Let's go boost a car."

The first three vehicles parked along the darkened street were outfitted with biometrics. He could bypass the sensors, maybe even rekey them to his own prints, but they didn't have that kind of time. The longer they lingered, the more likely they were to run into trouble.

He kept looking.

The fourth car was an older model—with both back tires missing. Finn stopped by the fifth, a huge, four-door monstrosity with pitted beige paint and a cracked windshield. But the interior was spotless, and the tires looked new.

Best of all, it had an old-style manual lock.

Finn passed the bag off to Trix and knelt to tug at one of the laces on his boots. Her shoes caught his attention, black-and-red two-tone pumps with straps around the ankles, and he mentally kicked himself for not having noticed sooner. "How the hell are you still walking in those things? Your feet must be killing you."

She avoided his eyes as she shifted her weight and leaned against the car. "If I can pull a double and still dance a set in them, I can certainly walk."

The lace almost snapped beneath his fingers. "O'Kane's making you dance?"

"No one's *making* me do anything," she shot back. "I'm damn good at it."

Something else that was new—Tracy had never had a temper. Finn concentrated on dealing with his bootlace and tried not to picture Trix on stage in O'Kane's bar, burning up with all that new fire.

Fuck, with that body and those smiles, she wouldn't

even *have* to be good at it.

She was still glaring at him when he straightened, but his apologies would have to wait. He looped a sturdy slipknot into the bootlace and worked it under the edge of the car door, finessing it until the loop dropped over the lock. The first tug pulled the knot tight, and the second dragged the lock up with a soft *click*.

"That's resourceful." Trix hauled open the door, tossed the bag inside, and climbed in after it.

"Life in the sectors, baby doll." He slid into the driver's seat and reached beneath the wheel to pry off the plastic covering on the steering column. "We work with what we have."

She watched him as he teased out the bundle of wires that led to the battery. "There's no back seat. You think the owner's a smuggler?"

"Probably. Smuggling food to other sectors is this hellhole's second biggest industry. Grab that flashlight, would you?"

She flicked it on and aimed the beam toward his hands. "Can you get it?"

He'd hotwired dozens of cars in his youth, plenty under less optimal conditions than this—but he'd also punched a lot of faces. It didn't matter how steady he could keep his hands when the cold made his joints stiff and his fingers had always been too big for delicate work.

Pride was nice. Weighed against her safety, it meant shit. "Get your tiny fingers over here and separate the wires, huh?"

Trix laughed softly and passed him the flashlight. "Hold this." She leaned over, her head almost in his lap as she peered beneath the steering column.

Great, now *all* of him was getting stiff.

She shifted closer, her arm rubbing his leg as she fiddled with the wires, and he didn't have to imagine what it would feel like to sink a hand into her hair while she opened his jeans and slid those lips around his cock.

She'd done it before. Fuck, she'd done it in a *car* before, laughing before taking him deep, not caring if she fogged his brain with so much pleasure that he ran them both off the road.

She'd never cared about much of anything, as long as he handed over her next fix.

The engine turned over and rumbled to life, and she straightened with a satisfied smile. "I remembered how. Rachel's gonna be proud."

Finn gripped the steering wheel, the guilty arousal of his memory clashing with a newer, simpler sort of appreciative lust. She'd always looked good, but it was so much hotter to watch her be a little bad. "Nice trick."

Her gaze flicked to his lap and back up, so quickly he might have only imagined it. "Life in the sectors, baby doll."

The urge to laugh—really, honestly fucking *laugh*—hit him for the first time in months. Years, maybe. He let himself as he pulled away from the curb, the engine rumbling quietly. "You're about to see a whole different side of it. How much do you know about this sector?"

"They grow things, right?"

"Most of them. Some people who live along the reservoir fish, but that's a special privilege. 'Cause it'd be a city-wide crisis if a fancy lady in Eden wanted to serve fish at her dinner party and the day's catch ended up in the belly of a starving sector brat instead."

Trix looked out the window. "Some things are the same all over."

"Bad," he agreed. "When they're not worse. The farms here aren't much better than the communes. A bunch of farmers, taking as many wives as they can knock up, everyone spitting out kids as free labor. Everyone works fifteen-, maybe eighteen-hour days. I used to move more stimulants through Six in a month than all the other sectors go through in a year. Combined."

"Is that where we're headed? To one of the farms?"

"Technically." He took a left turn onto the road that followed the reservoir out to the edge of the sector. "We're going to the people who moved the stims."

"Drug runners?"

Finn imagined Shipp's outraged expression at being called something so distasteful and almost laughed. "Moving product for me was more of a sideline to fund their real passion."

She nudged him. "Which is...?"

Teasing her felt good. Sharing Shipp's place with her would feel better than good, even under shitty circumstances. How many times had he taken the long ride out to this outlaw village and wished he'd discovered it before she was gone, so he could share the magic of midnight races across the desert and the blinding shine of lovingly polished chrome under the noon sun?

Words couldn't describe the oasis of peace Shipp and his old lady had built, so Finn didn't try. It would be more fun to watch the delight in her eyes when she got her first good look around the compound come dawn tomorrow. "Let's just say they like cars. They *really* like cars."

Finn had a talent for understatement.

He'd told her they were going to a farm, but it turned out to be a loose cluster of cabins and workshops that looked more like a small settlement. He'd also said they liked cars, but nothing prepared her for the roar of engines echoing through the still desert air out past the buildings. More cars were parked in a large circle, their headlights shining toward the center, blocking out the darkness of the night.

"They have so many," she whispered. Dozens of cars—classic, cherry. The kind Dallas would have drooled over.

"They fix 'em up. Trade for them. Shipp's got some guys who range all the way out to the old cities. Vegas, Reno...places I can't even remember." Finn threw an arm around her shoulders and led her closer to the circle of light. "I think anyone in the sectors who really loves cars probably ends up here, sooner or later."

Some of the people at the edge of the gathering had turned to look, and Trix was suddenly acutely aware of the fact that she'd been tromping through the tunnels. She'd cleaned up, but she couldn't do a damn thing about her bruised face or her hair or the blood and dirt smudging her torn dress.

"Finn!" called a voice from their left, and a woman strode toward them through the swiftly parting crowd. A beautiful woman, lean and tough in jeans and a leather jacket, with her brunette hair tied up in a long ponytail that swung with her swift steps.

She stopped abruptly in front of them, hands on her hips, her expression darkening as her gaze swept from Finn to Trix. "I know you weren't about to drag this poor girl into the middle of a rally."

Finn's eyebrows drew together, usually his first sign of irritation. "Trix, meet Alya. This is her farm."

Trix held out her hand. "Nice to meet you."

Alya clasped Trix's hand and turned it over, studying the hint of ink peeking out from beneath her bandages. But she didn't comment, just smiled. "Come to the main house with me, honey. We'll get you fixed up. Finn can tag along, I suppose. Shipp'll want to see him."

The woman made it sound casual, but Trix had lived in Sector Four too long not to recognize what it meant—they wanted to check her out, and they had questions for Finn.

Not that he seemed worried. He reclaimed Trix's hand and followed Alya around the edge of the crowd. "I was just gonna show her the cars."

"And they'll still be there in the morning."

The woman moved deeper into the darkness, past several small, squat adobe structures and a few greenhouses. They reached a gentle rise, and Trix picked her way gingerly up the dirt and stone path.

The main structure was several stories tall and made of wood, wide boards cut from what must have been huge trees. A generous porch wrapped around both sides that Trix could see, and the glass-paned double doors sat open.

Two men dressed in denim and leather stood by the doors, smoking. One nodded to Finn. "Little early, aren't you?"

"Situation's changed." Finn's voice stayed relaxed, but his fingers tightened around hers. "I need to call in that favor."

The man brushed his dark blond hair out of his face and studied Trix. On the surface, it was a lazy perusal, slow and indifferent, but his gaze was sharp, and she knew he missed nothing.

Finn tensed as Alya reached over to pluck the cigarette from Shipp's fingers. She took a hit, exhaled toward the porch ceiling, and crushed it out into an ashtray. "Hawk," she said, nodding to the second man. "Head over and get things started. We've got business."

"You got it." He lumbered off into the darkness, but not before Trix got a good look at the giant handgun strapped to his hip. It looked like a cannon, for Christ's sake.

Whoever Finn's friends were, they were deadly.

Shipp tilted his head toward the open door of the cabin. "You hungry?" he asked Finn.

Finn exhaled slowly and relaxed, as if the offer had answered a silent question. "We could use a decent meal."

"We've got leftover stew. Some bread and cheese." Alya waved them into the cabin after her. "You both look like you could use a drink."

"Just water, please." The last thing Trix wanted was to feel groggy again, out of control.

Shipp took the chair at the head of the long table. "Introduce me to your friend, Finn."

Finn hauled out a chair and held it while Trix sat. "Shipp, meet Trix. I knew her back in the day, but for the last few years she's been running in Sector Four. With Dallas O'Kane."

"Is that what those are?" He nodded to the ink peeking above the tops of the bandages on her wrists. "His cuffs?"

Trix fought the urge to hide her hands in her lap. "Yes."

He grunted in response.

Alya brought a pitcher of water to the table and set it down beside two glasses. "If you're waiting for us to fill in the blanks, honey, we'll all be here a while. You know we don't hear shit out here. No vid network, no wireless."

Finn rubbed a hand over his face. "You're not gonna like it."

"Probably not. As I recall, that was a damn big favor."

"I know." Finn met Shipp's gaze. "I need to get word to Four, let them know she's here. And we need a safe place to stay until they can come and get her."

Shipp's jaw clenched. "Who's after you?"

"Most of Five."

"Must have really pissed off your boss this time."

Finn snorted. "Something like that."

Alya thumped a bowl of stew down in front of Finn so hard that a little slopped over the edges. Then she slid a second one in front of Trix. "How do you expect us to send a message? I just told you, we don't have access to the network."

"You could send someone."

Shipp laughed. "You make it sound easy. Maybe you

forget that it isn't, not for everyone."

Finn pressed his lips together, one big hand clenching his spoon until Trix thought she saw it bend. "Not easy, but you could do it. All they have to do is get to Four, and O'Kane will come get her. I know he will."

Shipp reached for the glass in front of him, but instead of filling it from the nearly empty bottle of O'Kane whiskey at his elbow, he spun it around on the table. "What aren't you telling me?"

Tense silence. Finn slanted Trix a look, but jerked his gaze away the moment her eyes clashed with his. "Mac Fleming was trying to start a sector war between Four and Five. Kidnapping her was part of it. I put him down."

"Put him..." Shipp blinked. "You fucking *killed* him?"

"Shit got complicated."

"No kidding."

Alya sank into the chair next to Trix. "They'll do this all night, you know. Dance around what happened one sentence at a time. Finn's drugs are more affordable than his words."

"We don't have to dance around what happened," Shipp said lazily, with no trace of humor to match his light tone. "Our buddy Finn killed a sector leader and came here. But what's done is done."

"What's done is done," Alya agreed. "I won't turn you away from the farm, but you'll have to let Shipp decide when it's safe to send a messenger."

Shipp rubbed his chin and sighed. "Tomorrow's soon enough. We'll have to spend tonight on guard, just in case."

A muscle in Finn's cheek clenched as he finally looked at Trix. "Is that okay?"

As if her input mattered to Shipp and Alya—but at least it did to him. She smiled gently, grateful for the chance to pretend, if only for a moment, that her answer carried weight. "It's more than generous. And I'm sure

Dallas will show his gratitude."

"I wouldn't mind a little." Alya leaned across the table to snag the whiskey bottle. "You wouldn't believe what we have to pay for a bottle of this stuff."

Dallas's appreciation went far beyond free liquor. "He'll take care of you."

"And we'll take care of you." Alya rose and circled the table, brushing her fingers along the back of Shipp's neck. A casual touch, soothing, the kind Trix had seen Lex give Dallas a hundred times. "I'm going to start the water heater. Trix, love, when you're done eating, follow the hallway to the stairs. I'll have a bath and a med kit waiting."

"Thank you." She avoided Shipp's gaze as she picked up her spoon.

He had danced around things, all right—like the fact that harboring them, even overnight, was dangerous. It was impossible to know how far Beckett would go to catch Finn or recover her, but they had to assume the worst—that he'd tear apart the sectors, not to mention anyone who got in his way.

4

FINN DIDN'T BLAME Trix for rushing through her meal. Shipp looked perfectly amiable, sprawled in his chair—but she had spent her life around dangerous men. She wouldn't miss the tension in Shipp's eyes.

It didn't explode until she'd vanished down the hall. They both listened to the old wooden stairs creak gently as she climbed, and Shipp lit another cigarette as the sound receded.

Then he swore viciously. "You put me in one hell of a goddamn spot here, Finn."

"I know." He reached for the empty glass by Shipp's elbow and poured himself a generous helping of whiskey. "I'm sorry, man. I am. If I'd had any other option—"

"Forget Fleming's men," he interrupted. "Or Beckett's, or whoever the fuck took over. The other sector leaders could want your head."

It was true enough. For the first time in forever, the

thought of dying stirred a twinge of regret. He'd been barreling toward death for so long, it was hard to believe he could still have a reason to live. But there she was, upstairs in a bathtub, trusting him to get her through this.

"My head, yeah." He knocked his glass against the whiskey bottle. "If it comes to that, they can have it. But if you keep Trix safe, O'Kane'll keep you safe. Believe me, Shipp. That man has more pull with the other sectors than anyone else."

"If you're so ready to die—if you're not after that pull yourself—then what are you doing with Ginger up there?"

"You know that favor you owe me?"

"No need to be delicate," Shipp shot back. "You saved my life. I remember."

It hadn't been a big deal—for Finn. He'd been cold already, still grieving the loss of Tracy. But he'd been in the wrong place at the right time, and so fucking tired of watching good people die. "Yeah, well, I didn't save hers."

"Did you take a whack to the head? Because you..." Shipp trailed off, his confused expression easing as realization dawned. "That's her."

Finn drank his shot. Then he poured another and drank that, too. The physical burn helped to distract him from the one in his chest, the rising tangle of grief and rage he still couldn't face dead on, because it was fresh again. Raw.

He hadn't saved Trix's life. She'd saved her own. "Fleming gave her enough of the good stuff to OD a half-dozen times over. He did it to trap her. To take her from me, because he didn't like me having anything beautiful in my life."

Shipp muttered another curse, this time under his breath. "That's a lot of history. Lot of baggage."

"That's a lot of debt," Finn corrected. But it was his, not Shipp's, so he sighed as he poured a third shot. "No one inside Five has any reason to look in this direction, unless one of your clients admits who sells him his illegal stims. I wouldn't bring danger down on you and Alya."

"Someone always talks."

"Only if someone asks the right questions. Last I saw, they were all waiting for us to make a dash for O'Kane's territory."

Shipp nodded and took a long drag off his cigarette. "What's your plan?"

He only had one—the one that would redeem and break him at the same time. "Get her home."

"*After* that, big guy."

That was the question, wasn't it? If there could be an *after* in a world where Trix was alive but he wasn't welcome in the home she couldn't—and shouldn't—leave. "Fuck if I know."

"Fair enough." Shipp shoved the nearly empty bottle of whiskey at him. "Does she know you don't know?"

He'd already had enough liquor to fuzz his nerves, but he dumped the rest of the amber liquid into his glass anyway. "We've been running for our damn lives. Not a lot of time for chats about our hopes and dreams."

"Doesn't take long to say, 'Don't make big eyes at me, honey, I'm kinda planning on dying,' does it?"

No time at all. The real killer was all the time they would waste arguing about it afterwards—time she'd spend distracted from the goal of getting her ass safely home. "You're an asshole, you know that?"

Shipp laughed. "Of course I am. If I was a nice guy, you wouldn't come around anymore."

"Doesn't explain why Alya puts up with you."

"She loves me. That makes up for damn near anything."

Oh, that was a dangerous fucking thought. Like waving a prime cut of steak under the nose of a starving dog. "Now you're just bragging."

Shipp sobered, a muscle in his jaw clenching. "Shit,

Finn. It's no kind of life to live, not knowing how true that is."

That summed up his existence: no kind of life. Even those few, bright years when Trix had painted his dull world in colors had been a kind of torture. He'd never been good for her, and the more she shined, the more he'd hated himself for hurting her.

He finished the whiskey and stared at Shipp over the edge of the glass. "Anyone who finds love in the sectors is beating the odds. Count yourself lucky."

"Is that really what you think?"

Christ, Shipp would get along with Dallas. He even sounded like an O'Kane—high on pixie dust and fairy tales. You could point out all day long that life was a shithole full of shit people who'd step on your face to get out of the muck, and those bastards kept on grinning like the world was made of rainbows.

"Maybe it's not as bad here as it was in Five," Finn said. "But don't tell me you haven't seen ugly things out there. The world hasn't been a decent place since the lights went out, and you're not old enough to remember that."

"No," Shipp conceded, "but Alya does. You get her waxed up on a little of O'Kane's finest, and she'll tell you the truth—the real truth." He leaned forward. "The lights went out, but they also came on. The ugly shit isn't new, Finn, just out in the open now. That's better, don't you think?"

He almost disagreed before he remembered Logan Beckett. Sleek. Civilized. Evil wrapped in the illusion of decency, and a far greater threat than Mac had been even at his craziest. Because Mac couldn't hide the rage seething beneath his skin.

Beckett could. And if you didn't know it was there, you wouldn't see him coming.

"You're right," Finn said. "This makes it easier to know what you're up against, at least."

Shipp grunted and nodded as he finished his cigarette. "I thought of a reason you should make a plan. I managed to get my hands on that car you wanted, but it's basically a shell. Needs a lot of work. You might want to consider coming back and making that happen."

It felt like a hundred years had passed since the afternoon he'd spent under the hood of one of Shipp's latest restorations. Helping the other man put the final touches on the newly rebuilt engine had been the first good feeling since Trix slipped from his life. A few hours where he'd been building something instead of smashing it into pieces.

The lingering satisfaction had faded almost as soon as he crossed the border back into Five. More of Fleming's messes to clean up. More lives to ruin, people to kill. Destruction was in his blood. He was good at it. On his worst days, he liked it.

The idea of having a car of his own had been a stupid fantasy, but Shipp's words weren't about the car, not really. They were a peace offering. A rope thrown to a drowning man. Whatever went down with Dallas O'Kane, Finn had someplace to go. People who would welcome him. All he had to do was turn his back on the mess he'd made and let it be someone else's problem.

Not so hard. He'd been doing it all his life. "Maybe we can take a look at that car tomorrow."

"It'll give us something to do while the boys make their run out to Four." Shipp reached under the table and came up with a new, unopened bottle of whiskey. "Tonight? We drink."

Sometime between slipping into a hot bath and letting Alya scrub the dried blood from her hair, reality began to crash down on Trix.

She'd been living in surreal fantasy since the moment Finn had shot Fleming. The painful danger of their situation had intruded, of course, but only in brief flashes she could barely grasp. It was easier to let it slip through her fingers, to shove it away. To not think about the truth.

Finn had shot Fleming.

Finn had shot a sector leader.

People had been killed for far, far less, no matter how justifiable their reasons.

She shivered in the bath as Alya poured fresh, warm water over her neck and shoulders, rinsing away the last of the soap with gentle fingers. "You've had a shit couple days, haven't you, honey?"

"I've had better," she admitted. "Also had worse, though."

Alya shook her head and rose. "Too many of us have. But not on this farm, not anymore. You and Finn will be safe here."

No one would be safe there—not if Beckett showed up, intent on revenge. "You'll all be better off once we're gone. That doesn't hurt my feelings, it's just fact."

"Someone could come looking for you," she agreed, shaking open a fluffy towel. "But it's not likely to be tonight. It's one of the nice things about living this far from Eden. People tend to forget you're there."

"Sounds peaceful."

"It can be. Have you ever looked up at the stars without the lights from Eden's walls getting in the way?"

Just once, when Finn had taken her to his cabin beyond the outskirts of Five. She'd expected it to be dark, so far away from the fires and electric lights, but it had been brighter, somehow. Luminous, with the starlight and the soft glow of the half-moon shining through the windows.

She'd spent her second visit shaking from withdrawal, in too much wracking pain to notice anything else. But she could still hear his voice, with its grating edge of surrender. *"Fuck me, Tracy. I can't watch you die, not like this."*

"No," she whispered. "I never have."

"Well, we'll fix that. Maybe tomorrow night." She gestured Trix out of the tub and held up the towel. "We're far from the city, but the main farmhouse has a few luxuries. You can take all the hot baths you want, and we have electric heating, though we usually lay a fire in the bedrooms at night to save power."

She took the towel and wrapped it around herself before tucking in the edge to secure it. "Thanks, Alya."

"It's nothing, honey." Alya ushered Trix out the door and across the hallway, into a cozy bedroom with a stack of clothing and a med kit laid out on the bed. "Finn saved Shipp's life, you know. That's a debt I feel just as much as he does. Maybe more."

"I think I understand." The place clearly belonged to Alya, but Shipp seemed right at home.

"Wouldn't blame you if you didn't. I can only imagine the stories you've heard about Sector Six. Probably as wild as the stories they tell about Dallas O'Kane."

"Biggest difference?" Trix smiled as she picked up the nightgown, a floor-length confection of peach-colored satin and white lace. "Half that shit is actually true."

"Is it, now?" Alya sat down and opened the med kit. "Well, most of the shit you hear about Six is true, too, and it's not half so entertaining. My husband claimed this farmstead when the lights went out. I was fourteen when I became his third wife, and he took seven more before Shipp finally put him in the ground."

Trix nodded. "There's a girl from Six—she tells stories. When she feels like talking, I mean. A lot of them sound like that."

"Not a lot of good stories come out of this sector. Hell, Shipp could have been another bad one. The leader of a gang of outlaws on a farm full of women and children and men too beaten down to fight..." She trailed off and nodded to the ink around Trix's wrists. "You ever tell people stuff and they don't believe you, because they think it's too good to be true?"

It was all her life was—a collection of things that should have killed her but somehow hadn't. "Every day."

"Then you understand perfectly." She patted the bed next to her. "Sit and let me look at those wrists."

Trix draped the nightgown over her arm and shook her head. "No, I'm fine, really. Just a few scrapes from the handcuffs. I didn't even need the bandages, but Finn—he needed them."

"Ah." Alya tilted her head, studying her with a curiosity she didn't bother to hide. "That's a side of him I never thought I'd see."

"It's all I've ever seen."

"I'm glad someone has." She closed the kit and rose. "I don't know how long Shipp will keep Finn up. Should I make up a second bed for him?"

The denial died on her lips. What she wanted was immutable—and irrelevant. She wanted Finn, always had...but that didn't make it safe, and it didn't make it right. Especially here.

"Lex would have my ass if I went into someone else's house and tried to dictate the sleeping arrangements," she said instead.

Alya paused with one hand on the door, her expression still serious. "No one will be offended if he shares your bed, honey. But if you need a night to yourself, Finn'll sleep where I put him."

Would he? "He spent the last four years believing I was dead," Trix confessed. "I could be wrong…but, somehow, I think he'll wind up here."

"He—" Alya bit off the words as her eyes widened, and she closed the door with a soft *click*. "Well, that explains a lot. You're the one he lost."

That made it all sound so innocent, so harmless, as if it was something outside of her control that had just happened instead of a calculated decision. "No, I'm the one who left him."

Alya went still, her dark eyes suddenly wary. "Are you with him willingly now?"

"It's not—it wasn't like that. I had to get out of Five, and Finn..." She searched for the words. "He wasn't ready, that's all."

After a moment, Alya nodded. "Maybe he wasn't. I didn't know him before he lost you, but the man I've seen these past few years isn't the man who showed up tonight. He's alive."

Trix shivered, chastised and reassured by the words all at once, and she found herself trying desperately to explain. "We were both fucked up. It wasn't—wasn't good. But if I had had a choice—" She swallowed hard. "Leaving hurt him, I know that. But staying would have hurt him worse."

"Shh, no." Alya abandoned the med kit and crossed the room. She gripped Trix's shoulders, her fingers warm and strong as she urged her to sit on the bed. "Girl, I've been there. I've been fucked up. I put Shipp through hell before I let him love me."

Love. They had to focus on staying alive right now, nothing else. "If we can make it home, I can show him things are different. But we have to get back to Four first."

"He doesn't care about a new world right now. He cares about you." Alya tilted Trix's chin up and smoothed her hair back. "But that doesn't make him your burden to carry. You can go back to Four and know we'll take care of him."

She nodded, even though it wasn't true. She couldn't leave without him, not because he was a burden or a responsibility, but because he was Finn.

5

THE STAIRS CREAKED under Finn's boots, but he didn't care if his hosts heard. Alya had dropped a stack of pillows and blankets on the couch downstairs before dragging Shipp to their bedroom, but the suggestion had remained unspoken. Since the woman was fully capable of parking her ass on the stairs with a shotgun and telling Finn to stay away from Trix, an unspoken suggestion damn near equaled permission.

He still knocked on the guestroom door, because *damn near* wasn't good enough, and only one person could make it okay. "Trix?"

Silence—until the lock clicked and she pulled open the door. "Come in."

He couldn't move. He couldn't do a damn thing but stare. The lights in the room were off, but firelight suited her. So did the nightgown Alya had dug up, something floaty that made her seem as insubstantial as a dream.

Maybe she was. Maybe he'd never wake up.

She gripped the edge of the door and stared back at him.

Touching her was wrong. She was clean from her bath, her skin soft and smooth under his fingers. A bruise stood out on her cheek, vivid even in the uncertain light, and his other hand clenched until his fingers ached. "You okay?"

Trix tilted her face to his touch. "I was waiting for you."

No, this wasn't a dream. He'd never be delusional enough to conjure up a world where she leaned into him. Wanted him. This was a stolen moment, cut off from the truths of both of their lives. A *might-have-been* or a *could-have-been*, and it would sting like a bitch when reality tore her away from him again.

Bad choices. His past was littered with them, so he made another one, sliding his hand to cup the back of her neck. Not a rough grip, but firm enough to guide her into the room as he edged one boot over the threshold.

She slipped her hands beneath his vest and clenched her fingers in his T-shirt. "Finn..."

Letting go of her would kill him, but he made himself ask. "Yeah?"

Her eyes locked with his. "Close the door."

He took another step, and this time she didn't move. Her body brushed his, so close her breath blew warm across his throat as he found the edge of the door with his heel and kicked it shut.

"I'm sorry." She was already tugging at his shirt, and she whispered the words again as the fabric pulled free of his pants.

She'd be touching skin any second, and his dick was past ready. He could lay her out, strip her bare, bury his face and his fingers between those lush thighs, and make her beg him for it. It wouldn't be the first time—hazy, drug-fueled memories assured him of that.

But it would be the first time either of them remembered clearly.

He caught her wrists, stilling her hands against his sides. "Why are you sorry?"

Trix froze, then a low laugh burst free. "You want to hear something stupid? I don't even know anymore."

Anger came out of nowhere, leaving him unbalanced. Raw. "Fuck that. You don't apologize to a single fucking person in Five, least of all me."

"Okay." She leaned in and pressed an openmouthed kiss to the side of his neck, short-circuiting his righteous anger with one brush of her tongue. "Okay."

He released her wrists and grabbed her waist instead, then gave in and slid his hands down, over that perfectly rounded, fucking *gorgeous* ass. Her body rubbed along his as he hoisted her, and her tits thrust against his chest, firm and pouting for his attention.

He'd give them plenty. Soon. If he ever got done with her lips.

He covered her mouth with a groan. She met the kiss eagerly, parting her lips beneath his with a low noise as she wound around him—her arms around his neck, her legs around his hips.

Even with the liquor burning through his veins, he could fuck her like this. Get his pants open, get beneath that nightgown, sink deep into her and lose himself. He'd made his body into a weapon after he lost her. Strong, hard. Unshakable. He could stand there and help her ride him, let the pleasure of it wash over him until she came.

It would be hot. And over too fucking soon.

So he kissed her and tightened his grip on her ass, rubbing her up and down, rocking her against his cock until she tore her mouth from his with a shuddering gasp.

Her eyes were glazed already, hazy and unfocused. This time, it was sheer pleasure at his touch, and knowing that drowned his lingering guilt in pure, primal satisfaction.

Fuck the drugs. He could make her feel good just like this.

"Look at me," he whispered, waiting until her sleepy eyes locked on his before grinding his hips into hers. "That's it. Feel it."

A little of the haze cleared, replaced by undeniable heat. She dug her nails into the base of his neck, beneath his collar, and picked up the rhythm, rocking with him.

He gritted his teeth against the pleasure, so much sharper with the kiss of pain. It was hot like this. Dangerous. A kidnapped O'Kane straddling his cock was stupidly self-destructive, even for him—but fuck.

What a way to go.

She moaned, and he pressed his forehead to hers. "Quietly, doll. I'm not sharing you with the whole damn farm. Bite me if you have to."

Trix rubbed her cheek over his, her mouth close to his ear. "You like that, don't you? Something just for you."

If you listened to the stories, the O'Kanes fucked each other on every available surface, in public and private. He'd never given the rumors much thought because he'd never cared, but now he had to imagine *her* there, her limbs tangled with another person's, her face alight with pleasure—

Jealousy wasn't nearly as hot. He tried to bite back a growl, but it rumbled free as he tightened his grip on her. "I never was good at sharing."

Her whimper turned into a sigh that teased over his skin. "You're the one I want, Finn."

It was more than he deserved, but he still took it. He took *her*, claiming her mouth again as he spun blindly and pressed her to the door.

She dug her teeth into his lower lip and arched her hips, harder than before. She was trembling, clutching at him for purchase as she shifted in his arms.

So close. So close to coming apart for him.

He braced her with one hand and slid the other up her body. She'd always had a nice rack, but her curves were killer now. He cupped one breast through her nightgown and worked her nipple with his thumb. "I can't wait to get my mouth right here."

"Finn—" She slipped her fingers into his hair and pulled—hard.

Pleasure raced down his spine, reminding him how long it had been since he'd had a woman's hands on him. "Tell me how to get you there, baby. Tell me what you need."

Her hand dropped to cover his, and she met his gaze as she dragged his fingers up to nestle around the base of her throat.

She felt fragile under his hand. She always had, but so much more like this, with her pulse fluttering wildly beneath his fingers. If he tightened them at all, he could cut off her air, leave her struggling to draw breath as he drove her toward release.

Mac Fleming had done it all the time. It had been one of his favorite games, and a surefire way for a junkie to get her hands on the good stuff. Sometimes he fucked her himself, sometimes he told someone else to, but it was always Mac's fingers around her throat, his whim to let her gasp in air or taunt her with the possibility that he might never let go.

It was hard to tell which ones genuinely liked it and which could fake anything for the drugs Mac gave them as a reward, but that had always been the ugly truth seething beneath the surface of Mac Fleming's sector. His men didn't force women. They didn't have to. Women ran to them with flattering eagerness—because most of them were hooked on the shit that had nearly killed Trix, and would do anything to keep the high rolling one more day.

So *willing* was a word that had lost meaning a long

time ago in Sector Five. The reminder should have killed Finn's hard-on, because his only high ground was that he'd never lied to himself about it. He'd known touching Trix was wrong, from start to finish.

The fact that it hadn't stopped him then should really stop him now.

But it didn't.

He rubbed his thumb up and down the side of her throat and met her gaze. "I'm not going to hurt you. Not even if you ask."

"I don't want you to." He felt her swallow beneath his hand. "I need to know that you could, but you won't. Not ever."

"Never again." He knew what she needed now. Bracing her weight, he caught one wrist and dragged it above her head, pinning her in place as he rolled his hips. "But I'll give you anything else. Anything."

She closed her eyes, and her breasts pushed against his chest as her breathing sped. A shudder wracked her, then another, and a moan vibrated up her throat. She bent her head and muffled it by closing her teeth on his wrist, but the sound broke through anyway—low and tortured, sharp and relieved.

Watching her come, her mind clouded by nothing more than pleasure, was the best fucking thing that had ever happened to him.

Anything.

Trix struggled for breath as she drifted down. It had nothing to do with the careful hand around her throat—and everything to do with it. His control was an illusion, betrayed by the fine tremor of his fingers. A seductive illusion, but not nearly as alluring as what lay past it.

He'd lost control before, and she knew what that felt like—intense, rough. Wild. What she didn't know was what would happen if he let go. If he relaxed his iron grip and set himself free.

But she could find out.

She opened her eyes. He was watching her, utterly focused, as if she couldn't feel his cock straining against her. "You come so pretty."

A fresh flash of hunger twisted in her belly, and she freed one hand to touch his mouth. "Are you going to watch me like this all night?"

He bit the tip of her finger. "Depends."

"On?"

His lips curved into the rarest thing of all—a lazy, warm smile. "How many more times you get off on riding my cock."

"Depends," she echoed, then arched off the wall to grind against him.

Groaning, he hoisted her away from the door and turned toward the bed. "Undress me."

Another thing that skated along the edge of familiarity. She had done all of these things before—undressed him, seduced him, come apart in his arms—but never with this sort of clarity. Everything before was like a dream, but this was solid, clear. Sharp as a blade.

She shoved his leather vest off his shoulders and dragged it with her when she slid to the bed. She reached for his shirt next, tugging at it as she came to her knees.

He stripped it over his head, revealing his chest. It was just as broad as she remembered, but leaner, his muscles cut in stark relief. Tattoos covered him from shoulder to shoulder, the familiar intricate shapes and flames bisected by new scars—scars that shouldn't have been there at all, especially on a man who worked for the leader of Sector Five. Med-gel might be a luxury for some, but it had been readily available on Fleming's compound.

She touched one pale, silvered line. "What happened to you?"

"Shit's been dangerous." He caught her hand, holding it to his skin. "The scars were to remind me of my place. Mac needed me alive. He didn't need me whole."

Her throat ached as she gently freed herself and caught his belt. "They're beautiful, like the rest of you."

He snorted roughly and ran his finger over a flower Ace had tattooed on one of her arms. "I'm as beat as my ink. And it was never all that pretty. Not like this."

"I didn't say pretty." His skin beckoned, and she kissed the flat of his stomach, just above his navel. "I said beautiful."

He shuddered. Her nightgown pulled tight against her arm as he fisted one hand in the fabric at her hip. "Take this off. Fuck, Trix, let me see you. All of you."

She was naked beneath it, and the fabric whispered over her skin like a caress as she lifted it over her head.

For one silent moment, Finn simply stared at her. His gaze swept over her, tracing from her face down to her knees and back up, so she smiled and wrapped her fingers around his belt again.

The worn leather was supple under her fingers, warm from his body, and goose bumps prickled up on her skin as she drew the belt free.

His hand dropped to her shoulder. Drifted. He grazed his knuckles along the line of her throat and down, the back of his hand brushing one breast. "This is a bad idea. You deserve sweet. Gentle."

He could be both, in his own way. "Other things, too. Hard and rough, if I want it."

"Do you?"

"Honestly?" She slipped the button on his pants free and drew her fingertip over the bulge straining his zipper. "There isn't much I don't want from you."

He hissed in a breath and froze with the back of his hand pressed against her stomach. "I told you, Trix. Anything. Name it, and I'll do it."

Metal clicked and rasped as she tugged at the zipper

pull, slowly parting the teeth. "Let me?"

That made him move. He shuddered and plunged both hands into her hair, tilting her head back as he loomed over her. "I said you could have anything. It doesn't have to be— You don't have to—"

"Shh." He'd never understood how touching him could bring her pleasure. Hypocritical, when she'd seen the same sort of satisfaction light his eyes at her moans and cries.

The thought of watching him shudder with more than anticipation sparked breathless need. She dragged at the heavy denim until she bared his cock—proud, hard, straining toward her with a hunger that gave lie to his denials.

She wrapped her hand around the base, gasping when he thrust into her touch with a groan, then slid lower on the bed. Lower, until she could draw her tongue in a slow circle around the head of his cock.

"*Trix.*" His fingertips pressed hard on her scalp, hands trembling with restraint. "Jesus Christ, woman."

She flicked her tongue against the spot beneath the crown, and his hips jerked in response.

He flexed his fingers, tugging lightly at her hair. "Look at me."

She closed her lips around the tip of his cock before tilting her head just enough to meet his gaze without pulling away. He stared down at her, every beautiful muscle tensed as he rubbed small circles on the back of her head.

His fingers tightened. Hardly at all, but enough to guide her head forward, and he watched her lips inch up his shaft with dark hunger.

It could have felt like a demand, but Trix could see the truth burning in his eyes. This was acquiescence, not force.

Surrender.

She shivered and took him deeper, moaning when

the movement yanked her hair taut in his grip. He bit off a curse and pulled harder, dragging her back. "Is this what you want? To suck me off?"

Yes. But that was too simple, not quite right, because what she really wanted was to give him everything he'd offered her. So she swallowed the answer and rose, shifting to her knees and stretching up to draw him into another kiss.

That trembling control inside him snapped.

He dropped his hands to her ass and hauled her up into a brutal, starving kiss. His teeth scraped her lower lip before closing in a harsh bite, taunting her with the vibration of his low growl. He hoisted her higher, off the bed entirely, only to bear her back down.

Her back thudded against the mattress and he pinned her there, his cock grinding between her legs, his hands tangling in her hair as he gripped the bed sheets and rocked. "Do you want this? Do you want me to fuck you?"

She arched beneath him, helpless to do anything but beg. "Please, Finn. No more waiting—"

He smothered her words with another tongue-tangling kiss. He hooked one hand under her thigh and lifted her leg, spreading it wide. "Tell me," he demanded as his shaft slicked between her pussy lips, working her clit with tormenting friction. "Tell me to fuck you."

"Fuck—" Another flex of his hips sent a shock of pleasure racing up her spine, cutting off her words. "Fuck me."

Every muscle in the arm next to her cheek flexed as he raised his body. He loomed above her, half of his face in shadow, half illuminated by the firelight.

He sought her gaze, held it. The fingers of his free hand brushed her pussy as he reached between them to grip his shaft. "Tell me how hard. Tell me how deep."

She whispered the only two words that came to mind, words that contradicted her pleas. "Tease me."

One smooth push and he was upright, standing above her with his hand still curled around his dick. "Roll over."

She obeyed, and it wasn't until she braced her elbows on the mattress that she caught sight of the mirror in the corner, across from the bed. "Finn..."

"Watch," he whispered, smoothing one hand over her hip.

He pushed against her, and she looked down in time to see the blunt head of his cock spread her pussy wide. The sensation slammed into her a split second later, and she whimpered as she tried to rock back, to take him deeper, faster.

He stilled her with one iron hand on her hip. "Not like that. Watch in the mirror."

She lifted her head, and her gaze clashed with his. She was vaguely aware of everything else reflected in the mirror—naked flesh and twisting ink, all gilded by firelight and darkened by shadow—but all she could really see was his face.

His eyes.

"Don't move." Quiet words, skating the edge of something wild. "I can't fuck you slow if you move."

She didn't *mean* to, but sheer quaking need made her clench around him.

In the mirror, she watched his eyes close and his lips part. His hips rolled, driving him deeper, and then he was over her, the hot skin of his chest pressed to her back, one strong hand under her chin, tilting her head. "Tell me to stop," he hissed against her ear, even as his body caged hers.

Never. She wrapped her fingers around his forearm, relishing the play of hard, tense muscle beneath his skin. He kept asking her what she wanted, telling her she could have anything—

"Give me this," she whispered.

He did.

His next thrust was hard, forcing her to feel every inch of him. He muffled her shocked cry with his hand over her mouth, and Trix's head swam, not because she couldn't breathe, but because she couldn't process the dichotomy of it all. How she could be caged but free, at the center of such a storm of need and yet still in control.

And she was. Even as he thrust into her again, twisting the tense pleasure in her belly with impossible speed, he watched her. Carefully, so carefully, and she knew that one hint of distress and he'd stop.

She clung to him instead.

His beard scratched her skin as he pressed his cheek to hers. "Touch yourself. Get yourself off on me."

Christ. She slid her hand from his arm, down over her throat, stopping to cup her breast. She met his gaze before pinching her fingers tight enough to hurt. The pain bowed her back, and she shuddered as the position tilted her hips for his next pounding advance.

She must have been so *numb* the last time he'd fucked her, cut off from everything. Surely she would have remembered this, the longing and lust. The ravenous look in his eyes as she dropped her hand lower to tease her clit.

Pleasure deepened, and Finn snarled his approval as her pussy clenched tight around him. "That's right, baby. Let me feel you."

I can't. The words came out unintelligible, muffled by his hand. It was overwhelming, far too fast. She was hurtling toward release, and she'd barely had a chance to savor the aching stretch of his cock inside her. It couldn't last, not like this, and the very thought broke her heart.

What if this was all they had?

She pulled her hand away.

Finn curled his fingers around the column of her neck, gentle but heavy. "Is this what you want?"

She opened her mouth to answer, but she could feel a wild cry building in her throat, so she sank her teeth into her lower lip to hold it back. When her gaze fell on the mirror, Finn was still watching her. Not her swaying breasts or the erotic sight of his cock plunging into her, but her face. Her eyes.

His hips flexed, driving him deeper. "Don't hold back from me. Don't fucking hold back."

He'd told her he wouldn't share her, not even her screams, and suddenly she felt it, too. This was a moment just for them. No one else had to understand or approve, as long as they knew.

He had to know. "I missed you so much," she rasped. "I wish—"

He smothered her regrets with another kiss, forcing her head up and back with one shaking hand on her chin. It was messy and raw, a tangle of tongues and teeth and low, animal noises, as he fucked her in short, rough strokes.

He held her like that, wrapped in his arms, grinding against her, as if he couldn't bear to pull away for even a moment. She could feel his heart pounding, thumping in time with hers, and Trix gave in. Finn had always stripped away her resistance, and never more than now, when he was all over her, touching her like he couldn't get enough. Like he could breathe *her* instead of oxygen, live forever on the panting moans he drank from her mouth.

She was an O'Kane. Getting off was easy, simple. This was more, her body drawing him in and holding him as the first pulses of orgasm wracked her, and the world dissolved in a white-hot rush of pleasure until there was nothing left but Finn.

And when he stiffened above her, surging deep with a final, guttural noise, there wasn't even him. Just *them*. Trix grabbed on to it like the stolen moment it was, digging her nails into Finn's rigid, trembling arms, willing time to stand still.

But it couldn't. Finn exhaled slowly and eased his

grip on her chin. "You okay?"

Not even close. "Yes."

His gaze clashed with hers in the mirror, and the lazy pleasure on his face faded. "Don't lie to me, Trix."

She lifted her hand to his cheek. "Not okay. Better."

He was still stiff. Wary. Hell, that edge in his eyes was damn close to fear. "You're good?"

How could she possibly explain? Here, like this, she finally understood how disconnected they'd been from each other before, and it terrified her. If being with him had felt like this, she wouldn't have had the strength to leave, to save her own life.

They'd both be dead.

"This is good," she told him instead. "I'm just...remembering."

He pressed a kiss to her palm before pulling away, straightening his pants as he rose. "Better makes sense, then."

She stretched out on the bed and rolled over to watch him. "You should hate me. I don't know why you don't."

Finn grunted. "I told you to cut that shit out."

"Why?" She swallowed hard. "It's how I feel."

He dropped to the edge of the mattress and bent down to unlace his boots, giving her a glimpse of the scars decorating his back. "Fleming gave you drugs, right? The good shit?"

"The best." Vial after vial of his own personal stash, the stuff they didn't even sell on the streets.

"You know what that means, right?"

"I'm not stupid," she snapped. There had always been only one reason Mac Fleming would summon a woman to his office. Only one reason he'd bend her over his desk and rape her, all the while daring her to cry.

Trix clenched her teeth. Of all the goddamn things in her life, that had to be the one memory that haunted her with crystal clarity—tears streaming out of her eyes to soak into the papers stacked on Fleming's desk, smearing the ink. *Knowing* he'd look at the blurred words later and be so very, very pleased with himself.

Finn's boot thumped to the floor. "I could never hate you for anything that got you away from him before he—" He ground out a low curse. "I'm glad you left. You could have put a bullet in me on your way out, and I'd be saying the same thing."

Before. Nausea roiled in the pit of her stomach. She'd left to save herself, but also to save Finn. If she'd gone back to him, he would have known the truth, and he'd have gotten himself killed. Better that he didn't know, even now that Fleming was dead. It would only hurt him.

"That's not what I meant," she said instead. "I should have found a way to let you know I was all right, that's all."

His other boot hit the hardwood floor, and he stretched out beside her. "And maybe Mac would have found you sooner if you had."

She curled into his arms. "Mac wasn't looking for me. He was looking for the woman who got Dom kicked out of Four."

"Fucking Dom." Tension tightened his body, but he stroked her arm gently. "I don't know what Beckett will do with him."

Nothing compared to what Dallas would do when he found out what had happened. "I'm spun, and I killed the mood. I'm sorry. When we get back to Four, I'll have my head on straight."

"Hey." He gripped her arm and waited until she met his eyes. "It's important, okay? That you get this in your head. I don't hate you. I could never hate you."

"I know." For her, he had risked his life to kill the most powerful man in his world. He'd say anything, do anything.

Forgive anything.

6

ENGINES BEFORE DAWN weren't unusual on Alya's farm.

Panicked shouts were.

Finn rolled from the bed, glad he'd kept his jeans on the night before. Behind him, Trix scrambled for the folded dress on the chair beside the bed. "An attack?"

"I don't think so. Not enough cars." He glanced out the window as he hauled on his boots, but the guest bedroom overlooked the backyard. "But Shipp said he was sending out a messenger."

"This early?"

He might have thought it would be easier to sneak by in the dark. Or he might have just wanted Finn and his baggage the hell away from the people under his protection. Finn couldn't blame him—but he'd fight him, if he had to. "You should stay here."

"You've got to be kidding." She smoothed the dress

into place down over her hips and reached for her ridiculous shoes. "No way. Not if there's trouble because of me."

He slipped on his shirt and stared at her, searching for any trace of the biddable, obedient Tracy he'd known.

An O'Kane stared back at him.

"Fine," he grumbled, hiding the smile that tugged at his lips. She'd complicate shit, but it was hard not to love the new spark of life in her. "Let's go."

Downstairs was sheer chaos. Someone had left the front door wide open as people rushed around in the kitchen, and Finn realized why when Shipp and Hawk hurried up the porch steps, carrying a bloodied man between them.

Shipp's jaw was set, hard and angry. "Big John," he grated out. "He took a bullet on the run to Four."

Dishes shattered to the floor as Alya swiped everything off the table. "What about Slider?"

Hawk shook his head in stony silence.

Numbness descended over Finn as he watched Alya cut away Big John's shirt. The man was one of Shipp's oldest friends, a smart, no-bullshit driver with quick reflexes and a lead foot. And Slider had been young. Cocky but skilled, with a whole damn life ahead of him, a life he'd just lost because Finn had called in a debt.

Shipp turned, avoiding his gaze. "They ran almost all the way out to the mountains. Beckett's men must have the whole border covered."

Finn had been prepared for a chase, but Beckett's resources were limited. If he had his men patrolling the line that far past the edge of the sectors, it meant he had a very specific priority—keeping Finn away from Dallas O'Kane. "Did they try to follow your men back?"

"They tried," Shipp confirmed grimly. "They failed."

And it had cost Shipp. One man this morning, maybe another by the end of the day. A decent man—a *friend*—would forgive the debt. A life lost for a life saved was already too much to demand.

Finn couldn't be a decent man. Not until Trix was safe.

A groan of pain rose from the table behind him, and Shipp flinched. "It won't be safe to try again until tonight. Hawk can head the—"

"No." Trix stood in the doorway, her hands clenched in fists at her sides.

Finn ignored the pain in her voice and the pain in his chest. Harder to ignore was Alya's stricken look, but he locked down everything but the goal. "We have to get you back, Trix."

"Not like this," she argued. "It isn't right."

Yeah, she was an O'Kane now. Someone who had the luxury of worrying about *right*. "You have a better idea, doll?"

She stared at Big John for one endless moment, then shrugged helplessly. "No, but I can't sit here while Shipp's men are risking their lives. While they're dying. We should be taking that risk, too."

She was an O'Kane, so he bit back his knee-jerk denial. Trying to break her through to Sector Four was a risk, but nothing in her life there would be safe, either. Not with Beckett staring across the sector line at Dallas O'Kane. War was coming for her family as surely as it was coming for Finn.

"We could go the other way," he whispered. "Drive west and keep going until we hit the ocean."

Trix gazed up at him, shaking her head so gently that he knew she wasn't even aware she was doing it. "I have to go home, Finn, not run away."

The words shoved him past numb, straight into frozen. It stung. Fuck, it burned, without the comfort of heat. She had always been the closest thing he'd had to home. What a sick fucking delusion—one she didn't share.

"Okay," he said, forming the word with stiff lips.

"Then we'll get you home."

"No, you don't—" She reached for him, wrapping her hands as far as they would go around his upper arms. "I want you with me."

"I know."

"Do you?"

He did, that was the hell of it. Trix wanted to drag him home like a stray dog, oblivious to the fact that he'd already bitten plenty of the people in her life. She'd do it, too, because she wanted him in her life.

He wanted to *be* her life.

Fucking sick, for real. "I get it, Trix. Just...one thing at a time, right? First we get out of Shipp's hair."

The man scrubbed his hands over his face, leaving streaks of sticky, drying blood behind. "Hawk can take you. I'll have some of the other guys ride out, draw them away from you. Give you your best chance."

Trix pressed trembling fingers to her lips. "Thank you. And I'm sorry."

Shipp's voice grew hoarse. "We all are, honey."

Everyone except Finn.

Hawk drove like a crazy man.

He stared straight ahead, his hands clenched on the wheel, and Trix had to shake away the sick suspicion that he was looking *at* the windshield, not through it.

She gripped the back of the front seat and leaned up as Finn double-checked a handgun. "I want one, too," she told him.

To his credit, he only hesitated a moment before handing her his. "If something happens, try to cover Hawk. I don't want to crash."

"Not planning on it," Hawk murmured. "But if something happens, you'd both best hold the fuck on."

"I know how to handle a firearm." It wasn't something Trix could ever have learned in Five, but with Lex, lessons were mandatory. "I learned from an ex-Eden sniper."

Finn lifted a second gun and glanced back at her. "Donnelly?"

"Yeah. You've run into him?"

"More like he ran into me. When Lex killed that councilman in Five."

Trix froze. No one had ever mentioned it to her, not even Jade, who had been at the center of it all. She was the one being abused and drugged, the one Lex had killed to save.

Then again, why would they tell her? No one knew anything beyond where she'd come from and the fact that she'd been a junkie herself. She'd never breathed Finn's name to a soul in Sector Four.

"Oh," was all she could think to say.

He studied her face warily. "You didn't know."

The scrutiny left her feeling like she'd fucked up somehow. "I wasn't a member then. They didn't exactly invite me to discuss what happened."

"Dallas O'Kane almost killed me." Finn turned to face forward. "But we struck a deal. I framed the leader of Sector Two for the murder. He let me live."

A sudden turn nearly pitched her against the door, but it didn't rock her as hard as his words. "Why?"

"Why'd I frame her?" He bit off a dark laugh. "So she and Mac would stop playing nice. So I wouldn't have to drug any more of her girls."

A chill shook her, and she let go of the seat to rub her hands over her upper arms. "I didn't know it was you."

"Yeah." He braced an arm against the window as the car careened again, and she barely heard his question over the roar of the engine. "Did the last girl make it?"

"Jade," she supplied. "Her name is Jade. She just took her ink."

"Yeah? Maybe O'Kane's good at pulling off miracles, after all."

"No, just more lies," Trix countered. "The biggest one Mac ever told. Getting clean doesn't kill people." It only made them wish they were dead sometimes, especially in the most stinging, desperate throes of withdrawal.

Finn stared ahead in silence, his jaw clenched. He had to be thinking about those days in his cabin, when he'd endured everything from her crying to her angry, accusatory screams, all with stone-faced acceptance.

It was what came after that he hadn't been able to handle—the uncontrollable shaking, the hallucinations. The crying and screaming of an entirely different sort.

She had to say something. "You tried—" A distant rumble cut off her words. At first she thought it was thunder—

But then Hawk swore under his breath. "Shit." He looked out at a dust cloud rising in the distance to their left. "At least two. This'll get ugly."

Trix tightened her fingers around the gun in her hand and tried to recall what Bren had told her about shootouts. Precious little of it had had to do with moving vehicles, but she remembered his admonition to aim for windows instead of tires.

The engine revved, and the car shot forward. "Hang on," Hawk ordered.

Her heart pounded as the dust clouds resolved into two distinct trails, coming in fast and hard.

Hawk's hands flexed on the wheel as he angled the car to the right, skimming past their pursuers as gunfire echoed over the roar of the engines. Metal dinged, and Trix had only a moment to realize they were bullets before the back windshield shattered above her head.

"Get *down*," Finn roared as the car lurched again. He turned as if to shoot out the back windshield, but Hawk made a sharp turn, slamming them both against the side of the vehicle. The shiny black car behind them skidded, trying to follow, gravel and dirt pinging skyward in a huge cloud as the wheels lost traction.

The car behind flipped in a cacophony of crunching metal and shattering glass. Hawk let out a short whoop, but his satisfaction died when the second car sped out of the dust, quickly closing the distance between them.

"Can you get a shot off on this motherfucker?" he asked tersely.

Finn rolled down his window and twisted to lean out, ignoring the wind whipping at his hair and clothes. Gunfire erupted behind Trix, and she ducked down in the seat. She wanted to drag Finn back in along with her, but he only grunted when Hawk swerved again, then returned fire.

She leaned up and caught a glimpse of the passenger and back seats loaded with armed gunmen. There were too many of Beckett's men pursuing them for them to win a firefight—

—which meant Hawk had to outmaneuver them.

"I thought you were a bunch of gearheads," she muttered. "Fucking *drive*."

Hawk grunted. "Finn?"

"Yeah?"

"Grab the wheel."

Finn lunged back into the car and seized the steering wheel. Hawk reached down into the front floorboard and hauled up a massive weapon, something that looked like a two-foot metal tube with handles fused to the sides. He slid a smaller canister inside it, casting a glance her way.

"Keep your head down," was all he said before swinging out the window and lifting the tube to rest on his shoulder.

It looked like the kind of thing that would be loud, but it fired with little more than a whistle. Trix uncovered her ears and peered through the ruined window in time to see the projectile make contact with the second car.

It *exploded*, raining fire and shrapnel on the desert.

Finn bit off a curse and gripped the wheel until his knuckles stood out, stark and white. "You're a crazy motherfucker."

"I know." Hawk slid back into the car and reclaimed both the gas pedal and the wheel.

But the relative peace of the moment fractured with a grinding slam as a third car sideswiped them and sent Hawk's car spinning. The gun flew out of Trix's hand, and she scrambled for it as the car whirled in dizzying circles.

Shots fired, and the window above her head exploded. Glass rained down on her as Finn swore again. The car shuddered through another impact, metal screeching against metal.

Trix lifted her head. The other car was close, close enough to reach out and touch. Instead, she raised her weapon and fired off a shot at the driver. It found its mark, snapping his head to one side as the car careened out of control. It went reeling, scraping in two full revolutions through the dirt before crashing into a boulder.

Hawk straightened the car and met Trix's gaze in the rearview mirror briefly before altering their course, cutting slightly back toward where Eden rose in the distance, its tallest towers reflecting the light above its pristine walls. "We're almost to the border."

Trix released the breath she'd been holding, but it came out on a sob. "Good." Her gun hit the seat with a thump, and she rubbed her shaking hands over her face. "Maybe we can—"

The sound of engines rose again, sending her heart lurching painfully into her throat. But these were motorcycles, not cars, sunlight glinting off chrome as they formed a line between Hawk's car and the edge of Sector Four.

Hawk tensed, easing off the gas as they coasted toward the wide, pitted road that marked the official boundary between sectors. "Friend or foe?"

"I—I don't..." Then one of the riders pulled off his helmet, and her heart dropped out of her throat and into her stomach. "Mad."

The car hadn't even stopped when she pushed at the back door. It swung open with an angry creak, dented and hanging from its hinges, but Trix ignored it, ignored everything as she tumbled out and ran toward the line of bikes.

Mad met her halfway, catching her against his chest in a rough hug. "Hey, sweetheart," he murmured, turning them to put his body between her and Hawk's car. "I got you. You're home now."

She clung to him, desperate to ground herself against the adrenaline-fueled rush of relief. "We ran, but Beckett—Jesus, I didn't know if we'd make it—" Her voice broke, and she shook her head and kept babbling. "And oh my *God*, Zan. Tell me he's okay. Please."

"Zan's okay," he said quietly, edging her toward the bikes. "Beckett lifted the embargo, and Dallas's regen tech got there in time."

The words sent a chill up her spine, and she jerked back. "Beckett tried to *kill* us."

Gravel crunched behind them, and Mad spun, drawing his gun so fast Hawk froze mid-step, slowly holding both hands out to his side. "I just gave the lady a ride."

"Stop it." Trix pushed at Mad's arm, driving the barrel of the gun toward the ground. "He helped us get here, me and Finn." She gestured toward the car, but Finn was still sitting in the passenger seat, the door ajar—

His face deathly pale.

He met her eyes and worked for a smile. He shoved the door wide and climbed out of the car only to crumple to his knees, and the last thing she saw before he hit the ground was the blood blooming across the front of his shirt.

doc

THE FIRST THING Dr. Dylan Jordan did was fill a syringe with enough potassium chloride to stop a fucking elephant's heart.

He didn't use it, but it was there, within easy grasp, and its mere presence made him feel better about digging a bullet out of a man he'd much rather kill.

"Why are we saving him?"

Adrian Maddox could move silently when he wanted to, that much was certain. Dylan tilted his head without looking up. "Because he brought Trix back."

Mad eased the door shut and crossed to the opposite side of the bed. "How do we know he didn't take her in the first place?"

"You saw her," Dylan answered absently as he reached for a pair of forceps. "Did she look like a woman who was scared of him?"

"No." It came out grudgingly, and Mad crouched

down to put himself on eye level with Dylan. "But we both know that doesn't prove a damn thing. Just means it'll hurt more when he betrays her."

Such a clever, beautiful, *vengeful* man. "Someone else might buy that...but I'm not someone else," he murmured. "You and I both know what this is really about."

Of course Mad denied it. He would always deny it, because he wanted to be the sainted hero. "It's about him posing a danger to the gang. It's about the people he could hurt."

It was about Jade, pure and simple, and the fact that Finn had been the one to hand her the drugs that had nearly killed her. Dylan embraced the knowledge, because owning it was the one thing that could keep him from lunging for that deadly syringe.

"Say we let him die," he mused aloud. "What then?"

Mad's gaze held a new edge, a darkness that had been there since the night he'd wound up trapped in that cave-in. "Then the people we care about are safer."

"Are they, Adrian? Or would it just make you feel *good*?"

"They're safer," Mad insisted, but after another heartbeat he squeezed his eyes shut with a whispered curse. "And I want him dead. I want him dead before he has a chance to hurt Trix. I want him dead before Jade has to look at him and remember what happened to her every time he drugged her. I want him dead."

Satisfied, Dylan confessed, "So do I."

"Then *why*?" Mad rose abruptly and paced away. "Why save him?"

The answer was simple, visceral. All-consuming. "Control."

"Control? Of what?"

"Of myself." Dylan stripped off his gloves and picked up the syringe. "Potassium chloride. A high enough dose causes hyperkalemia. It disrupts cardiac muscle function, resulting in fatal arrhythmia. I'm told it burns like a motherfucker going in, too. Real bad way to go." He set it down again, closer than before. "I have it here to remind myself—I could use it, but I won't. Control."

Mad's gaze locked on the syringe, his brow furrowing. "You already had the needle ready."

Dylan allowed himself a small smile. "It isn't much of a test of my self-control otherwise, is it?"

"No." Mad resumed his pacing, prowling like a wild creature trapped in a too-small pen. "You care. I wasn't sure before, but you wouldn't be this pissed if you didn't...care."

He cared too much. It had dragged him to the very edge of darkness, left him staring into an abyss so deep and hopeless that sometimes he thought death was the only escape. But he couldn't seem to stop, so he'd embraced that, too.

Control.

He put on a fresh pair of gloves and nudged the box toward Mad. "Help me dig this goddamn bullet out of him, and we'll continue the conversation over drinks. O'Kane's best, perhaps? I think he owes me."

Mad caught his wrist, strong fingers burning against his skin. "And if he gets out of that bed and hurts the people we care about?"

"Then we'll deal with it." He kept his voice low, a soothing, secret whisper just for Mad. "Trust me."

"Okay." Mad's thumb slid in a slow circle, the calloused pad scraping the inside of Dylan's wrist. "I do. I have. You know that."

The tiny touch sparked more than heat—warmth, curling low and spreading up to make his chest ache. Mad had always been tough, tough enough to survive, but there was a vulnerability in him, as well. Nothing as prosaic and delicate as fragility, but an openness. Holes in his armor, places where things touched him so deeply they could shatter him from the inside out.

Dylan almost shuddered, but he locked it down—just like everything else. "Put on the gloves and help me," he said quietly. "Then we'll go get that drink."

7

IT TOOK TRIX less than five minutes to learn what a treacherous, lying bastard Logan Beckett really was.

She stared at Dallas, dumbfounded. "He told you *what*?"

Dallas leaned back in his chair, the sprawling, easy posture belying the tension in his dark eyes. "That your friend out there got real pissed when he realized Fleming wasn't planning to hand you over to him, so he put a bullet in his boss's head and kidnapped you himself."

It was just close enough to the truth to be not only plausible but probable. But she knew better. "Finn didn't have anything to do with it. Fucking Beckett."

"So who killed Fleming. Beckett?"

"No, he—" She dragged her hands through her hair with a frustrated groan. Nothing she said came out right, and it was all because Dallas didn't know what had happened before, years ago, when she'd lived in Five.

When she and Finn—

She drew in a deep breath. "Finn shot Fleming, that much is true. But none of the rest of it makes sense unless I start at the beginning."

Dallas reached for a cigarette and took his time lighting the tip. It flared brightly as he snapped the lighter shut and studied her. "Lex knows some of it. When we brought Jade back, she told me you'd been hooked on the same shit and had survived. But I imagine she doesn't know who gave it to you, or she wouldn't have let Finn walk away in one piece."

"No." She had to swallow past the lump in her throat. "That was one thing Finn always kept me away from. Someone else gave it to me first, and then he didn't exactly have a choice."

The harsh edge of his expression softened, just a little. "So tell me the story, darling. From the beginning."

The beginning. She'd suggested it, and she realized with a start that she didn't even know what that meant. When she'd first met Finn? Or when she'd first set foot on that collision course?

She took another deep breath. "Things in Five are different. Messy. If you don't have a factory job to inherit, you're shit out of luck when it comes to earning straight. And women don't have a lot of options either way. So if you're young and pretty, you party with the dealers. Hope one of them likes you well enough to take you home, make you his girl."

Dallas's scowl returned. "Yeah. I've seen their kinds of parties."

The girls all gave themselves different names, considered themselves different things—girlfriend, mistress. Wife. But it all boiled down to one thing, a transaction older than any other industry in Mac Fleming's sad little sector.

"It's a peculiar kind of prostitution," she whispered. "They consider it uncivilized, trading sex for money. So the men in Five find other ways to pay their whores. They buy them clothes, a place to live. Give them drugs. It's how things are done."

"It's shit," Dallas said, voice quiet but vicious. "Civilized is giving a woman something she can spend. Something she can own. Anything else is about fear and control."

A laugh bubbled up, and Trix pressed the heel of her hand to her mouth to hold it back. "No kidding."

"So, Finn. What did he give you?"

A drink and a smile, the first bit of his grudging attention. Everyone knew about Finn, that he didn't keep women, but his interest kept the worst of the predators at bay.

And then it had turned into something more.

She steeled her spine. "What do you want to hear, Dallas? That he drugged me? That he made me fuck him for my next fix? He did and he *didn't*, because none of it was that simple."

"I just want to hear the truth, Trix." He stubbed his barely touched cigarette out in the ashtray and leaned forward. "Especially the ugly parts. Because lying won't protect him, love. There're a few dozen O'Kanes out there who will take him apart and put him back together inside out if they think he'll hurt you."

"I know." She looked away. "Once I was addicted, it was like things spiraled out of control. Finn tried to get me clean, but it didn't take. And then I caught Mac's eye. So I left, and everyone in Five thought I was dead. Even Mac." She couldn't sit still anymore, so she rose out of her chair and crossed her arms over her chest. "Don't you get it? It was Dom. He convinced Mac to send his men after me, some sort of sick revenge thing."

She'd seen death in Dallas O'Kane's eyes before, and it was there as he rolled out of his chair to brace both hands on the desk. "Fleming kidnapped you for *Dom*?"

"He was after Trix," she confirmed, "but he got Tracy. And he couldn't wait to shove that in Finn's face."

"So Finn shot him."

The memory—the relief and revulsion, all at once—made her shudder. "Yeah."

Sighing, Dallas pushed himself upright. "I believe you, darling. A hell of a lot more than I believe a word out of Beckett's mouth. But Finn..."

She dug her fingernails into her skin to suppress another shudder. "He's done everything he could do, Dallas, and it almost got him killed. Don't you think he deserves a chance?"

Dallas reached for her, covered her hands with his own. They were warm, strong—and as tough as his words. "He's been the monster chained in Fleming's basement for twenty years. If I give him a chance, will he know what to do with it?"

She *wanted* to say yes. She even opened her mouth, but the bleak memory of the hopelessness in Finn's eyes stopped her cold. Despair was no different than drugs or booze or gambling—it could become a habit, just as easily as anything else.

"Maybe not," she admitted hoarsely. "But what kind of people would we be if we didn't try?"

Dallas didn't answer. He circled his desk and drew her into a tight hug, with one big hand cradling the back of her neck and his chin resting on her head. "I'll figure something out, love. I fucked up by underestimating how much danger you were in, and he fixed it. We all owe him for that."

"It's not just that." She tilted her head back to meet his eyes. "Finn can't stand what goes on in Five. He lived there and worked there, but he *hated* it all so much."

"Good. My gratitude gets him in the door, but the rest he'll have to earn." He caught her chin, his gaze serious. "You know what that means, right?"

All the new guys had to deal with a little hazing, even the ones who'd come in under the best of circumstances. Finn would have it worse. "I understand."

And she did. No, the part that left her blinking back tears was how much Finn would relish the abuse, all because he thought he deserved it.

Finn hadn't expected to wake up.

For a few disorienting seconds, the only thing he could muster was disappointment. He'd hit the dirt with his last glimpse of Trix etched into his brain—her standing behind Adrian Maddox, protected as the man burned with a righteous fury more suited to Eden's deity than the benevolent God they worshiped in Sector One.

As last images went, it wasn't the worst. His girl safe, his mission complete. Dying was the coward's way out of the mess he'd made, but fuck if he wasn't *tired*.

And sore, too. Sore enough that even opening his eyes seemed like too much effort. But he did it anyway, and disappointment shattered as Trix's face swam into view.

Trix, at his bedside. Thank fucking *Christ* he'd woken up.

Her lips tilted in a gentle, brilliant smile as she tugged his hand up to the soft curve of her cheek. "Hi."

"Hey." Funny, how things didn't hurt as much now. The magic of touching her. "I guess you rescued me, huh?"

"Yeah?" She turned her head to press a quick kiss to his palm. "Now we're even."

Not even close. Not in a million years. But he wasn't ready to lose the brightness of that smile, so he didn't argue. "What happened after I passed out? Is Hawk okay?"

"He's fine. Dallas and Lex are gonna put him up while they figure out this whole mess."

"And me?"

A little of the light in her eyes dimmed. "You can stay. No one's jumping for joy about it, though. But you knew that was coming."

He'd known. He just hadn't realized how much it would sting. Not the disdain of the O'Kanes—anything short of putting him in the ground was the next best thing to an open-armed welcome—but watching her joy fizzle.

Trix still saw something shiny and new underneath the grime of Finn's life, and he didn't know if he wanted to shake her until her vision cleared or wrap both arms around her and never let go.

Not that he had the energy to do either right now.

"It's okay," he whispered roughly, contenting himself with rubbing his fingers over her cheek. "No one's gonna hurt my feelings, doll. They can't say anything I haven't heard before."

"I don't have to like it." Her lips pressed into a thin line, and she sighed. "And you don't have to stay for me. Soon it'll be safe enough for you to go back to—"

He rested his thumb against her mouth, silencing the offer. "If I stay, it'll be for you. If I go, that'll be for you, too. There's no *back* for me."

Her lips trembled under his touch. "It won't be easy."

Finn smiled and stroked his thumb along the sweet, full curve of her lower lip. He knew what it tasted like now. He knew how she moaned when he caught it between his teeth, how she melted when he growled against it. "Some things are worth it."

"They're all afraid you'll hurt me."

He couldn't blame them. He *had* hurt her—by mistake, with neglect, by being too fucked up to do the right thing. "I only care what you think."

For a moment, she only stared at him as a wave of sadness swept over her features. "I think...I'm not ready to let you go."

"Then I'm not going anywhere."

She kissed him again, this time a soft, quick caress at the corner of his mouth. Even an aching body couldn't keep him from driving his fingers into her hair and pulling her back for another kiss. Slower. Deeper. No teeth, no tongue, just his mouth on hers, and all the time in the world to memorize the way she felt.

She shivered, then gingerly braced her hand on his shoulder and pushed away. "You scared the hell out of me. Are you okay?"

"I'm still breathing." He lifted a hand to the bandage wrapped around his torso. "Everything hurts, but not nearly as much as it should."

"Doc patched you up." She stroked her fingers over his shoulder, over bare skin instead of gauze. "He says you're gonna be fine."

He'd met their doctor once. He'd been there when O'Kane had come for Lex, redefining *high on his own supply*. Finn knew an addict when he saw one, and he'd bet his last credit that Doc spent most of his time tripping higher than Eden's walls.

Finn wasn't just glad he'd woken up. He was apparently lucky, too. "Don't suppose he left me something to wear."

"Not hardly. His clothes wouldn't fit you, anyway. But I sweet-talked Flash into letting you borrow some things." She turned to a small table by the bed and lifted a stack of folded items.

Yeah, everything ached, but that had never kept him down before. So he shoved the sheet to his waist and swung his legs over the edge of the bed, ignoring the dizzy tilt of the room and the burn blooming in his chest. "Does O'Kane want me staying put?"

"Hey, hey." Trix dropped the clothes and caught him by the shoulders, steadying him. "Take it easy, all right?"

He bit back his instinctive protest—*I can't.* Weakness was alive inside him, and it was hard as hell to tolerate. Here, surrounded by her friends who wanted to be his enemies. He needed to be strong enough to weather the abuse headed his way, and that meant shoring up his vulnerable spots. "I promise I will. Just point me to a bathroom."

"No. You're going to hurt yourself even worse."

Adding pain to the list of things he was ignoring, Finn reached for her. Closed his fingers around her waist and jerked her off her feet, into his lap. She landed straddling his thighs, one knee pressed to the mattress, and Finn curled one hand around the back of her head. "I know from bullet wounds, doll. Soft bed. Med-gel. Compared to the last few times I got shot up, this is a goddamn dream."

She framed his face between her hands with a wry laugh. "Is that supposed to reassure me?"

"Only about my ability to put my own damn pants on. Unless you're trying to distract me..." He flexed his fingers on her waist and in her hair, savoring the feel of her beneath his hands.

Being distracted wasn't so bad. The real world stood beyond that door, but here, like this, they were still living in his dream. The one where he'd fucked her slow and deep and then quick and hard, watching honest-to-God pleasure paint her features. Nothing vague or lost or distant, not anymore.

Staying naked and vulnerable was worth a few more moments of playing pretend.

Her gaze fixed on his mouth. "Maybe I'm still scared."

"Don't be." He slid his hand up and spread his fingers wide between her shoulder blades. "You're home. Safe. And I'm hard to kill."

"Not that." She leaned closer, resting her forehead against his. "I want you to love it here like I do. I don't know what I'll do if you don't."

Even if he could—even if he *did*—it wasn't likely the O'Kanes would ever love him the way they loved her.

Truth, maybe, but it wouldn't soothe the tension stiffening her body. So he stroked her spine and lowered his voice to a rough whisper. "Show me. Show me the things you love."

"Really?"

Not quite enough of an edge to qualify as disbelief, but Trix was wary—and he was glad. Blind trust was too much damn responsibility for him right now. Too much guilt, because fuck if he could stop stroking her, stop touching her. "Really, baby. If anyone can make me a believer, it's you."

She closed her eyes and exhaled. For a moment, he thought she'd close the distance and kiss him. But then she straightened—and grinned. "You've never seen me dance."

He fought the urge to tighten his grip on her, to choke back the dark thread of possessiveness unwinding in his gut. "Dancing, huh? I've heard stories about the Broken Circle's style of dancing."

"Mmm." She slipped her fingers into his hair. "I've got my own style."

She always had. Even now, in her sassy little polka-dot dress and whatever the hell she had on underneath it. Miles and miles of some sheer, crinkly fabric the same color as those polka dots, and the sweet primness of it made that knowing look in her eyes so much more dangerous.

He skated a hand down to her bare knee. "I like your style."

The look she flashed him was stern, but he still heard the catch in her breath. "I meant my act. It's all feathers and fans. Old-school striptease."

He tried to picture it, but with the softness of her skin under his fingertips, all he could think about was working his hand higher. He brushed his thumb along the inside of her knee just to hear her breath catch again. "You trying to make me jealous?"

"Oh, I could make you jealous." She tilted forward, rocking toward his hand. "Noelle and Rachel have been talking about putting together a show. Blonde, brunette, and redhead—and a whole lot of skin." Her fingers clenched in his hair. "Is that the kind of dancing you've heard about?"

His brain spun, trying to match the names to faces. His mental dossier covered most of O'Kane's men, but other than Lex, the women were a mystery. Though fuck, hadn't the councilman's daughter who'd ended up with O'Kane had an *N* name? There'd been a video of her going around for a while, all brown hair and pale skin and screaming her way to messy, gleeful orgasms—usually with Lex's face between her thighs.

He imagined Trix in her place and damn near groaned. Jealousy and arousal—a more potent cocktail than anything Mac Fleming had ever bottled. "I didn't think you liked girls."

"That depends on the situation," she murmured wickedly. "Almost everything naked does."

Growling, he slipped his thumb higher, brushing her inner thigh. "Congratulations, doll. I'm jealous."

"Bullshit. You're curious." Her breathing sped up. "But you'll figure it out. It's fun, and it feels good, but it doesn't mean I want you less."

That made him smile as he stroked the edge of her panties. "How much do you want me?"

"A lot." Trix kissed his forehead and slid off his lap. "And I'm going to show you. I promise."

Half the sheet went with her, slipping to the floor. Finn refused to lunge for it, even if it bared all of his scars—and the prominent hard-on that was well on its way to aching as much as the rest of him. "Does that mean I can get dressed?"

At first, she kept her eyes locked on his face. Then, as if she couldn't help herself, her gaze drifted down, and she licked her lips.

He bit back a groan, but he couldn't stop the mental image—that tongue, gliding over his cock. Those lips parting wide as he pushed between them, savoring the slickness, the heat, the *sight* of her sucking him off, as eager and hungry as he was.

Watching her face, he wrapped a hand around his shaft and pumped once, slowly. "Or I could stay like this."

She gasped, her chest rising with her sudden, in-drawn breath, her breasts pushing against the low-cut bodice of that damned dress.

Something wild slid through his veins, sweeping away exhaustion and discomfort. The sounds she made were better than adrenaline. Better than any drug Mac Fleming had ever created.

And suddenly they weren't enough. "Come here, Trix."

She was shaking her head even as she stepped forward. "You're injured."

He grabbed her flouncy skirt and used it to draw her in, close enough to get his other hand under all those layers of ruffled fabric. He caressed the outside of her thigh and savored another hitching breath. That was what he wanted, what he *needed.* More of those noises. "You're not."

She closed her eyes and swayed toward him. "Tease."

He hooked a finger under the edge of her panties. "Take these off, and you'll find out if I'm teasing."

Trix shivered and reached beneath her skirt, her hand brushing his. "You always used to tease me. That's one thing I do remember."

It had never been meant as a tease. More like an offering, a way to assuage his guilt every time she climbed into his lap and he didn't push her away. *It's not so bad if it's all about her,* he'd tell himself, knocking her hands away from his belt and sliding his own beneath her clothing. Paper-thin rationalizations that shredded with her first moan.

As if getting her off could ever be penance.

"It's not a tease if you follow through," he said, already dragging the fabric off her hip. "Eventually."

She braced her hands on his shoulders and breathed a sound that was half moan, half strangled sigh. "Not fast enough."

Another day or two and he'd have the stamina to take her fast and hard. The twinge of soreness in his muscles as he guided her panties down her legs was a reminder that tonight was about slow. Careful.

Thorough.

The dainty fabric fell to the floor, and Finn used one foot to urge her stance even wider. "You look so proper in this get-up. So sweet."

"Is that good or bad?" she asked, innocence edged with something a little wicked, because she already knew the answer.

Or she thought she did.

He had never let her see all the dark places his mind wandered. Or the twisted, beautiful, fucked-up shit that got him hard. "It's bad," he whispered, brushing the backs of his fingers over her pussy. "It makes me think bad things."

Her nails dug into his shoulders. "Like what?"

Like bending her over his lap, flipping that ridiculous skirt up over her back, and spanking her until she writhed her way to orgasm against his leg. Like dragging the scoop neck of her bodice down until her breasts spilled free and fucking her like that, disheveled and half-clothed, debauched perfection.

Her pussy lips were bare. Smooth. He parted them and slid one finger over her, relishing the slick glide. She was already wet for him, already eager. Not afraid, not even a little. "How many of those stories they tell about the O'Kanes are true? Ropes and chains and people on their knees, sweet and submissive?"

She shuddered, her hips bucking against his hand. "All of them, and more that no one ever hears."

The prick of her nails was all the encouragement he needed. He pumped one finger into her, shuddering as she clenched tight around it. "Do you know why I teased you, Trix?"

"Because—" Her voice broke on a whimper. "Because you wanted to make me crazy."

Because only a sick motherfucker made demands on a woman when her life depended on him giving her another fix. "You couldn't say *no* before. But you can now."

She looked at him, her gaze slowly sharpening as she focused on his face. "Oh."

"Yeah." He cupped her ass and dragged her closer. "That's how selfish I am. It's not enough to watch you ride my dick. I want you to love it. Need it. Choose it."

"Shh." Her fingers skipped up his neck to thread through his hair. "I understand. You don't ever have to worry about that, not anymore."

Because the minute he pissed her off, her friends would tear him to pieces. It was fucked up to find that soothing, but Finn was past caring. He hauled her astride his lap, her slick pussy rubbing along the length of his shaft as he rocked their hips together. "Then do it. Ride me."

"You're still hurt—"

He slapped the curve of her ass with a growl. "I said *ride me*."

Then she said it, the one thing he needed more than her pleasure. Clear, firm, fingers still stroking through his hair. "No."

There it was, that defiant spark that was all Trix. Tracy had never had it—or, if she had, it had been ground out of her by the time she'd rolled into Finn's life. But Trix wouldn't fall obediently to her knees. He'd have to coax her there. Put her there. If she stayed, he'd know she was as hot for it as he was.

Fuck, if she stayed, he'd never be able to leave.

Finn was hard, ready. Trix shifted slightly, and a bolt of undeniable pleasure raced through her as the movement ground the base of his cock against her clit.

Easy, so easy. All she had to do was move again, slide up, position her body to take his, and let instinct do the rest.

But she wanted more than easy now, more than the simple, effortless drift. She wanted to be strong, to be *Trix.* To show him what that meant.

So she kissed him instead.

He groaned against her mouth, his fingertips digging into her hips. So impatient, but he didn't lift her, didn't force her to give in. Instead, he bit her lower lip with a hoarse laugh. "I like you like this. I like a challenge."

"I'm not being a brat." His mouth was soft, and she flicked her tongue over the center of his upper lip. "I'm taking what I want."

"So you don't want my cock?"

"Mmm." She rolled her hips slowly and hissed in a breath. Even with her arousal easing the friction of the caress, it was hot. Electric.

Bullet wounds couldn't shake him, but when she did it again, Finn shuddered, his head falling back. "I know you do. I watched your face when I took you. You made the hottest noises when I fucked you deep."

"No." She watched him, rapt, as she slipped her hands down over the hard, muscled plane of his back. "When you fucked me like you couldn't get deep enough."

He smiled, slow and dangerous. "Give me a couple days, and I'll get even deeper."

"Filthy." She moved more carefully this time, rising until the head of his cock nestled between her pussy lips.

"Tell me more."

"It'll be hard." He freed one hand from the tangle of her skirt and curled it around the back of her neck with his thumb resting heavy across her throat. "You want that, don't you?"

She wanted it all—hard and rough, slow and sweet. *Everything*. She whispered the word as she pushed down, taking him inside her inch by torturous inch. Dancing had left her strong enough to ease down gradually, but the sheer sensation rocked her, left her legs trembling as she fought not to slam down against him.

"Yes." His free hand found the zipper at her back, tugging it down with the same teasing slowness. "You were too fragile before. You couldn't take all of me."

The words meant something more than the obvious—she could feel it in the weight of his gaze. But she couldn't think about it, not with the already familiar haze of desire wrapping around her.

Her dress slipped from one shoulder. He eased it lower, burying his face against her revealed skin. "Take all of me, baby. Ride me."

She closed the last bit of space between them with a snap of her hips.

"*Fuck*." Finn's teeth closed on the swell of her breast, and the shock of it left her scratching his lower back hard enough to draw blood.

But she couldn't stop. She urged his mouth closer to her skin as she shifted her hips, grinding against him. "Don't let me hurt you."

"It's just pain." He licked the spot he'd bitten, sending shivers through her. "Pain won't matter when you're coming on my dick."

It had to, because they'd hurt each other for so long, and the only thing that would save them now was making it different. Doing it right. "It matters to me," she rasped.

His fingers twisted in her hair, tightening to the edge of pain. He pulled her back and pressed his forehead to hers. "Then I promise, doll. I won't let you."

It was exactly what she needed. She tried to take it easy, but slow and gentle gave way to a wilder grind as pleasure built. Finn only encouraged her, panting crude promises against her lips. Promises to woo her, ravish her, fuck her rough and messy.

To *be* there, which was the headiest promise of all.

She came with a cry, wrenched from her as surely as the sudden orgasm that curled her toes in her shoes. She clung to Finn, who grunted, slid his arm around her back, and hauled her down into a final flurry of short, hard thrusts.

When he came, it was with his face against her throat and her name on his lips. His breath blew hot across her skin, and she slid her hand up to rest on his mouth. "Say it again."

"Trix." His lips pursed against her fingers on the *T*, so close to a kiss.

So close.

8

FINN OPENED THE bathroom door and almost lost his grip on the towel wrapped around his waist.

O'Kane's woman was sitting on the edge of his bed, her leather-clad legs crossed and one dark eyebrow raised. "Good afternoon."

Retreating back into the bathroom was a coward's move. Walking into the same room as Lex Parrino with nothing sturdier than a towel to guard his dick was just asking for pain.

But hey, he'd always been an idiot.

Finn crossed the room and propped his hip against the small desk. "Lex."

She studied him slowly, a lingering perusal from head to toe. "You're looking better than you did when you came in here. Of course, to look worse, you'd have to be dead."

"Seems like I damn near was," he replied, keeping

his voice as easy as hers. "Thanks for that, by the way."

"Standard operating procedure. We don't let people die on our doorstep."

"Ever?"

"Nope." She rose and slid her hands into her back pockets. "Either they're worth saving, or they're worth saving so we can kill them more slowly later."

"The thought had occurred to me," he admitted. "But I'm guessing you wouldn't do that to Trix. Not for something petty like revenge."

"No. Hell, no." One shoulder lifted in a delicate shrug. "She seems to think you're a stand-up guy who was stuck in a bad fucking situation."

Phrased as a statement, but Finn recognized the question. Lex was waiting for an answer and looking at him like she'd know if he lied.

So he didn't. "All of Five is a bad fucking situation. I didn't do as much bad as I could have. But I didn't do as much good as I *should* have, either."

"Truer words." She rocked back on her heels. "What about now?"

"Now?" Finn met her gaze and didn't flinch, even when those too-knowing eyes stared right through him. This was a woman who wouldn't be fooled by bravado or graveyard humor. She'd see the darkest parts of his heart, and he had to trust that the woman who took Dallas O'Kane to bed had a soft spot for obsessive motherfuckers. "I'm here for her. Whatever she needs."

"Uh-huh." The first glimmer of a smile flashed across her mouth, only to vanish immediately. "You got any marketable skills, Romeo? Besides framing people for murder and pushing drugs, I mean."

"Sure," he replied easily. "I hit things. I scare the piss out of people. I fix problems."

"No offense, sunshine, but I don't think Dallas is ready to have you running point on any security operations just yet."

Finn grinned at her—the scary grin that usually sent his men stumbling back a few steps but had no damn effect on her at all. "You don't say."

"Mmm. Maybe I'll send you over to Bren, see if he's got any work for you to do."

Bren Donnelly. The Eden sniper turned O'Kane. "I thought you didn't want me killing people."

She scoffed. "Where's your imagination? There's more to life than snuffing motherfuckers out."

And there it was, stark as could be. The people in Sector Four killed readily enough to preserve their way of life, but then they put down their guns and their knives and *lived*. That was the part no one had ever taught him how to do.

Though Shipp had offered. "I guess I can fix things. Cars, engines. Plumbing. Real hero shit."

She seemed to miss the sarcasm completely. "No kidding? Huh. I guess I will have to stick you with Bren, then." She headed for the door. "Be at the garage bright and early tomorrow morning. Trix can show you where it is."

Jesus Christ. They were gonna let him wander around their fucking compound like he hadn't spent the last twenty years working for the enemy? Maybe the doctor wasn't the only one high as a kite and tripping over moonbeams. "That's it? No restrictions? No rules? You're not even gonna take me to your leader, lady?"

She stopped, looked back over her shoulder, then slowly turned to face him. "You just had that meeting, sunshine. Try to keep up. And the rules are simple—you mind your fucking manners. Got it?"

The message was clear. Dallas O'Kane wasn't the only leader in Sector Four, and if Lex decided she wanted to finish what Beckett's men had started, no one on this compound would stop her.

Finn tried to imagine Mac Fleming's wife standing at his side as an equal. It was almost as laughable as the idea of Beckett letting Lili Fleming be more than the pretty blonde trinket he'd married as a business strategy.

Finn was in unfamiliar territory. He couldn't afford to make assumptions or dismiss rumors. Dallas O'Kane didn't follow anyone's rules but his own, and if Finn wanted to avoid breaking Trix's heart, he'd have to learn those rules awful fast.

Starting with manners. "Yes, ma'am."

"Good. And, Finn?"

"Yeah?"

"You may not consider me much of a threat, but if you hurt her, that'll change. Fast. And I won't need Dallas or any other man to take care of my shit for me. You understand?"

Oh, he understood. He saw his death in her eyes, after all. "Loud and clear, boss."

Just like that, she smiled again. "It was good to see you. Take care."

She slammed the door shut, leaving him pondering the last time he and Lex had crossed paths. She'd been dolled up in virginal white lace and ruffles...and she'd just shoved a two-foot shard of glass through a man's throat.

A *councilman's* throat.

Lex Parrino sure as fuck wasn't the sort of woman you wanted to piss off, but Finn had the weirdest feeling that she kind of liked him.

Before inviting Finn into any of the O'Kanes' most intimate spaces, Trix had to talk to Jade.

She found her on the roof of the warehouse, standing inside the skeletal shell of their new solar greenhouse. Jade turned at the sound of the door swinging shut, her pensive expression melting into sheer relief. "Trix! Oh, thank *God*."

Trix barely had time to blink before Jade enveloped her in a desperate hug, and she rubbed her friend's back soothingly. "It's okay. I'm okay."

"Are you?" Jade pulled back and framed Trix's face, studying her with an interest that went beyond scrapes and bruises. Looking for signs of withdrawal, no doubt.

Trix shook her head. "They drugged me, but nothing addictive. I'm fine."

Exhaling roughly, Jade closed her eyes. "I was so worried. We all were, but... I'm just so glad you're home."

"Me, too." Trix hesitated, then forged ahead. "I need to talk to you."

Jade let her hands fall away from Trix's face and nodded. "Anything you need."

There was no gentle way to say it, no way to ease her over to the truth. "Finn's here. He's the one who brought me back."

No reaction marred her friend's open, easy expression. Jade was a master of masks, so good at hiding her feelings and her pain. But Trix had watched her writhe through the agony of withdrawal. She'd watched Jade rebuild those masks, one painful day at a time.

The lack of response betrayed her, and after the pause stretched on into awkwardness, Jade clearly realized it. "I never told you his name."

"I could say the same, I guess."

"You could say the same." Jade laced her fingers together and looked away. "You knew him?"

"I did. He was—" Christ, she still didn't know what to call him. "We had a thing. *Have* a thing."

"And that's why he brought you back?"

So she hadn't heard any of it yet. Trix squared her shoulders and met Jade's eyes. "He didn't just sneak me out. He killed Mac Fleming."

Jade clenched her fingers so tightly, her knuckles stood out like pale bruises on her dark skin. She dropped her gaze, stared blankly at her hands, and her rigid silence broke on a shaky laugh. "I always wondered if he hated his job, or if scowling was the only thing he knew how to do."

"Both, I suppose. He hasn't had many reasons to smile." Trix wrapped her arms across her midsection. "Do you hate him for what he did to you?"

"A little bit," she said softly. When she looked up, the pleasant mask had slipped. She looked haunted. Tired. "Do you hate me for admitting it?"

"No. But he can do good things here, Jade," she whispered, her throat raw.

"I know. I know, Trix." Jade turned away, staring toward Sector Two as if she could see it off in the distance, past the buildings. "I want to forgive him. I need to. Because I understand him all too well."

It was probably true. Jade had seen firsthand how Cerys had run Sector Two—all the people she had hurt, the lives she'd destroyed—but she'd been helpless to stop it. So she'd gone along with it, because of all the small things she could do to counter Cerys's madness.

Short of putting that bullet into Mac's head, Finn had been just as helpless. Just as stuck in a system that worked because one person standing against it could only die trying to change things.

Trix shuddered. "Sometimes we do what we have to do to stay alive. Until we can't do it anymore."

"Until we can't anymore," Jade echoed. A chilly breeze gusted across the roof, snapping the tarp that protected the lumber and grabbing at Jade's hair. She shook it out of her face and wrapped her arms around herself, looking more fragile than she had in weeks. "He'll stir bad memories. I can't change that."

And Finn would punish himself for every moment. "I thought you should know, that's all. That he'll be around."

"Thank you." She hesitated. Seemed to steel herself. When she turned, her walls were firmly in place, that raw pain swallowed as if it had never existed. "He brought you back to us. That's all the reason I need to make my peace with him. I can, Trix. I will. I just...need a little time."

She was trying so hard, but the truth was crystal clear—it wouldn't be easy, and it might never happen.

And Trix couldn't blame her. She'd bathed Jade's face, held her through the worst of the agony that had torn at her during the height of her withdrawal. Listened to her delirious ranting, her seething anger—and, worst of all, her hoarse pleas when fury had given way to desperation. When she'd begged Trix to make it all *stop*.

"I get it, Jade," she mumbled. "I do."

And then Jade's arms were around her, squeezing tight enough to bruise. "I love you, no matter what. Remember that. We all love you."

"I know." Support only went so far when countered by bone-deep worry, and Trix couldn't blame them for that, either.

She took that with her as she walked back inside and climbed down the stairs with Jade's unspoken words echoing in her head like her steps on the concrete. They loved her, and they'd protect her—even from herself.

She meant to return to her room, but her feet took her in the opposite direction, straight to the room Dallas had given to Finn. She knocked on autopilot, too, staring at her own hand as it rapped on the door.

She couldn't help herself, so maybe they were right to be so worried.

9

DALLAS O'KANE'S GARAGE looked like the sort of place where Shipp would feel right at home. Chances were pretty good Hawk would take one look at it and never want to leave.

Hawk would be a hell of a lot more welcome than Finn was.

Bren Donnelly barely glanced out at him from behind an open hood before returning to his task. "Lex said you'd be by."

Curt, cool, and dismissive. Finn supposed that was better than a fist to the face. "Lex didn't make it sound optional."

Bren grunted. "You know engines?"

"Well enough." Finn slid a hand across the top of the car. A newer model, probably one that hadn't even been driven before the lights went out. You had to baby those more than the older models, because the electrical system got glitchy, but the parts were damn near impervious to weather and time.

He'd stripped enough cars like this for parts to know.

"You like it?"

"What's not to like?" Finn quirked an eyebrow. "Where'd you get it? Reno?"

"Yeah." Bren straightened and wiped his hands on a grease-smeared rag. "I hear you might be here for a while."

"Guess that depends on O'Kane," he answered carefully. Finn hadn't survived this long through complacency. He was standing face-to-face with a potential enemy, and Brendan Donnelly wasn't your everyday sector bruiser. He'd been trained by Eden's Special Tasks force, trained to be a sector dweller's worst damn nightmare.

Finn could still remember the uneasy mutters when word had gotten around that Dallas O'Kane had acquired his own pet sniper. The delicate balance of peace between the eight sectors had always rested on the illusion of mutually assured destruction. O'Kane had been stacking the deck for years, collecting a private army of absolutely loyal killers.

Bren scratched his chin, leaving behind another smudge of grease. "I'm pretty sure Dallas would say it depends on you."

Yeah, there was the O'Kane fantasy. A world where a man's actions defined his destiny. The drunken mirage of control. "I can't change what's already done."

"None of us can." The corner of the man's mouth quirked up, a smile all the more chilling on the face of a trained killer. "Doesn't make you special."

"So what does it make me?"

"Staring down a chance." Bren picked up a wrench. "And you'd better not blow it."

Finn tensed, judging where to take the hit so it would hurt the least. He knew what a wrench swung with temper could do to an arm or a face, but Bren just turned back to the engine, leaving Finn pissed at himself for being so damn jumpy.

The O'Kanes weren't gonna swing a crowbar at his head or jump him in the garage. If they'd wanted him bleeding or dead, they'd had plenty of chances to make him that way. No, they were going to punish him with words and glares and by withholding their dreamy, sappy love.

As if he gave a fuck about being *liked*.

Feeling steadier, he swung around to stand next to Bren. "So why did Lex send me down here? You need help fixing cars?"

"What else are you gonna do to make yourself useful? Dance a set at the club?"

That was one way to sabotage O'Kane's business. Make everyone stare at his battered, scarred body. "For all you know, I'd be fucking fantastic."

"Your tits are too small. Your ass is okay, though."

"Thanks for noticing."

"You're welcome." The wrench clanged against the frame as Bren loosened one of the bolts securing the engine in place. "Some of the guys are gonna want to get you in the cage."

The momentary humor faded. Maybe the beatings were coming, after all. "I guess we won't be chatting about my ass in there."

"Not likely." Bren squinted over at him. "Want my advice?"

"Sure."

"Take your lumps. You've got it coming."

He couldn't argue with that. Hell, he could come up with plenty of reasons. "As Mac Fleming's enforcer? Or as the bastard who never did right by Trix?"

That drew a chuckle from Bren, something as out of place as his smile. "Take your fucking pick."

"Why wait for the cage?" he asked, watching Bren's

hand. Watching that damn wrench. "If I've got it coming, why isn't anyone dishing it the fuck out?"

"Because we have rules." Bren set the wrench aside and reached for the open beer sitting on the worktable next to the car. "If someone's got a beef, you take it to the cage. Nobody gets jumped."

"And do I walk out of the cage?"

"It wouldn't be a very sporting fight otherwise."

So they hated him for the things he'd done, disliked him for who he was...and they didn't want to jump him like an animal in the street. They wanted to be *sporting* about it.

Christ, he understood the fancy moralistic fuckers in Eden better than he understood these crazy bastards.

He blinked at Bren, who stared back at him for a long moment before finishing his beer in two long gulps. "Okay, then. Pep talk's over. Grab a wrench, soldier."

Relieved, Finn moved to the bench and studied the selection of shiny, well-loved tools. Nicer than anything he'd had growing up, but a wrench was a wrench. There were only so many kinds of screwdrivers, and they all matched a screw. Neat and tidy. Black and white.

Familiar, and right now that was the most soothing thing of all. A car engine was broken until you fixed it, and you knew you'd gotten it right when it started running. It made sense.

At least something in this sector did.

Lex encouraged her to take a few days off, but the Broken Circle was packed, and Trix couldn't stand to see them short-handed.

She wasn't the only one. Zan sat at the bar, his arm in a sling, glowering into a glass of whiskey as she bustled around, pouring an order. "Don't pout, honey." She leaned over and dropped a kiss to his forehead.

"We're both a hell of a lot better off than I thought we'd be a few days ago."

"Easy for you to say," he grumbled, though his gaze softened. "You're working."

She couldn't resist teasing him as she rubbed his cheek. "You should have asked Doc for a cast. Then you could still bounce. Just beat the unruly bastards over the head with it."

"Now there's an idea." The table in the corner yelled for their order, and Zan turned on his stool. "Shut the fuck up, or I'll boot your asses out of here!"

Wounded arm or no, he could still scare the piss out of people. The table fell silent, and Noelle slapped her tray down on the bar with a grateful sigh. "Thank you. They're driving me *crazy*. They want another round of Nessa's last batch, though, so at least they're rich and annoying."

Zan polished off his drink and pushed his glass out for Trix to refill. "Better than broke and annoying, but not as good as rich and polite."

"You been dipping into Doc's personal stash again?" Trix asked. The humor was a little forced, but she couldn't stop herself. Joking with Zan was the next best thing to wrapping him in a never-ending hug, and she'd dissolve into tears the moment she tried.

But he grinned at her, and it eased some of the tightness squeezing her chest. He was okay—not only alive, but up and walking around, drinking and glowering like any other day.

All the female attention couldn't be hurting. As Trix moved drinks to her tray, Noelle went up on her toes to kiss his cheek, just like she had the last five times she'd come to pick up an order. "Zan appreciates good manners. That's why we love him."

The tops of his ears turned pink. "I thought it was about my manly good looks and charm."

Noelle took off, balancing her tray on one hand as if

she'd been slinging drinks all her life instead of less than a year. Hawk's silent gaze followed her, so intense and considering that Trix almost warned him that Noelle was very, very taken. But when Noelle dropped the drinks off at the newly subdued table, his gaze didn't follow her back into the crowd.

It stayed on the liquor. "How much are they paying for that?"

"For one of Nessa's special creations? Way too much." Trix flipped over a glass, picked up the half-empty bottle, and poured him a double. "And not nearly enough. Try it."

He lifted the glass, squinting at the liquor as he swirled it around. He had the glass halfway to his lips when the music changed, the familiar strains of a low, primal bass rhythm pouring out of the strategically situated speakers.

Jeni danced out on stage, already naked. Instead of the teasing build of stripping off her clothes, she moved with the music, letting it guide the dip and sway of her body.

Hawk jerked his gaze from the stage, knocked back the drink, and slammed the glass to the bar. "You guys don't mess around."

Zan laughed and clapped him on the back. "Welcome to Sector Four. You're gonna like it here."

The words pierced Trix's heart. Not because Hawk didn't deserve the welcome—Christ knew he deserved that and more, not only for the risks he'd taken, but the people he'd lost—but because part of her couldn't help but wish that Finn could have the same.

Hawk was still trying not to stare when Noelle returned to the bar. She took one look at him and grinned at Zan. "Were my eyes that big the first time I saw Jeni dance?"

"Not quite, but cut the man some slack. He's new to the wonders of the Broken Circle."

Laughing, Noelle patted Hawk's cheek as if he wasn't a grown man with the first hints of silver in his beard—and probably old enough to be her father. "Poor baby. Be glad she's only dancing. Those shows she used to do with Ace would give anyone big eyes."

Trix picked up a towel and wiped a spill from the counter behind the bar. "Guess she'll have to find a new partner."

"Or keep doing what she's doing. They're eating it up." Zan arched an eyebrow. "What are you and Jas up to tonight, Noelle?"

"We're keeping Ace and Rachel company while Cruz is out on business." She leaned into Zan's good side and rested her head on his massive shoulder. "You guys should come. I think Nessa's going to show up, too."

"I'm there."

He turned to Trix, and she opened her mouth to agree, but stumbled over the words. If she showed up with Finn, everyone would be uncomfortable, including him. And if she left him out, she'd never forgive herself.

He'd come to Four—to her *home*—expecting to have the past shadow him like a ghost. So far, that was exactly what had happened.

"Another time," she said instead. "Thanks for the invitation, though."

"You sure?" Noelle ignored a drunk customer trying to flag her down and leaned across the bar. "If you don't feel up to it tonight, promise me we'll hang out soon."

God, she was so earnest that Trix couldn't even lie. "It's been a long couple of days. But soon."

"Okay. Hey, the old-timers at the back table are almost ready for another round. Get me set up while I go see what the drunk guy wants?"

Trix glanced down at the half-filled tray. "Already working on it. I got your back."

Noelle grinned and pushed away from the bar. "And I'll get us a badass tip."

She headed off into the crowd, and Zan eyed Trix over the rim of his glass. "If you're so beat, how come you're behind the bar, slinging drinks tonight?"

Trix avoided meeting his gaze. "Gives me something to do."

"Bullshit. You've got plenty to do."

It was Hawk who finally broached the one topic everyone in her life had been so carefully avoiding. "How's Finn healing up?"

She could have kissed him. "He's good. He spent the day helping out in the garage. I'm surprised he didn't drag you out there with him."

"I was with the other guy. Cruz?" Hawk slid his glass across the bar and shook his head. "I don't know how the hell he pulled it off, but he sent someone out to the farm and set up a vid link so I could talk to Shipp and Alya."

Knowing Dallas, he'd sent more than communications equipment. "How are they?"

"Relieved to hear from me, and doing okay. Big John made it, and no one got anything worse than bruises while we were breaking through."

"I'm glad." She refilled his glass and leaned over to meet his eyes. "Listen, Shipp and Finn might be square, but I owe you now."

He didn't disagree, just dropped his gaze and stared into his liquor as his thumb made a slow circle around the glass's edge. "Did you know Alya's my mother?"

"What?" Shock left her gaping at him, and she snapped her mouth shut.

The corner of his mouth kicked up, but he didn't look amused. "She was barely more than a kid. A third wife, with stepkids almost as old as she was. Half the people on that farm are either my stepmothers or my half-siblings."

Trix could hardly believe it, not only because of Alya's age, but because that meant she'd sent her *son* off on what could have been a suicide mission. "Why did she let you come with us? I don't understand."

"She didn't want to. She got overruled. Shit is bad out there, Trix. My mother loves that farm, because it was the first thing that was ever hers, but I don't think it'll be safe forever." Hawk sipped his drink and eyed Trix over the glass. "If I want to take care of my family, I need to start storing up favors."

Another flash of surprise widened her eyes. "You want to stay here."

He shrugged and finished his drink. "If nothing else, at least I'm not related to all of the women here."

The matter-of-fact words drew a helpless laugh from her, though she quickly sobered. "Does Finn know?"

"Hard to say. He's not big on small talk."

She shifted her weight nervously from one foot to the other and glanced at Zan, who was trying very hard to focus on Jeni's dance—and not on eavesdropping.

Not that it mattered. Her words weren't a secret. "He could use a friend."

After a moment, Hawk nodded his agreement. "He could. Maybe you'll be able to convince him that's true. The rest of us never had much luck."

"I can try." It was the only way he'd ever understand that he couldn't stay for *her*.

He had to do it for himself.

FROM A PROFESSIONAL standpoint, it was hard not to be impressed when Jared took off his shirt.

If Cruz had ever stopped to think about it, he might have assumed that being the living embodiment of female fantasy required a certain amount of physical discipline, but Jared's body crossed the line from attractive to lethal.

Ace had either seen it too many times to be impressed or was simply oblivious, too focused on setting up his workstation. Markers, needles, and ink, the only things necessary to change a man's life in Sector Four.

"Sit your fine ass down," Ace directed Jared without looking up. "I've been waiting to get some ink on you for years, brother."

Jared dropped into the chair, relaxing against the padded back. "Liar. You just wanted me at your mercy."

"Quit flirting with me," Ace chided. "You'll make

Cruz jealous."

Cruz met Ace's wicked look with an easy smile—and a peace he'd never imagined. "I know what's mine."

"Fabulous," Jared said dryly. "And vaguely disgusting. It must be love."

Ace laughed with his usual endearing obliviousness, too wrapped up in his newly won happiness to see that Jared was the one suffering the pangs of jealousy. Or maybe Jared simply hid it too well. Ace had always buried his vulnerabilities under a wave of manic cheer and filthy flirting. Jared was like the frozen surface of a lake—serene ice over dark waters you could only glimpse through the rare cracks.

It was the cracks that worried Cruz. Jared was a touchstone in Ace's life, a friend who had been family long before Ace had found the O'Kanes. Losing him would tear at Ace's heart in a way Cruz couldn't tolerate—and couldn't stop.

If the cracks weren't filled by something else.

Discarding subtlety, Cruz settled in for a little minor recon. "I heard Dallas made you another offer."

Jared's gaze sharpened. "He wants me to run that speakeasy in Eden, the one he and Liam Riley took over after the bootlegger attacks. If he had his way, he'd turn me into my very own well-dressed noir novel. All that's missing is a femme fatale to ruin me forever."

"Oh, we can find you one of those, easy." Ace braced a hand on Jared's chest and traced the first line in bright blue marker. "A refugee from Two, maybe. Orchids are the new femme fatale."

"A woman just like me? No, thank you."

That made Ace frown, so Cruz cut in before he could respond defensively and derail the conversation. "It's an interesting idea. We've mapped the tunnels to the warehouse across the street. Noah thinks he can arrange for the O'Kanes to purchase it via proxy. Establishing a foothold inside of Eden could change things."

Jared snorted. “No offense, but I’m not sure I want to be the vanguard of O’Kane’s invasion of Eden.”

In some ways, he already was. Jared sparked desire to life in the women who paid him, and Cruz knew how swiftly an addiction to *feelings* could take hold. Rachel and Ace had stripped him of a lifetime of repression in a few short months.

Sometimes, for those women, Jared did it in a single night.

Rubbing a hand over his neatly trimmed beard, Cruz studied Jared’s face, searching for any hint of unguarded emotion, any clue. “I think O’Kane just wants you to join up, period. He’d let you do damn near anything you want.”

“One wonders why.”

Ace snorted rudely. “One suspects it’s because you’re a brilliant, fancy fucker.”

“Since when has Dallas O’Kane had any use for fancy shit?”

Probably since the uneducated-bootlegger act had worn thin. Dallas had played it to the hilt for years, but Cruz had seen it fraying at the edges in the short time he’d been a member of the gang. Dallas couldn’t hide his shrewd mind forever, and the more power he gathered into his hands, the less he seemed to like playing ignorant barbarian.

But that was a private observation, something for O’Kane ears alone. Jared was as close as you could be without taking ink—but that line was still there, even if Ace ignored it. Maybe that was the reason Cruz couldn’t stop trying to sell Jared on the idea.

Ace’s heart was more easily bruised than most people realized, and it was Cruz’s job to keep it whole and safe. “O’Kane has always had a use for brilliance.”

He laughed and reached for a cigarette, causing Ace to push him back into place with a wordless noise of protest. Jared lit the cigarette carefully, exhaled, and looked at Cruz through the wreath of smoke. "I didn't know you had taken up recruitment."

Cruz made the mistake of meeting those dark brown eyes, and Jesus *Christ.* Jared had perfected bedroom eyes to a degree that was as chilling as it was affecting. It was hard to remember that the same man had trained Jared and Ace, when Ace's friendly, shameless lust came from a place of such warmth and Jared's—

The frozen lake again, only this time he was staring straight into the waters' chilly depths.

It was hypnotic, and uncomfortably seductive. That was undoubtedly what Jared intended, to use his desirability and Cruz's inevitable discomfort as an effective means of shutting down the conversation. It was a tactic that would have worked even a month ago, so Cruz paused to appreciate the effort.

And then he shut it down. "Ace, your friend's eyeing me like he wants to get his hands on my dick."

"Of course he does," Ace replied without looking up. He finished another part of his sketch and thumped Jared lightly on the chest. "Behave, brother. No one's allowed to touch Cruz's dick unless Rachel's here to watch."

The teasing words did what Jared's gaze couldn't—brought heat to Cruz's cheeks as his too-vivid imagination conjured Rachel into the midst of this scene, her eyes bright and eager as he put on whatever show she wanted.

"He still blushes," Jared murmured, low and dark. "I like it."

"Fuck off," Cruz muttered. But the darkness in Jared's voice stirred an echo inside him, a protective, possessive fury that should have risen up at the first sign of flirtation. He still struggled with the openness some of the other O'Kanes embraced so easily. Ace and Rachel were his, won through blood and pain, and he wasn't eager to share.

But something about Jared was different. He was dangerous, no doubt. A lethal man dressed in the trappings of refinement. But he was wounded.

And he was Ace's. Important to Ace's past, a strong presence in his life. That made him important to Cruz. Maybe that was how a man as possessive as Dallas O'Kane could watch with unconcerned appreciation when another O'Kane laid eager hands on Lex.

Dallas never shared Lex. He brought the people Lex cared about into the circle of his protection. They became his, because they mattered to her. Dallas shared *them* with *her*. A distinction as thin as a razor's edge, but Ace and Rachel were teaching him to appreciate the finer lines in love and sex.

Jared understood fine lines already. He'd be good for the O'Kanes, and they'd be good for him. Cruz knew it in his gut. Somehow, he'd convince Ace's friend before that ice grew so impenetrable no one could reach him.

The world wasn't doing any more damage to Ace's heart. Cruz wouldn't allow it.

10

SECTOR FOUR'S MARKETPLACE was a little ragged around the edges.

Finn eyed a broken stall as they passed it. The damage was so recent there were still splinters clinging to the wood on one side. A man stood on a precarious ladder leaned up against the side, nailing shingles into place on the tattered roof. He watched Finn as he passed, his lips tightening around his mouthful of nails, but when his gaze dropped to Trix's wrists, he looked away quickly.

"Is this from the fight?" Finn asked her, tilting his head toward a storefront with wood in place of its window.

"Minimal damage, but there was some." Her brow furrowed. "Was Fleming behind it—the bootlegging? Or did he just let it happen?"

"Honestly, I don't even know. That was Beckett's baby, and Beckett never liked me. Or trusted me." Finn didn't bother to hold back a scowl. "He had some crackpot idea about doing the same thing to the booze that he's doing to the drugs. That damn additive."

She stumbled to a halt in the middle of the street. "You've got to be shitting me."

Finn steadied her with a hand on her elbow. "Who knows if it would have worked? But I'm pretty sure Mac would have gone along with anything if he thought it'd hurt Dallas."

Her throat worked as she swallowed hard. "I'm glad it's over. For now, anyway."

"For now, yeah." Beckett's crazy would be slower in coming—and a hundred times more lethal. "I'm gonna tell O'Kane everything important. You know that, right? Anything that'll help him."

Trix shook her head and curled her arm through the crook of his. "Not right now, okay? We're shopping today, that's all. No business."

It was an invitation to ignore the sharp edges of life that kept trying to poke their way into this dream. If he'd had his way, they wouldn't have left the compound at all. Every moment outside of that room—that *bed*—felt like a wasted opportunity. There were so many ways he still wanted to touch her.

But Noah had showed up with Finn's personal stash of money, retrieved with God only knew what sorts of hacking magic, and Trix had seemed so excited to take him shopping. He couldn't say no when she got that look in her eyes.

So he'd shop. He'd shop all damn day, as long as she came home with him at night. "So what's on your list, doll?"

"Clothes, obviously. And I have to take you by to meet Stuart—he does amazing things with leather."

From what he'd seen, the O'Kanes appreciated leather, all types of it. The kind you wore, the kind you decorated with, and the kind only useful for kinky games of pleasure and pain. Not usually one of his vices, but maybe it was one of hers. "Leather, hmm?"

She laughed and bumped her hip against his. "Vests and jackets, smartass."

"Hey, baby, I wasn't judging."

"Uh-huh. Say that without leering, and I might believe you."

Smiling, he freed his arm and wound it around her waist, resting one hand on the lush curve of her hip. "Leering isn't judging. Leering is approving."

"It can be both." She slid her hand into his back pocket. Her fingers pressed against his ass, the tips digging into flesh just enough to serve as a delicious reminder. She clutched at him when he fucked her now, her nails scoring his skin, leaving marks of encouragement.

Just like that, he wanted to be in her again.

She blushed at his low growl, but she didn't stop walking—and she didn't move her hand. "Do you mind if we make a stop on the way? I need more shampoo."

His growing need to touch her didn't go well with extra stops, but he loved the way her hair smelled. Sweet and floral, a scent that lingered on his pillow long after she was gone. Way better than the utilitarian soap they shipped out of Sector Eight. "Sure, doll."

"You might find something you like in Tatiana's shop. She makes all kinds of things."

Her cheeks were pink and swiftly turning a red to rival her hair, which made him wonder what the hell someone could sell alongside shampoo that would make an O'Kane blush. "Just like the leather guy, huh?"

She laughed, soft and husky, and pulled him toward a storefront on the opposite side of the street. "Come on."

The little shop was bigger inside than it looked, with sturdy wooden shelves lining three walls and a large table in the middle of the room. Two women sat at one end, dozens of small bottles with handwritten labels spread out in front of them. The blonde rubbed at the inside of her wrist and lifted it to her nose, her eyelids drooping in pleasure. "Oh God, Tatiana, you're right. It's heavenly."

The second woman had long black hair, smooth brown skin, and a tired smile that brightened when she looked up to see Trix. She rose and patted the first woman on the shoulder. "Try the jasmine, if you want, but it costs ten times as much. And I think that blend suits you."

Trix grinned sheepishly at her approach. "I'm almost out of shampoo. Again."

"You're in luck. I think I have one bottle left." Tatiana hesitated before resting a hand on Trix's arm and lowering her voice. "Are you all right? There were rumors, but everything was so chaotic after the fight in the market square..."

Trix stiffened. "It's fine now. Zan got shot, but he's gonna be okay."

If Finn hadn't been staring right at Tatiana, trying to figure out why something about her face was so naggingly familiar, he would have missed the way her eyes and lips tightened. "I suppose that's why I haven't seen him since before the fight."

"He's gonna be okay," Trix repeated, more quietly this time. "But one of the other guys may be stopping in to check on you for a while."

"I understand." She squeezed Trix's arm briefly and tilted her head toward the far wall. "I put out a new batch with that iridescent glitter Ford helped me find. Take a look while I get your stuff from the back."

"Thanks." Trix wandered over to peer at the bottles and other containers, touching a few labels before finally picking up a jar. "The glitter looks good under the stage lights."

Finn stopped in front of the row of shelves next to it, where a carefully hand-lettered sign announced *Massage*

Oils. Beneath it were smaller signs affixed to each individual shelf. *Sensual, Therapeutic...*

Edible.

Sector fucking Four, man, where even the lube was pretentious. He picked up a jar labeled *Mint* and eyed Trix. "So this is the O'Kane corner of the shop?"

"Being an O'Kane has its privileges." She plucked the jar out of his hand. "Don't knock it 'til you've tried it. Though I prefer the warming oil."

He followed her gaze to another shelf with a row of even smaller bottles. The price listed beside them was outrageous, but he picked up two at random. "You'll have to show me why."

She dropped her hand to his, her fingertips teasing at the inside of his wrist. "I have some already."

"So I'll get this for my room."

"Or you could stay with me."

Yes.

It was the answer to a problem he hadn't realized he had, a way to smudge that final line between them. But it created a whole set of new problems, too. Everything about the room Dallas had given him screamed temporary. It was sterile, empty, full of furniture without personality. A roof over his head, but not a home. Trix made it home when she was there, and took it with her when she left.

If he started sleeping in her room, surrounded by her, it would be easy to forget he didn't really belong.

But he'd have her to himself. All of her. All the time. "You sure, doll?"

"I'm sure." She stared up at him, her fingers tightening on his wrist. "I want you there, Finn. Sharing my home with you didn't end at the sector border."

He covered her hand with his, stroking that soft skin that probably smelled so good because she rubbed some of the lotion from one of these endless shelves into it. "And sharing yourself with me? Where does that end,

Trix?"

Her fingers trembled, and she tugged her hand away. "I have to pay for this," she mumbled. "The shampoo, too."

Finn followed her more slowly, reaching the counter in time to add his two bottles to the stack and pull out his cash. Stubborn pride, maybe, but it felt good to be able to provide something other than dirty words and obligation.

It felt even better that she let him get away with it.

Trix fidgeted with the bag until the door closed behind them with a jingle. Then she grabbed his hand and pulled him around the corner of the building, into the shadowed alley, away from the bustle of the street.

She took a deep breath. "It doesn't."

They were almost entirely in shadow. When he braced an arm against the wall and leaned closer, it was like the rest of the damn world wasn't there. Just him and her and a moment that felt too heavy for sunshine and daylight. "What doesn't, baby?" *Say it. Say all of it.*

"Sharing myself. There isn't a place where that ends." Her eyes were huge, luminous. "Not with you."

Funny how the words could send satisfaction roaring through him but still leave him wary. Because she'd only seen his guilt, the side of him that gave and gave because giving felt good, and he was too damn scared to take. Even now, she was gazing up at him with total, endless trust.

Like she couldn't imagine a world where he'd hurt her.

And he never would. Never, even if it meant holding back forever. Touching the corner of her mouth with his thumb, he shook his head. "There should be. With all the shit you've had to survive, all the shit I didn't protect you from."

She laid a soothing hand on his cheek. "Not because you didn't try, Finn."

"I tried." He smoothed his thumb to the center of her full lips and pressed down to still any protest. "You promised you'd say *no* to me."

Her lips moved beneath his hand as she nodded.

He gripped her hips and spun her so quickly she gasped. The bag of oils and shampoo thumped to the cracked pavement as he penned her in by bracing his arms on either side of her. Still protected, still sheltered from the gaze of passers-by, but trapped.

His.

Stifling a groan, he nuzzled his way beneath her hair and found her ear with his lips. "What if I'm not so different from those Sector Five perverts? What if I get off on imagining you in a pretty dress and pearls, getting on your knees and begging me to fuck that perfect mouth until your lipstick's all over my dick?"

The breath she drew in was sharp, but her voice had gone soft around the edges, lazy with lust. "But you need me to get off on it, too. None of Fleming's men—Beckett's men—would care if I even wanted it. They'd take it anyway."

It didn't seem like enough for redemption. Fuck, it was just the bare fucking minimum of acceptable behavior, as if making her come in return was some trial or obligation. "Would you get off on it?"

"Maybe I don't want to tell you," she whispered. "Since you seem to think it's so perverse."

He slid a hand around her body, splaying his fingers across her abdomen to hold her in place as he rocked closer. "You know where I'm from, baby, and you know what it's like there. What would you think if you were me?"

"I'd think—" She shuddered, and her head fell back against his shoulder. "I'd think you can find beautiful things even in ugly places."

He had. He'd found her. "But you never learn how to take care of them," he murmured, toying with the button on her pants. "Teach me, Trix. Prove it can be beautiful instead of twisted."

Her head tipped forward this time, coming to rest on the dirty brick as her hand dropped to cover his. "It would get me off." Her fingers nudged past his and undid the button. "Your hands in my hair, holding me so you could take your pleasure. It'd get me off, because we'd both know the truth."

Finn was starting to suspect he'd never known any truths, or that they made truth different here in Sector Four. With the impossible softness of her skin under his fingertips, he groaned in her ear. "What's that, doll?"

"It's not about force, or about taking. It's a different kind of surrender."

"Yeah, it is." Her panties had a lace edge, and it was wrong to stroke them like this, in an alley, in broad daylight. He could hear people in the street, their shouts echoing across the market square. People going about their lives, bickering and laughing and living.

Everyone here was so damn *alive*. He could be, too, if he slid his hand a little lower and trusted her. "Don't let me hurt you, Trix. Promise me."

"I promise." She braced both hands on the wall above her head. "Please."

Not permission. A plea, and he'd never been good at denying those when they fell from her lips. So he cupped her pussy and growled in her ear when the damp fabric of her underwear rubbed against his knuckles. "So wet, already."

"Oh, God—" Her feet bumped his as she shifted her legs wider.

He slicked his finger over her clit, a testing brush that made her hips jerk into the touch. "Pearls. Someone in this marketplace must sell jewelry."

"Stuart—the leather worker," she gasped. "His—his sister."

He'd buy whole strands of them. He'd blow through

every credit to his name and wrap them around her while he fucked her. "That's all you're wearing tonight."

Trix whimpered. "You only want me wearing them?"

Oh, *fuck*. He growled against her ear and pumped one finger into her with a shudder. "Dirty, dirty girl. I wonder how loud you'd scream if I rubbed them right..." He curled his finger. "*Here*."

She shook in his arms, a low, desperate noise bubbling up in her throat as her pussy clenched around his finger. "More. Give me more."

"Shh." He clamped his free hand over her mouth, muffling her needy, approving cry as he worked a second finger deep. She squirmed, grinding back against his dick, and he had to bite back his own noise as he worked the heel of his hand against her clit, driving her toward a quick, hard climax.

"What the *fuck*?"

The words were the only warning before a fist twisted in the back of his borrowed shirt, dragging him back so fast pain exploded through his face before he got his hand out of Trix's pants.

His lip split against his teeth from the punch, and instinct took over. He swung back, trying to make room to get between the attacker and Trix, but he was too slow, his brain still sluggishly shifting gears. His face hit the wall, the brick scraping one cheek as the barrel of a gun dug into the other.

"You son of a bitch." Low words, vicious and deadly. "I should fucking shoot you right—"

"*Jasper*." Trix squeezed between them and shoved the other man back. "What the hell are you doing?"

"What do you mean, what am I doing?" Jasper's arm shook, but he lowered the gun. "The bastard was hurting you."

"No, he wasn't." She turned to Finn and winced as she reached up to gingerly prod at his lip. "Jesus Christ."

Finn steeled himself against the urge to laugh. The

worry in Trix's gaze was real, so she wasn't likely to appreciate it. But Jasper's fist crashing into his face was the first thing that had made sense in days, the realest, most comprehensible thing that had happened to him.

He had legitimately had it coming. For so many reasons.

Trix's thumb touched the split in his lip, and he hid a flinch and caught her hands. "I'm fine. Don't worry."

"This is horse shit." She tossed a glare over her shoulder at Jasper as she dug a lace-edged handkerchief from her pocket. "The next time you're giving it to Noelle in some dark corner somewhere, I'm going to come kick you in the balls. See how you like the interruption."

Jasper tucked away his gun and snorted. "I'm sorry, Trix. It looked fucking bad, okay? I didn't think to stop and ask about safe words."

It was perversely reassuring, knowing that Jasper McCray would eagerly blow a hole in anyone who laid a rough hand on Trix. Maybe he and Jas had something in common after all. "Leave him alone, doll. I get it. Better safe than sorry."

She grimaced, shook her head, and dabbed at the blood on his face. "Don't you start, too."

"Sorry." He turned his head enough to spit the taste of blood out of his mouth—and didn't even aim at Jasper's boots.

"You're both impossible." Trix pushed the handkerchief into his hand, buttoned her pants, and snatched up the fallen bag. "Fucking impossible."

She pivoted and stalked away before he could come up with a damn thing to say, leaving him in the alley with a bleeding mouth, an uncomfortable hard-on, and the man who'd tried to shove a gun barrel through his cheek.

Jasper pressed his lips into a thin line. "She's pissed."

"Sure seems that way." Finn stared after her, even

after she vanished into the crowd. “I get it, McCray. I’m a sick SOB capable of damn near anything. But the one sure thing you can count on is that I’ll do whatever it takes to keep her safe. Even let you assholes beat the shit out of me daily until you get it out of your systems.”

“I don’t know you, that’s all.” He relented with a half shrug. “But Trix does, and that should be enough. Under any other circumstances, it would be.”

“These circumstances are pretty fucked up,” Finn agreed. “I didn’t expect you all to greet me with hugs and cuddles. Maybe she did.”

“Or she wanted to, because it’s that important to her.” Jasper held out his hand. “Reason enough to try, right?”

His cheek still throbbed, and he hadn’t managed to clear his mouth of the metallic taste of blood. If it had just been him, he would have shrugged off the gesture. He didn’t need approval, especially from a man so ready to assume the worst about him.

He didn’t need it—but Trix did. So Finn slapped his palm against Jasper’s and resisted the urge to turn their clasped hands into a pissing contest by crushing the other man’s fingers.

11

SHE HAD TO go looking for Finn.

Trix checked the likeliest places first—his room, the bar, even the courtyard in the middle of the compound. She finally spotted lights burning in the garage and found him, alone, bent over the engine Bren had ripped out of one of his pet projects. He was bared to the waist, his skin smudged with engine grease and sweat. She watched, her mouth dry, as he tightened something deep inside the tangle of metal, the muscles in his arm and back bulging.

She leaned against the workbench. "You're working late."

He glanced up just long enough to flash her a smile. "Turns out I'm no good at sitting on my ass, twiddling my thumbs."

There was plenty of work, and Finn could do it all—if Dallas and the others ever learned to trust him. She shoved the thought away. "I went back to the market this afternoon and picked up some things for you. My way of apologizing for this morning."

"I thought I was the one who needed to apologize." He hefted a clean cylinder head and set it on the engine block before carefully nudging it into place.

"I lost my temper," she explained. "Jas overreacted because he doesn't trust you, and that made me angry."

For a silent moment Finn concentrated on his work, starting to bolt the head to the engine block. "Jas doesn't trust me," he said finally. "That means he didn't overreact. In his place, I might have pulled the trigger."

Her chest ached. "What does that mean for us?"

Finn tossed the wrench aside and reached for a rag, wiping one hand clean before touching her cheek. "For starters, we don't play that game again without a locked door between us and the world."

She hadn't been talking about sex, but about the rampant distrust. She understood the sentiment from her friends—even expected it, in some ways—but from Finn himself... It sliced at her a little more every time he spoke of himself in that damning way, as if he wouldn't blame any of the O'Kanes for leaving him to die in an alley.

She swallowed past the pain and nodded. "I put your new clothes in my room, but I didn't ask if you still wanted to be there."

His thumb made a slow circle, tracing along her cheekbone and back down, so close to her lips. "Take me home, Trix."

She almost bit his thumb—but he was right. Not out in the open, where anyone could stumble across them and jump to the wrong damn conclusions again.

So she pushed off the workbench and took his hand. They made the walk in silence, through the shivery night air of the courtyard, into the other building and up the stairs, all the way to her apartment.

She hadn't expected to feel so nervous, but he'd never been here before. He filled the space as he took a few steps inside, his gaze sliding over the furniture and decorations, over all the little things she'd collected that made it the first real home she'd ever had.

"I'm on the list for a bigger one," she said, anything to break the silence. "I was up next, but then Flash and Amira had their baby, and they needed the space more than me."

"It's still nice." He stopped next to her four-poster bed and ran a hand up one of the columns. "Really nice."

It was impossible to see him that close and not imagine him on her bed, *in* her bed. Waiting for her. Watching as she stripped off her clothes, piece by piece—a private version of the shows she put on downstairs, and all the more gripping because of it.

Here, it was just the two of them, in orbit around each other, with nothing else in the universe.

Trix gave in to the magnetic pull and reached out, brushing the backs of her fingers over his hip.

He sucked in a breath, the muscles of his hard abdomen flexing in a hypnotic dance. "Have you got a shower? I'm dirty."

Goose bumps rose on her arms. "It's big enough for two." She slipped two fingers through one of his belt loops and tugged him toward the bathroom. "I'll show you."

Finn smiled as he followed her, a smile that lingered as she reached into the shower and he bent to haul off his first boot. "You gonna wash my back, doll?"

She pulled the decorative pin out of her hair and turned so he could get her zipper. "Is that really your best request?"

His other boot hit the floor with a *thud* followed by a tug on her zipper. The teeth parted with soft clicks, baring her spine to the heat of his breath. "Not my best. Just my first."

Steam began to fill the shower and billow out into the bathroom. "How filthy do these requests get?"

Instead of answering, he left her dress half undone and slid a hand down her thigh. "You changed. I love these damn dresses."

"It's too cold to wear them outside right now, but they're fine for shifts at the bar." When she moved, his hand rubbed the satin of her slip against her bare skin, and she moaned.

"Do you want to get dirty before we get clean?" he murmured, stroking the back of her leg. "I could finish what I started."

Temptation almost overwhelmed her. But she couldn't keep letting things happen to her, even things like delicious orgasms at Finn's beautiful hands. So she shook her head and turned in his arms. "No. Not yet."

Still smiling that dark, hungry smile, he reached for his pants. "Then get naked with me."

A pulse of hunger left her wet and aching as she dropped her dress down over her hips and stripped her slip over her head. Finn was naked by the time it hit the floor, and he twisted a hand in her panties and ripped them off one hip with a satisfied noise that weakened her knees.

It didn't matter. Once they'd stumbled into the shower, Finn pressed her against the tile and claimed her mouth, kissing her hard and deep as the water splashed against his back and ricocheted to cling to her cheeks.

Here, shrouded in steam, it was safe to take what she wanted. Trix stroked his slick, wet skin, every inch she could reach. Up to his shoulders, down his sides, to the hard swell of his ass. She dug her fingernails into his clenching muscles, delivering on the teasing promise from that morning.

Then she gentled her hands again and slid them around to where his cock nestled between them.

Finn broke from her mouth with a groan and pressed his lips to her ear. "Is that what you want, baby?"

"Your dick?" A helpless laugh escaped her as she wrapped her fingers around him. "Hell, yes. All the time. Any way I can get it."

He braced his palms on the tile on either side of her head and pushed back just enough to block the spray. "Show me."

She released him and reached for the soap instead, turning it over and over in her hands before smoothing the suds across his chest.

His eyelids drooped. Closed. His chest heaved with his sharp inhalation, but he let it out on a long sigh of pleasure. She let her hands follow the lines of his body, massaging lightly as she moved up to his neck and shoulders, then down to his stomach.

But the silence made it seem too much like a dream. "Talk to me," she murmured.

"Let's forget the rest of the world for a while," he whispered. "Just stay here. In your shower. In your bed. I never thought I'd see you again, and now I don't want to let you out of my sight."

Left to her own devices, she'd take it even further. She'd pretend they'd never met before his arrival in Sector Four, that every touch, every whisper, was brand new. That none of it had to be second-guessed or framed with the baggage of the past.

That he could be *hers*, without doubt or reservation. "I could stay here." Water sluiced down over his skin, washing away the soap, and she followed it with her fingertips. "Or here."

Barely a touch, and every inch of his powerful body shuddered. "Or lower."

"Horny bastard." She teased him with the soft brush of her palm over the head of his cock. "Tell me what you want."

Another shudder. And a moan this time, a low, hungry sound that felt like triumph. Even more when he spoke. "I want your mouth on me again. And this time, I don't want you to stop."

She slid down the tile, all the way to her knees, and stared up at him as he loomed above her, blocking the water but not the light, not entirely. It cast one side of his face in shadow, but his eyes...

He was watching her like she could bring him to *his* knees with a single touch, and she never wanted it to stop.

She touched his thighs, drawing her fingernails lightly over his skin, relishing the answering flex of muscle. A scar cut across one leg, thin and raised, and he hissed as her fingers traced over it. "If I'd known I'd see you again, I wouldn't have gotten so banged up."

"Do I look disappointed?"

"You look perfect."

The words shivered through her as she wrapped her hand around the base of his cock, and she held his gaze as she stroked him. Slowly, up to the head and down again, alternating a light tease with a firm grip.

His jaw clenched. His hips flexed, thrusting his shaft into her hand. "You don't take orders, do you?"

She'd learned this from him—how to draw out the moment until it sharpened into the finest knife's edge of anticipation, just before it tipped over into frustration. "I take pleasure," she whispered, then leaned in and traced her tongue over the tip of his cock.

He groaned, one hand slipping on the tile. And then it was in her hair, his fingers twisting through the damp strands to cup the back of her head, a warning but not a demand. Not yet. "Take more of it. Take *me*."

She did, licking him one more time before parting her lips. He trembled with restraint, and she drew him in gently, slowly.

At first. But the moment he tightened his fingers—just a little, and probably not on purpose—she sucked him deep into her mouth. Hard.

"*Fuck.*" His fingers dug in, holding her in place as he panted. "Just like that. Don't fucking stop."

She obeyed, keeping up the same pressure even as she deepened the caress. But her hand was in the way, so she dropped it and clutched at the back of his calf.

"I remember this," he said hoarsely, rocking back and returning, fucking her mouth in slow, careful strokes. "I remember trying to pull you back so I wouldn't hurt you. And you'd take all of me."

Because he made her greedy. No matter what he offered, she knew in her heart that she would always want more.

Always.

She met his next thrust eagerly, and the head of his cock hit the back of her throat. Trix fought the urge to tear away and swallowed him instead. He rewarded her with another tortured, pleased noise, with his fingertips rubbing encouraging circles against her head.

"Just like that." He held her there for what seemed like forever before drawing back, only to push deeper the next time, his grip edged with the same roughness as his voice. "You can take it, can't you, baby? You can swallow my whole damn cock."

Yes. When he tried to retreat again, she followed him, pulling against the hold he had on her hair. She kept him in her throat as long as she could, until her lungs burned and her head began to swim, until she had to break away and gasp for breath.

But when she tried to take him again, he tightened his fingers, wrenching her head back with the rough edge of command she'd started to think he would never show her. "Where do you want me to come, Trix?"

The answer sprang to her lips without thought. "All over me."

His gaze locked with hers. His lips curved slowly. "You want your pearl necklace, baby doll? Take it."

It was more than permission. For once, it was a demand, and Trix took it. She grasped his cock and pumped her hand, slow and hard.

"Faster." He released her hair, returning his hand to the slippery tile wall. Every muscle in his body seemed tense, but his gaze didn't fall to her hand. It stayed locked on hers. "You know what gets me off."

Her body responded automatically, from the renewed rush of heat to the way her hand sped. She twisted her fist lightly as she reached the tip of his cock, just enough to flick her thumb roughly over the sensitive spot beneath the head.

Finn's eyes glazed. His breathing sped. Then he bit off a curse and covered her hand with his own, squeezing her fingers almost painfully tight as he jerked them over his shaft, faster and faster until he came with a choked noise and a hot spurt that painted her chin and open mouth.

Before, he would have watched her with a vague look of shame and recrimination as come dripped from her chin to her breasts, as she licked the taste of him from her lips. Now he followed her tongue with his thumb, stroking her swollen lips with a smile of unchecked satisfaction.

Fuck, it was hot.

Then he twisted his hand. Gripped her chin. "Stand up."

She rose, sliding her body against his as she moved, and reached to wrap her arms around his neck. But he caught them and twirled her, pressing her to the tile with her hands above her head. "I never got to finish what I'd started."

Everything in the shower was slick and steamy, but the tile was still cool, and Trix shivered as her nipples hardened at the contact. "No, you didn't."

"And you were close, weren't you?" His hand edged between her body and the wall and slid down to cup her pussy. "So wet and tight around my fingers. You would have come right there in the street. For me."

She bit back a whimper, tried to turn it into a noise of agreement. In the street, everything had been quick and hard, overwhelming. You had to move fast when you were getting off in an alley—but the shower was different. Private, enclosed, a whole little universe of its own where nothing existed but them.

They had all the time in the world, and Finn would take it.

And he did. Slow. Painfully gentle, one fingertip ghosting over her clit so lightly it almost wasn't there. As if to contrast it, his grip on her wrists tightened, pinning her in place as he worked her over with gradually deepening circles.

The spinning pleasure left her dizzy. She turned her cheek to the tile and closed her eyes. "I'm so hungry, Finn, all the time. It never stops."

"I know." His fingers parted, opening her to him. A third pushed into her with a shallow, easy stroke. "It doesn't have to stop."

Except that the idea terrified her. Their relationship had once been based on that sort of loss of control, on the fact that, no matter how hard either of them tried, they couldn't stay away from each other.

It had almost killed them both.

The thought shuddered through her as surely as his touch. "Tell me this is different," she begged.

"I don't have to." He pressed his forehead to her temple, his breath hot against her cheek. "You can feel it. You know it in your bones. Nothing's the same as before."

Because he wasn't fighting her anymore. Fighting himself. They were sober, clear-headed, free to do what they wanted—and this was it. More than anything else, more than *breath.*

Another jolt of heat burned up her spine, and she couldn't stop her hips from moving, seeking more profound contact. He gave her that, too, one broad finger pumping deliciously deep. "I came on your tongue. I want you to come on mine."

The mental pictures evoked by the words—riding his tongue, watching his eyes as he drove her toward the edge—twisted the need even tighter. "*Finn.*"

He laughed—probably at the scandalized edge in her voice—and turned her, pressing her back against the wall before sliding to his knees. "Don't turn shy on me now, doll."

"I'm not. I'm—" She tangled her fingers in his wet hair. "The things you say. It's new, that's all. You never talked like this before."

"Didn't do a lot of things before." He laid a hand on each leg, tracing his thumbs up along her inner thighs. "I used to wonder, every time I touched you, if you really wanted it."

I would have stopped you. The protest died, unspoken. The truth was that she would have done anything. The fact that fucking him had always been pleasurable was incidental. In the end, all that had mattered was knowing when her next hit was coming, because that was what addicts did.

She told him the truth instead. "You were the only thing I ever wanted as badly as the drugs."

He coaxed her legs wider, steadying her when her foot slipped. "I'm going to tell you every filthy fucking thing I want to do with you and to you. Because I only know what gets you off. I want to learn what turns you on."

She almost laughed, but then he bit her hip and cut off her breath. She leaned her head back and arched off the tile. "Fuck."

"Go on," he rumbled, the words tickling over her abdomen as he stroked her pussy with both thumbs. "Tell me what turns you on."

"I don't—" His tongue touched her, tracing lightly

over her outer lips. She hissed and braced her hands on his shoulders. "Rough. I like it a little rough."

He hummed, shifted his grip to her ass, and swiped the flat of his tongue over her clit. Sensation splintered through her, and she rocked against his tongue instinctively.

So he did it again. And again.

And *again*.

The sheer abandon of it wrenched a cry from her throat. She rode his mouth, eager to take what he offered—not just the physical release, but the passion, pure and untouched by anything but their desire.

It built until her legs were shaking and he had to hold her up, until she wasn't sure she could stand another moment. Then his lips found her clit, a gentle kiss that turned rough as he lashed her with his tongue.

She tensed, but there was no denying the command in his caress—or the orgasm that shattered through her. She came *hard*, oblivious to everything but the pressure of his hands on her skin and the heat of his mouth.

She was still shaking when he eased her down the wall to straddle his lap. "You with me?"

Blood roared in her ears, and her hands fumbled as she brushed her wet hair out of her face. "Barely."

Finn's fingers joined hers, coaxing the tangled strands back from her forehead. "I got you, baby."

"I know." She always had, even in the depths of her addiction and the lowest points of their fucked-up relationship.

He rose slowly, lifting her to her feet, as well. He didn't speak as he steadied her against the wall and reached for the soap, or when he'd lathered his hands and was smoothing them along her skin.

If only the others could see him like this. The way she did.

His earlier words came rushing back, and Trix stroked his cheek. "We'll stay here. The rest of the world will get along fine without us for a while."

He turned his face into her hand with a smile. "Then hurry up and help me get clean, so I can get you into bed and get you dirty again."

lex

DALLAS ALWAYS LOOKED at his map when he was trying to think, planning moves and countermoves in his head. Thinking about possibilities, and sometimes even inevitabilities.

Lex shut the office door behind her and leaned against it, watching him. "I knew you'd be here."

He glanced up long enough to spare her a smile of welcome before going back to his staring. "Better enjoy it while I can. If I turn my back for too long, Noelle and Mia will be in here putting everything on a computer."

"You'll never give up your maps." She crossed the space between them and rubbed his back between his shoulder blades. "Have you seen Trix around lately?"

"I saw her in the bar," he said absently, still squinting at the notations he'd scribbled over Sector Five. But he caught up with the question a few seconds later, his back tensing under her hand. "Shit, that's the *only* place

I've seen her since she came back."

"Mmm. She works, and she goes home." Lex leaned down and kissed the back of his shoulder. "I don't really blame her. It's one hell of an awkward situation. But something to watch."

"Something I haven't been doing." Dallas sighed and sat back in his chair. "When did I get so damn soft?"

"You're not." He didn't want to deal with Finn—didn't want to hate him, and especially didn't want to like him. It could only make his hard decisions even more difficult. "I talked to Noah. He was there back in the day. He knows what they were like together."

Dallas flexed his fingers. Formed a fist. "I already know I'm not gonna like it. Finn's always been a cold bastard."

It had certainly seemed that way during the brief contact they'd had with him in his capacity as one of Sector Five's enforcers. But Noah's words had painted another, possibly more dangerous picture.

Best to get it the fuck out there. "He's not cold. He's crazy, and Trix is his trigger point."

Dallas twisted to stare up at her. "So that's how Fleming got his head blown off?"

"It wasn't the first time, either." Noah had told her the story, and relaying it to Dallas now raised the fine hairs on the back of her neck. "He killed the guy who got her hooked on the addictive shit. Walked into a meeting, shot him in the face, and told everyone else to stay the fuck away from her."

From the dark look in his eyes, Dallas found it utterly reasonable, and his words confirmed it. "Doesn't seem all that crazy to me. I would have done worse if someone had doped you up with that trash."

"I know." She stroked her fingers through his hair. "It's not that. It's the question, you know? What else he might do, and whether it could hurt Trix in the end."

"Is there any way out of this mess where Trix doesn't

end up hurt?"

He had more pressing concerns than her emotional welfare. "Is Beckett still making noise about wanting Finn to come back to Five and *face justice*?"

"Yeah." Dallas yanked the map closer and ran his hands over it. "I keep doing the math, and it's not coming up pretty. If he hauls me up before the other sector leaders... Sector One sides with us. Two will be with Five. Six and Seven cancel each other out because they'll never agree on a damn thing. No vote from Three..." He slapped his hand down on Sector Eight. "I don't like our odds, gambling on Jim Jernigan's mercy."

Fuck. "Are you going to tell Finn?"

"I don't know." Dallas traced a finger along the dividing line between Four and Five, and she could almost see the wheels spinning in his head. "Beckett's still playing good cop. Wanna hear the latest offer?"

"Christ, I don't even know. Do I?"

"Our own personal regen tech, fully equipped. Hell, Lex. After what happened with Ace and Zan..."

He had to be tempted, and for good reason. It was a trade that outweighed Finn's supposed value exponentially. "Makes you wonder why he really wants Finn back, doesn't it?"

"It sure as hell isn't because of justice." Dallas groaned and rubbed his hands over his face. "Beckett's cold, no doubt about it. But if he wants to play nice and stay out of our way, can we afford to provoke him? Shit'll come down either way, but we're more likely to survive it if we have some time to prepare."

She shook her head. "He's tipping his hand. This is important to him, and it isn't because he wants to avenge Fleming's death. That makes Finn one hell of a trump card, and we can't afford to hand him over too easily." *Or too soon.*

Dallas caught her hand and hauled her into his lap. "Promise me something, love."

She settled across his legs and wound her arms around his neck. “Anything.”

“Don’t let me lie to myself.” He pressed his forehead to hers. “Last time I was staring down this many tempting bad decisions, I almost lost you.”

“Okay.” She hesitated. “There’s one way I can see that we can get through this without Trix getting hurt. And it’s not the easy path.”

“Tell me.”

“We keep him,” she said softly. “And to hell with what Logan Beckett wants.”

“He’ll never belong,” Dallas replied just as quietly. “Not if he spends all his time hiding under Trix’s skirts.”

“We all have things we run to when shit gets tough.” Dallas had his maps, and Finn had Trix. “Bren says he seems to know his way around under the hood of a car.”

“That’ll do for now, I guess. Think he’ll show up tomorrow night?”

“He has to. He’s got a lot to prove.”

12

WHEN THE FIRST man went down spitting blood, Finn finally understood the O'Kanes.

The warehouse behind the Broken Circle was all sex, booze, and violence, distilled into one perfect storm of emotional release. Fight night, the night the O'Kanes stepped down from their holier-than-thou pedestals and punched each other in the face for giggles.

It was easier to believe the rest of it when you saw them like this. It was easier to believe that Dallas O'Kane could be ruthless enough to rule a sector and decent enough to rule it well. Because he wasn't some naïve dreamer about to be clobbered by reality, or a sociopath who'd learned how to hide his darker nature.

O'Kane didn't hide from his inner darkness. He embraced it. Channeled it, and taught his men to do the same. And one night a week, they took it out on people who could handle it.

An outlet and a statement. *Fuck with us at your own risk.*

And Finn was about to fuck with them.

Bren stood beside him, a sweating beer in one hand. "You look like you've got the itch."

"Maybe." At least it would get the shit out in the open. Half of the O'Kanes were probably dying for the same chance Jasper had already enjoyed—the chance to make him bleed. "Seems pretty inevitable either way."

"No one's going to make you fight."

"Doesn't mean I don't have to."

"Truth." Bren took a long swallow of his beer. "Question is, how do you handle it?"

Finn shrugged and watched as two men hauled the loser to his feet. He was swaying, staggering even with support, but he was alive. As long as the fights weren't to the damn death, nothing that happened within the chain-link walls mattered. "I'm more worried about how Trix is gonna handle it."

"She's used to the fights." Bren tilted his head. "It'll be different watching you go a few rounds, though."

"Because Trix and I have a fundamental disagreement on a few things."

Bren snorted. "Like the acceptability of you taking a couple of hits to the face?"

"And the fact that I have them coming." Finn rubbed the knuckles on his left hand. "Absolution's not always a bad thing."

"You do what you gotta do," Bren advised solemnly. "It's no good doing what makes her happy if it drags you down at the same time."

Trix wouldn't be satisfied until he found a place with the O'Kanes, and that couldn't happen until he met them on their turf and let them pound out a few rounds of frustration on him. "So let's make everyone happy. Dance with me, Donnelly."

"Want to jump right in with both feet, huh?" Bren

raised both eyebrows and grinned as he shrugged. "Hell, yeah. I'll play."

Finn stripped off his shirt before turning to find Trix in the crowd. She was standing beside the cluster of couches and chairs where the O'Kane women were watching the proceedings, for once dressed in the same leather and denim as the others.

She stared back at him, her features set in an inscrutable mask, but one hand was clenched into a fist at her side. A tiny blonde laid a hand on her shoulder, and she relaxed immediately, though her expression didn't change.

No, Trix wasn't going to be pleased with this, but he'd have to make it up to her when he stopped bleeding.

Another fighter was already headed for the cage, but he stopped abruptly when Bren stepped up to the door. Silence fell in their immediate vicinity and rippled outward. Heads turned, curious gazes fixing on Finn.

He weathered the assessment and tried not to let it injure his pride when the silence broke on the first shouted bet. "Two hundred credits on Donnelly!"

Other voices joined the first, a flurry of bets being placed and taken, money and credit sticks flashing under the harsh lights. Then another voice rose above the din, familiar and firm.

Jasper. "Five hundred on the new guy."

Dallas O'Kane himself appeared at the cage door, holding it wide in expectation. It was the first time Finn had come face-to-face with the man since he'd arrived in Sector Four, and his expression now—

Resignation. Challenge. They wouldn't have gone together without Jas's words hanging in the air, words that amounted to a statement of acceptance. Finn was *the new guy* now, and Dallas didn't know whether he liked it or not. Maybe Dallas knew something Jasper didn't. Something Finn's gut had been telling him all along.

His escape from Five had been too easy.

Finn watched Dallas, but the man's face gave nothing else away. He was the king now, the lazy, confident leader of Sector Four, and he smiled as he waved Finn up into the cage. "Don't hold back. Bren'll just make you pay for it later."

"I never hold back," Finn replied, letting the words fall like a warning. "Not anymore."

Dallas inclined his head once. Understanding. "Get in there and make Trix proud."

Nothing else to do but climb into the circle of steel and concrete and get ready to bleed.

Bren shed his shirt and tossed it out the open cage door. A brunette waiting on the other side of the bars caught it with a scowl. "Don't let him hit anything important," she called out as the door clanged shut. "I got plans for you tonight."

"Don't worry, sweetness." Bren stretched his back and arms, moving with deceptive laziness. "This is a clean fight."

"It better be," she muttered, shooting Finn a glare that made him wonder if she'd be the next one into the cage to pound on his face. She probably would be, because that was the truth about Sector Four he couldn't afford to forget—the women were as deadly as the men.

Even Trix. Hell, for him, *especially* Trix. He could see her from here, her red hair standing out amongst the blondes and brunettes clustered around her on the couches. He flexed his arms, feeling the gentle ache that warned him he had to go easy after this. He'd been abusing his body more than usual, which was saying something.

But tonight was for Trix, even if she'd never believe it. So he shook his arms and met Bren's gaze with a smile. "Let's do this."

There was no music, but the sound of stomping feet and shouted encouragement filled the cavernous warehouse. He and Bren circled one another, but only for the span of a few pounding heartbeats.

Then Bren lunged, driving straight toward his midsection.

Finn wrenched his body to the side, turning a powerful punch into a glancing blow that still drove a grunt from him. Bren had the muscles and bulk Finn had always associated with someone strong but slow, but the fucker recovered with a speed that would make an acrobat envious.

In the streets, Finn wouldn't have messed with someone like him, not with his bare hands. Maybe with a bullet to the back of the head, if it had to be done. Quick and neat, because fists were for intimidating people, and there was nothing to be gained from trying to scare someone you were planning to kill.

In the time it took that thought to form, Bren had circled around and swung again, opening the split Jas had left on Finn's lip and giving him another taste of his own blood.

Fuck. *Focus.* He shook off the pain, ignored it the way he had his whole damn life. He punched this time, driving for that slab of rock Bren called a jaw.

Bren took the hit. His head snapped back, but he shook off the blow with a bloody grin that looked anything but dismayed.

The crazy bastard was having fun.

Finn felt his own mouth curving up in response almost in spite of himself. Energy zipped through him, riding the realization that nothing about this was life or death. Just two guys taking a few swings, accepting the pain as the price of being alive and relishing the knowledge that the stakes were low.

It was like putting down a weight he hadn't realized he'd been carrying. His next punch went wide as Bren twirled out of the way, nimble as a dancer, but Finn was moving faster now, too. He avoided a jab and went for the other man's midsection, catching him with his shoulder and driving him back against the cage bars.

Bren's chest heaved, and it took Finn several terrifying seconds to realize he was laughing. "That is fucking creepy, man."

"Who cares?" Bren shook him off amidst the roar of catcalls and encouragement. "You're in O'Kane territory now. We do what we want, and fuck whoever doesn't like it."

Now there was a motto he could get behind. One he could embrace wholeheartedly, because he'd been living by it his whole damn life already.

We do what we want, and fuck whoever doesn't like it.

Bren's laughter was contagious. Grinning like he was as crazy as the rest of them, Finn swung around and punched his new friend in the teeth.

It took almost five minutes for Trix's jaw to unclench enough for her to speak. "They look like they're having *fun.*"

"Well, Bren probably is," Rachel mused, swirling the whiskey in her glass. "You know, getting pounded on?"

She made it sound so filthy, and Nessa laughed, nudging Rachel with an elbow. "He better not like it too much. Six gets possessive."

They were trying so hard, and Trix had to blink away tears. There was no mistaking the intention behind Jasper's bold, outspoken bet, or Dallas's pep talk before the fight.

As far as the crowd gathered in the warehouse tonight was concerned, Finn was a brand-new O'Kane, hanging out with his friends, a breath shy of getting his ink.

An ache of longing twisted in her chest, and she

reached for Rachel's whiskey, gulping it down to brace herself.

Rachel chuckled. "Help yourself."

"Forget the whiskey." Nessa leaned over the edge of the couch and came up with an unlabeled bottle. "I brought this for you and your man, Trix. Celebrate his first fight night."

If it didn't have a label, it had to be from one of her tiny premium batches, the stuff you couldn't buy. "Thanks, Nessa."

Nessa smiled and squeezed Trix's hand. "Bring him around the warehouse some time, huh? If he's gonna stay in Four, he needs to know his liquors."

"You bet." Still struggling to maintain her composure, Trix turned her attention back to the cage.

The men were grappling now, slicked with sweat and even a little blood. She watched as Finn slammed Bren against the side of the cage and broke away, getting enough space to take another swing at Bren's jaw. Bren let it land and returned it, driving a fist into Finn's gut so hard they ended up against the opposite side of the cage.

Finn was grinning like Trix had never seen before, his face alight with pleasure as he took advantage of Bren's momentary hesitation to land a solid left to the jaw.

Bren fell to his knees. A hush rippled over the crowd, obliterated by protests and cheers when he reached out and slammed his hand on the concrete beside him.

Rachel stared, openmouthed. "Bren tapped out. I don't fucking believe it."

"I do," a new voice said. Noelle dropped to the arm of the couch and squeezed Trix's shoulder. "Jas and Bren know what they're doing."

Jas was showing acceptance by making sure everyone saw him put his money on Finn. Bren was acknowledging that he'd fight him and yield, because he was worthy of the concession.

Not-so-tiny gestures, and they screamed almost as loudly as ink.

In the cage, Finn swiped blood from his lip and held out a hand, offering Bren help he didn't need to climb to his feet. The man took it anyway, grinning as he rose.

Trix was halfway to the cage by the time Dallas opened the door, and she didn't stop until she was inside, stumbling into the circle of Finn's arms.

"Hey, hey." Finn caught her with one arm around her waist and used the other hand to tilt her head back. "I'm still in one piece."

"You're bleeding. Again." But, in her heart, she knew this time was different. He wasn't bleeding *because* of her family, but *with* them.

"Only a little," he rumbled. He smiled, and winced when it tugged at his split lip. "My knuckles are worse. That bastard's face is like a rock."

"That's why people don't hit Bren," she said through a laugh. "Rookie mistake."

"I'll remember that next time." Finn rubbed his thumb along her jaw. "That girlfriend of his isn't gonna knife me, is she?"

"Better stick close to me, just to be safe."

His hand slid to her lower back, pressing her hips to his. "How close?"

Before she could answer, Dallas slammed a hand against the side of the cage. "All right, Trix, make way for the next show. Unless you want to *be* the next show."

She grasped Finn's hand, turned, and stopped short. Mad stood in the open doorway, tension lining his body in stark contrast to his casual posture. "My turn."

Mad didn't want to show tacit approval by facing Finn in the cage. He wanted to beat the hell out of him, exact some measure of vengeance for everything that had happened to Jade. But if Trix protested, said any goddamn thing at all, it would be a statement of weakness—not hers, but Finn's, and he couldn't fucking afford it.

He never could.

She squeezed his hand harder, and Finn stroked a soothing thumb over the back of her hand. When he spoke, the words were light. Lazy. "Sounds fun. Bren let me off too easy anyway."

"Okay." She had to edge past Mad, and she couldn't resist stomping one boot down on the bridge of his bare foot.

Mad didn't flinch.

Dallas swung the cage door shut with a *clang* and slung an arm across Trix's shoulders as the men within began to circle. "Better to get it out now, love. Clear the air."

"And if it doesn't?"

"You know Mad better than that," Dallas chided. "He's worried. About Jade *and* about you. It's not making him very smart right now, but it means he'll get over it."

Under normal circumstances, she'd have agreed in a heartbeat. Mad was one of the most decent people she'd ever met, with a solid, unshakable code of honor that made Dallas's look lax sometimes.

But these circumstances were anything but normal. "Would you feel that way if he had hurt Lex, even if he hadn't wanted to?"

Inside the cage, Mad took his first punch, moving with lethal speed. He connected solidly with Finn's jaw, snapping his head around, but Finn shook it off and swung back.

Dallas tightened a hand on Trix's shoulder and turned her away from the fight. His eyes were deadly serious, his expression unusually grim. "Honey, I feel that way because he hurt *you.*"

She had never explained, never talked to anyone about her life in Five. "He's the only reason I'm not dead, Dallas."

"And that's the only reason *he's* not dead." Dallas sighed and pulled her into a loose hug. "You're too new to remember, but this is how it goes, darling. You think the boys were eager to hug Bren when he first showed up? A goddamn MP in the heart of our compound? Everything we hated and fought against."

The dull thud of fist hitting flesh behind her made her wince, even as the rest of the gathered crowd cheered. "It's still hard to watch."

"Because you think it's hurting him." Dallas shook his head. "Some people have a darkness in them. They don't want it, don't want to give in to it. But it comes out, one way or another, and it feels *good* to let it out. Ask Six sometime why she keeps climbing into the cage. She doesn't have to. She doesn't have shit to prove. But it feels good to let it out without hurting anyone who isn't asking to get hurt."

She'd never know if this was what Finn wanted, not really. Even if it wasn't, he'd hide it from her, just like everything else.

The cage rattled loudly, metal scraping metal as two bodies thudded against it a few feet away from her. She turned in time to see Finn slam Mad into the steel mesh, and he wasn't smiling this time.

Neither was Mad.

He wasn't holding back, either. With a quick twist of his body, he broke Finn's hold and jerked him off balance, sending him staggering back with a rough punch to the gut. Finn regained his balance and straightened, but he didn't advance on Mad.

So Mad punched him again, driving Finn to his knees.

And Finn let him.

"I can't," she whispered. "He might need this, but I can't watch it, Dallas."

Dallas didn't answer. His brow furrowed as he watched Finn climb to his feet and hold both hands out to his sides.

When Finn spoke, his words carried beneath the shouts of the crowd, digging hooks into Trix's heart. "Here I am, Maddox. Whatever debt I owe, you keep collecting until it's paid."

Mad flexed his fingers, his face twisted with anger. "Stop fucking around and fight."

"If that's what you want." Finn shrugged and took another halfhearted swing. Mad slapped it away and drilled Finn again.

"Stop it." Another whisper, one she knew was too low for Mad to hear, but that was okay. It wasn't meant for him, anyway.

"I don't have to," Dallas said, looping his arm around her shoulders. "Finn's got this."

The words sounded ridiculous as she watched Finn drag himself to his feet and hold out his hands. Mad growled and shoved him. "Fucking *fight*."

"You don't want a fight," Finn replied, his hands still loose at his sides. "You want some righteous vengeance. So take it."

Mad trembled, and his chest heaved as he clenched his fists. But he didn't move, and Trix realized that he *couldn't*. It went against that code of his to beat on a man who wouldn't fight back, and she watched as he spun and shoved the cage door open with such force it rebounded and slammed into his shoulder on his way out.

Dallas squeezed Trix's shoulders. "Go kiss some bruises, darling. I'll deal with Mad."

At first, she wasn't sure she wanted to. She felt raw, exposed, like one false step or word could cut her, and that sort of vulnerability scared the hell out of her.

Then Finn looked at her with the same rawness, as if he wasn't sure of his welcome, and she held out her hand.

Ignoring the shouts of the crowd, he stepped from the cage and slid his hand into hers. "Wanna get out of here?"

"Yeah." She swallowed hard. "Yeah, I do."

Finn let her lug him back to her rooms. He let her examine the cuts and bruises, let her clean the blood from his face and hands with a warm washcloth. But when she reached for the med-gel, he caught her wrist in a steely grip and shook his head. "Let it be."

She thought about the darkness Dallas had mentioned and sighed. "Why?"

"Because it's nothing." He dragged her closer, until she stood between his knees. "If you want to kiss everything better, I won't argue. But if you want me to stay here, you can't be so damn worried all the time. This is still some soft living."

"I'm not worried about the fighting, Finn." Her lungs burned as she fought to breathe. "I'm scared, okay? I don't know what it means. Because you keep saying you don't give a damn what anyone here thinks of you, so maybe you're self-destructing, and I can't even *tell*."

"Hey." He used his grip on her wrist to press her palm to his bare chest, over his heart. "Feel that?"

Her fingers curled hungrily, as if she could capture the quick, reassuring thump of his heartbeat and hold on to it.

"That's me waking up, doll." His palm slid up her arm, all the way to her shoulder, where he brushed his thumb over the sensitive spot on her throat where her pulse raced just beneath the skin. "Dallas O'Kane isn't a saint. He's a sinner like all the rest of us. A dark man with violence in his heart."

She tried to pull away and his fingers tightened, curling like steel around the back of her neck. "He's a sinner," Finn said again. Lower. More dangerous. "But he made a choice, didn't he? He does bad things to bad people. I don't have a hope in hell of being a saint, but maybe I can make a choice, too."

Mac Fleming had attracted violent men to his organization, but even the ones who didn't start out that way had sometimes embraced the opportunity to indulge their darker urges. There was no one with the power to stop them, no one who cared as long as the job got done.

Finn was different. Every day she'd known him, he had defied Mac's authority. Some of those rebellions had been tiny, but others had skated the edge of what Sector Five's leader would tolerate.

Still, every day, he'd fought.

"You made your choice a long time ago," she murmured. "I know you did, Finn. I was there."

"I made a choice not to be as evil as Mac told me to be." He tilted her chin up, baring her throat. Even watching him lean in didn't prepare her for the heat of his mouth over her pulse, his teeth scraping a dangerous counterpoint to the tease of his tongue. "Now I can make a different one—to be as good as my lover believes I can be."

His touch sparked the same heat as always. It swirled together with her anger and fear until the battling emotions coalesced into something as dark and dangerous as the look in his eyes. "Only the truth from now on, no matter what."

"The truth? Sometimes I like to fight. And win." He closed his teeth on her skin again, streaking fire through her. "Sometimes I like to take."

She could barely breathe, much less speak, but she managed to whisper, "Show me."

He moved fast, flowing to his feet, crowding her space. His hands landed on her shoulders, and he spun her in a dizzy circle, stopping her when she faced the bed. "Put your hands on it."

Her hands sank into the mattress, and she anchored herself by clenching her fingers in the coverlet.

He gripped her hips first. His fingertips found the

edge of skin between her jeans and her corset, blazing heat along them. "You're the only person in any damn sector that I've never wanted to hurt. Not in my darkest fucking fantasies."

He had never been able to stand the sight of her in pain, even when it was necessary. Inevitable. "I know that."

"But I always wanted this." Warm fingers traced around her side to tug open the button on her jeans. "You. Under my hands."

Trix shivered.

Her zipper rasped, but he didn't tug her pants down. Instead he stroked upwards, fingers tracing the chains crisscrossing the front of her corset. "Is that where you want to be?"

Don't you want to be more than an enforcer's woman? The words echoed in her memory, but her body reacted as if they'd been whispered in her ear. Her skin crawled, her heart thudded, and her upper lip grew damp with sweat.

She wasn't looking at her own bed anymore, but the papers strewn across Mac Fleming's desk. She was small, helpless, and her brain stuttered to a halt, paralyzed by her options—make herself smaller, fold in until nothing could break through the shell at the center of her being.

Or fight.

Trix struck out with a whimper, panic eclipsing everything but the need to flee. She scrambled over the bed and slid off the other side. Pain exploded in her side as she fell, hitting the wall on her way down.

Floorboards creaked under soft footsteps. A huge figure crouched a few feet away—but didn't touch her. Only his voice, low and gentle. "Trix. It's okay."

The words swam in a haze, and it seemed like an eternity before she understood them. Finn's voice, her new name. Safety.

"Oh, God." She still couldn't breathe, but she covered

her face and gasped out an apology. "I'm sorry. I'm sorry, that was stupid—"

"Shh." Careful fingers brushed her hair. "You hit the wall pretty hard. Can you get up?"

"I'm okay." But when she tried to rise, her knees wouldn't hold her.

"Let me—" He touched her arm, but pulled away when she stiffened.

"No, I'm..." She caught his hand. "I'm okay."

"I'm gonna get you off the floor," he said, moving with heartrending caution. One arm behind her back, one beneath her legs, until she was cradled against the heat of his chest. He rose and carried her not to the bed, but to the couch.

He sat, leaving her on his lap but dropping his arms to his sides. Trix swallowed hard and leaned her head against his shoulder. "It's not you," she whispered.

Finn wrapped her in a hug then, sinking his fingers into her hair to hold her head. "Something happened to you."

She winced. The straightforward words were undeniable, a statement of fact. She'd spent years telling herself that nothing much had happened, nothing special, just the inevitable violations that came along with being a junkie whore on Mac Fleming's compound.

Now, she said it aloud for the first time ever. "Something happened to me."

"After you left Five?"

She couldn't look at him, so she squeezed her eyes shut. "The day I left."

"The day Fleming gave you the drugs." Every muscle in his body tensed, every part of him except for the fingers stroking gently though her hair. "I should have killed him then."

"I had to get out of there." The confession burst forth, a flood of words she couldn't stem. "I didn't take anything with me. I didn't even go home. I knew I could sell the drugs anywhere, so I walked out and I didn't stop. And you—" She bit her tongue.

He tilted her head back. "And I would have shot him."

He would have gotten himself killed going after Fleming. It was the truth, and it had been one of her reasons for leaving without him, but only one of them. The smallest one, because she could have begged and pleaded and Finn would have left it alone.

But he never could have stood by and watched while she struggled to get clean.

Christ, it was tempting to lock that down, keep on hiding it, but she'd made him swear—only the truth from now on. What kind of a hypocritical asshole would she be if she couldn't give him the same?

"That's not all." Her eyes burned, but she forced herself to form the words anyway. "I had to quit, Finn. I couldn't do that with you around, breaking down when things got bad."

All the stoic strength in his expression shattered as he closed his eyes. "You were dying on me. I didn't know what to do."

"I know." Her throat ached. "Mac said I made you weak because I made you feel, and then you couldn't get your shit done."

"Bullshit." He tucked her cheek against his chest, wrapping her in his warmth again. "I wasn't weak, and he knew it. I was more brutal than ever, because I had someone to fight for. It just wasn't him, and that scared him."

"Everything about you scared him, Finn. Maybe even some things about me, too." That was the thing about tyrants. They'd always be terrified of people they couldn't control.

"But you're the one he hurt."

She straightened and looked down to meet Finn's tortured gaze. "He raped me. Sometimes I still have nightmares. But that doesn't mean he didn't hurt you, too. He had enough cruelty to go around."

"You should have told me," Finn said, his voice rough. Fractured. He shifted his hand to cup her cheek, skin barely making contact with hers. "I scared you."

"It happens. Sometimes it's a word or a sound, or I'll remember something new, but it—" She wove her fingers into his hair. "It's not about you. I swear."

"But it hurts you, doll." His hair was soft under her hands, the only soft part of him as he wrapped her in a protective wall of hot skin over hard muscles. "What was it this time?"

"Something you said, it reminded me of him. It doesn't matter."

He wanted to argue. She could feel it in every tense line of his body. He wanted to demand every detail, drag every bad memory out of her so he could be sure he'd never, ever brush against those wounds.

And she knew what would happen next, too. He'd pull back into himself, slam the door on those real, raw bits of himself. He'd deny himself the things he needed out of fear of hurting her, never believing that she could need them too. Because the one way Finn had always failed her was by not believing she was strong enough to endure.

His fingers flexed on her lower back. He wet his lips, and she braced herself for his withdrawal.

"I should have let you kill him," was all he said.

She shook her head, blinking back tears. The moment was so tenuous, and having Finn watch her cry, thinking he'd been the cause of it, could snap it in half.

She kissed his cheek instead, then rested her forehead against his temple. In spite of the pain of her old scars ripping open and the anguish of telling him the truth, she felt lighter already. Free. "He asked me if I wanted to be more than an enforcer's woman. And I hadn't even considered it, you know? It wasn't how I thought of myself—your woman. I was someone you didn't want to care about, no matter how much you did. But as soon as he said it, it felt *right*."

"Right for Sector Five," he murmured. "I'm not an enforcer anymore. I'm an O'Kane woman's man."

His breath shivered over her skin as he spoke, and she smiled. "Even better."

13

TRIX KNEW THAT, sooner or later, she'd have to talk to Mad.

He was in the main warehouse, packing bottles into crates that had the O'Kane logo burned into the side. His shaggy, shoulder-length hair was scraped back from his face in a tight knot, leaving a clear view of his fierce expression—and the bruise decorating one sharp cheekbone.

He looked pissy, but when his gaze snagged on her, the tight set of his eyes still softened.

Under all his anger, Mad *cared*, and that just made it worse.

Trix crossed her arms over her chest and stared at him.

After a tense moment, he curled both hands around the wooden crate and looked away. "I'm worried about you, Trix, and I'm not the only one."

"Bullshit."

The wood creaked under his grip. "We miss you. Since when do you spend every night hiding in your room?"

She couldn't keep the sadness out of her voice. "Since if I come out of it, I have to deal with you being a bully, and then telling me it's for my own good."

He flinched. "That's harsh, sweetheart."

"So own it." She stepped forward. "He hurt Jade. He didn't want to, but he did, and that's why you're so angry."

"Damn it, it's *not all about Jade.*" Mad shoved upright and ran his hands roughly over his hair. "It's about the choices he made, and trusting someone who'd go that far to save his own skin. I know we're all survivors here, but some lines a man shouldn't cross."

Her throat burned. "Is that what you tell Bren? Cruz?"

"You weren't here when Bren joined up," Mad countered. "No one trusted him at first. He earned it. Like Cruz has been earning it, bleeding for us damn near every day."

"Cruz didn't have to put up with this shit. Bren vouched for him, and he helped us out, and that was enough."

Just as her attempts to vouch for Finn hadn't been. She didn't need to say it—it was stark in Mad's expression, riding hard alongside his own shame at not being able to trust. Mad would never want to hurt her by doubting her, but he was doing both.

And he knew it.

"I want to be wrong," he said finally, letting his hands drop to his sides. "I hope I am. If it makes it easier, I'll tell Dallas I need to take another tour of the sectors. You won't have to deal with me, and neither will Finn."

"Why? You think it'll be easier to look at him when

you get back?" she asked softly. "Or do you think it won't matter, because he'll fuck up and be gone by then?"

"Or maybe he'll prove himself. He can't do it from your bedroom."

She didn't want to cry anymore. She wanted to hit him, slap him right across the bruise on his cheek. "Six did it just fine from Bren's."

He recoiled as if she had hit him. "That's not the same thing."

"Yeah?" She shrugged and took a step back. "I guess I could stand here and let you *explain* to me how it's different, but you know what? You don't deserve it."

"Trix—"

"You consider yourself a champion of the wounded, but the truth is that it only counts when someone fits your idea of what that means. You don't give a damn about what Finn had to go through, what he had to do, how much it hurt him. You don't care, because he's not staring up at you with big eyes, asking you to fix the world."

She took another step back and stumbled over a crate sitting on the floor beside a packing table. Mad lunged to steady her, but she shook him off. "No, Adrian. I don't need you to rescue me, okay?"

She and Mad had always been close, and the anger tearing through her brought an even deeper sadness. But she turned and walked out, her head held high as her heart thudded a painful rhythm. Because he was *wrong*—she felt it in every cell, every fiber of her being. Wrong about Finn, wrong about her.

Worst of all, wrong about himself.

Finn spent an hour working alongside Bren in silence before he finally came out and said it. "I don't know how to make friends."

"Yeah?" Bren swiped a hand across his sweaty forehead. "Can't imagine it was a highly valued skill in Five."

"Not really." The best part of working in the garage with Bren was the ever-present bucket of beer. Finn pulled a bottle out of the melting ice and swiped water off the side. "I had one friend, but that was more his idea than mine." And for all he knew, Ryder had only made friends with him to further whatever goal kept him in Five.

"It's not that hard. Find people you like and be yourself," Bren advised. "If they don't appreciate that, they'd be shitty friends anyway."

It felt too much like what he was already doing. Floating by, letting things land however they fell. It would be easier to lock himself in a room with Trix and lose the key, but *easier* wasn't what she needed. She needed her family.

And he needed her family's forgiveness. "Mad pretty much hates me. Is that all about the girl from Two?"

Bren kept working for a moment, then straightened and looked at him. "Hard to say for sure. It's part of it, a big part. But there's also Trix."

"The shit from our past?"

"I'd be lying if I said we didn't all wonder," Bren admitted. "Why you didn't get her the fuck out of there."

The most damning question, the one Trix never asked because she already knew the answer. He'd been too weak to do what needed to be done. He hadn't believed in her inner core of strength or her will to survive. "I thought about it, early on. Maybe someone could tell, because one of my dealers gave her laced product. The first prototype of the addictive additive."

"So then she was hooked." Bren searched his face. "You tried, didn't you?"

"Once." His gut still twisted when he thought about those horrible days in his cabin. He'd almost gone back after he'd lost her to burn the thing to the ground, but leaving it standing had seemed like the punishment he deserved. A painful memorial to all the many ways he'd fucked up. "I watched her crawl to the edge of death. When she begged me to save her, I broke. I couldn't do it."

"She's never talked about it."

"Would you?"

"Nope." Bren went back to his task.

Finn drank half of the beer, as if he could wash away the bitter taste of his failure. He couldn't change the past, but he could make amends. And trying to settle this with Mad was the choice of a man still stuck in Sector Five. A man who believed the hurt he'd put on a woman was a debt he owed the men in her life.

Time to shake free of that bullshit and start thinking as crazy as an O'Kane. "I want to do something for Jade. Give her something she needs, without getting in her face."

Bren wiped his hands on a rag as he considered that. "She has a garden—up on the roof of the main building. She's having a bitch of a time figuring out how to water it without using up our fresh stores."

There were hundreds of creative ways to catch and filter rain, even more ways to play with the water filtration system common in any of the sector buildings built before the Flares. "Can you show me?"

"Sure."

He finished his beer while Bren put away his tools, then followed him out the garage door and across the open space in the middle of the compound. You could still see the roads and sidewalks, evidence of what had been a four-way intersection before Dallas claimed the buildings on every street corner.

A bar and offices. A garage. Two warehouses, a huge building full of living quarters, a workshop, and a storage room. There was chaos and life in the sprawl, signs of an organization that had outgrown itself again and again.

They'd had to make do, more often than not, repurposing what a building was meant for, using the tools at hand to create what they needed.

It was the sort of problem that had always fascinated him, so maybe it wasn't surprising that he felt interest stir when Bren led him up a set of exterior stairs and onto a wide roof.

The skeletal base of the greenhouse was already there. It covered half the available space, with a stack of lumber and tools crowding another third of the roof. With the right reflective material on the tops and sides and a little clever engineering, they'd be able to capture the sunlight and cultivate plants even in the cooler months.

They needed irrigation, insulation. Energy, but solar power was easy to come by in the desert, if you had the resources to install the right equipment.

Finn crossed the roof to grip the metal frame, testing its strength. "My mother was a mechanic. Before the Flares, I mean."

"No shit? What'd she work on?"

"Sustainable tech. She was one of the contractors they hired to complete the city, I guess." It was why she'd been there during the Flares, even though she'd been heavily pregnant with him. "That's how she fed us, those first years. She could take garbage someone else had thrown away and make something out of it."

Those first years. A man like Bren, a soldier trained by the elite forces of Eden, wouldn't miss the words—but he didn't ask.

Instead, he nudged a pile of boards with his boot. "We have lots of stuff stored here. Dallas collects things. Or, if you listen to Lex, hoards them."

"I can probably rig something up, then." He hesitated, flexing his fingers. "Should someone warn her? Don't want to make it look like I'm trying to buy her off, but she might not be anxious to look at my face."

"What do you think?"

That Jade would be within her rights to stab him in the balls, since the last time he'd seen her, he'd been advising Lex and Dallas to help her with a soft, quick trip out of the world. It had been the only mercy he could imagine, sparing her the agony he'd watched Trix suffer for those miserable days of withdrawal.

His habit of underestimating women was clearly going to haunt him for a while. And maybe that was the answer. "I guess I should nut up and ask her, in case she wants to tell me to fuck right the hell off."

The corner of Bren's mouth curved up in a smile. "Now you're catching on."

Only by going against every damn thing he'd ever learned. But those lessons had been ill-fitting, driven into him with pain and punishment. Some had never really stuck at all, and some had lingered only as long as the pain had before his own stubborn nature reasserted itself.

He'd been fighting against the current for so damn long that letting it push him in the other direction was a relief. And it was lazy.

Enough floating. It was time to swim.

lili

AFTER FIVE YEARS as a token wife, Lili knew the proper tempo of a supplication.

Not before dinner, of course. And not without preparation. Every detail mattered, though her husband would never acknowledge the hours she spent buffing and polishing. She had come to appreciate makeup, because clever application could add life and warmth to her face, even when she felt frozen solid beneath the skin.

The illusion was enough, as long as it was perfect. Perfection was invisible. Expected. It was the flaws that distracted, and she couldn't afford distractions. Not tonight.

She set a pristine table. Soup and freshly baked bread. His favorite fish, marinated in the last of the bourbon. The price of liquor seemed to increase as tensions with Sector Four did. It had cost her a diamond bracelet to secure one bottle of O'Kane whiskey, but she counted it worth the loss.

Logan liked a drink after dinner, and it was her job to provide Logan Beckett with the things he liked—and to thank all the gods that existed that she wasn't required to provide him with her body, too.

She poured his drink herself and only then settled into her chair. Gracefully. Silently. The opening movement of the night's performance. *A dutiful wife. Tempo di adagio.*

He ignored her completely.

Most nights, she would have considered the lack of attention a relief. There was a certain safety in knowing she'd done her job so well that he'd forgotten she was even there. She was like a lamp or a hutch—decorative and useful, but otherwise unworthy of note.

But tonight she wanted something, so she sipped her wine and waited until he'd finished his soup. "I hope you like the fish. It's fresh from Sector Six."

This time, he replied. "Make sure my charcoal suit is pressed."

She had too much practice to frown, but the charcoal was his best. The one he only donned when he intended to make an impression. "Of course. Will you need anything else?"

"My blue silk tie."

He wasn't going to make this easy. Lili drew a careful breath and put everything into making her voice soft and respectful. "If you're going to be busy with important matters, perhaps I could visit my mother."

Logan paused with his fork halfway to his mouth. "Why would you want to do that?"

Because her mother was a widow, grieving or no, in ill health, and trapped on a remote estate with Lili's terrified brothers and sisters. "I thought I could help her with the children."

"She has staff to help her."

The wise course would be to bite her lip and subside.

Her petition had been denied, after all, and that should be the end of it.

God, she was tired of *subsiding*. "Staff isn't the same as family."

Logan blew out an annoyed breath. "My answer is no. You have other things to focus on at the moment."

She felt some vague stirrings of disappointment, somewhere beneath the chilly numbness offered by the pills she took every morning. The emotion wasn't strong enough to break through, though. Nothing ever did, except for her exhaustion. "Where should I turn my attentions, then?"

He cast a sharp glance her way. "I don't like your tone, darling."

"I'm sorry," she lied blandly. That was the blessing and curse of numbness—no real fear. "I didn't realize I had a tone."

He picked up his drink. "Be more mindful of it in the future."

The future. It stretched out before her in perpetual sameness, and she felt something now. Claustrophobia, as if the walls of the house were shrinking in around her and one day would swallow her whole.

She pushed her chair back and rose. "Perhaps I should leave you in peace."

"Sit."

The ice fractured, just enough for rebellion to seep through. "I'm really not feeling well, Logan—"

He swept out his arm, and his plate crashed to the floor, shattering on the polished wood. But his voice was soft. Deadly. "Have a seat, Lili."

No one would notice or care if her husband murdered her, so Lili sat.

Logan picked up his napkin and wiped the corner of his mouth. "I've indulged you too much, it seems."

"I just wanted to see my family."

"Our children will be your family." He dropped his

napkin. "We'll start your drug therapy now. That way, you'll be ready."

Oh, there was the fear. The first stirrings of an old terror, the one that had made her reach for the drugs to begin with. She'd been fifteen, her mother's wedding-night advice ringing in her ears like a curse. *If you close your eyes and stay still, it can be over quickly. It will hurt, but you'll recover.* And then, most terrifying of all, *Be sure not to struggle. It will only encourage him.*

The unfamiliar strength of the emotion made her voice shake. "You promised."

"I promised you time," Logan retorted. "And I've given you five goddamn years."

Five years of making his dinners, entertaining his guests, pouring his drinks. Five years of donning makeup and jewels like armor. She'd played wife like a child playing house, because innocence was safety.

Or it had been.

She met Logan's eyes—those cold, chilly eyes. He didn't sample pharmaceuticals to enhance the icy unconcern in them. It was there all the time, a warning she ignored now. "I'll start the therapy willingly if you let me see my family."

His lips curved in an indulgent smile, and he pushed his chair back from the table. "Come here."

She wasn't stupid. His eyes were empty, still frozen. But there was no escape, so she rose, smoothed down her dress, and circled the table.

He patted his leg. "Sit down."

Spine stiff, heart pounding, she obeyed.

Logan lifted one hand to her hair, stroking carefully through the loose curls. "Lili. Beautiful Lili."

He never praised her in private. Compliments were useful only as a means of showing off, of rubbing his employees' noses in all the things they couldn't have. She couldn't trust the words, or the gentleness in his touch. "Please, Logan."

"You're a flower. *My* flower." His hand tightened, dragging her head back, pulling her hair so hard it burned. "And flowers don't argue, do they? They look pretty, they remain silent, and they *do what they're fucking told*."

She nodded her understanding, tears pricking her eyes as even that movement threatened to tear the hair from her scalp. Pretty and silent, tears sparkling on her lashes—the image would please him. Just like his gardens pleased him—gardens she labored over for hours every spring, because, contrary to Logan's silly, stupid words, flowers never did what you wanted them to.

No, he only saw the gardens after they'd been coaxed into life and submission. He only saw roses in vases, once they'd been cut and stripped of their thorns. So there was another thing he didn't know, would never see coming.

Flowers could be painful, poisonous. Even deadly.

14

THE VIEW FROM the VIP section of the Broken Circle was damn good.

Parked in the corner of one of the reserved booths, Finn could see the stage and the bar. As pretty as the brunette swinging her hips on the stage was, though, his gaze kept straying to the bar, waiting for the familiar flash of red hair.

There was a blonde working there now. Rachel, the one who brewed the beer Bren shared so freely. He was starting to match names with faces now, as the women dropped their wary defenses and came around to say hello.

The fact that he and Hawk were sitting with Jas and Bren probably didn't hurt.

Jas was talking about Sector Three. "Now that we have things cleaned up, we have to figure out what kinds of resources are there."

Hawk rubbed his thumb along the edge of his glass. "They provided electronics, right? Before Eden firebombed their asses, I mean. So what do they do now?"

"Not much of anything," Bren answered. "That's the problem."

Sector Four had always been heavily populated by crafters and artists, a legacy of Eden's original vision—a city where *handmade* and *organic* were more highly valued than the mass production of Sector Eight. Then the world had collapsed, and the pretentiousness had given way to practicality.

Trades were passed from parent to child, which made a place like Three a pit of hopelessness. All the jobs had been wiped out, along with most of the adults holding them. All that remained were stubborn orphans and opportunistic criminals.

Not exactly a prize, which made Dallas O'Kane even crazier for agreeing to take it on. "They need a purpose, then. One that makes them valuable but not so successful that Eden comes down on you. No small trick, huh?"

Jas lit a cigarette. "Not hardly. But Dallas took it on, and he'll make it work." He eyed Finn and Hawk appraisingly. "You two want to be in on it?"

Hawk slammed back his shot and met Finn's gaze. "You said you came up from the tunnels in one of the warehouses over in Six. You should tell them what you saw inside it."

He hadn't seen a damn thing—and Finn's stomach flipped end over end at the confirmation in the other man's eyes. He'd taken note of it at the time but had shoved it out of his mind in the chaos that followed.

"It was empty," he told Bren. A man who'd worked for Eden's government would understand the terrifying implications. "Harvest was only a few months ago, but it was scrubbed clean. And maybe it's the only one—"

"It's not," Hawk said. "Probably half of them are like that. And it's even worse in Seven."

The two O'Kanes at the table traded a sober look, and Bren picked up a bottle to refill their glasses. Casually, as if his next sentence wouldn't have gotten him shot in Eden. "Nothing sparks revolution like hungry people."

If the good folks inside Eden ever realized how tenuous their situation was, the rebellion wouldn't stay outside the walls, either. "Maybe we shouldn't stop with Jade's garden," Finn said. "We got resources, we got roofs, and we got a hell of a lot of useless folk needing work. Hawk can teach them to grow food."

Jas quirked an eyebrow. "I've done some farming in my time, too. Not a bad idea."

"Fifty-fifty," Hawk said. "That was the promise when the original stakeholders claimed the farms in Six and Seven. Everything was set up for them, all they had to do was work the land. Fifty percent of the yields went to Eden, the rest they could sell to support themselves and their workers. Now we have to give up close to eighty percent, and it's still not enough for them."

"Nothing ever will be," Bren muttered.

No, it wouldn't. And when Eden felt the pinch, they weren't going to worry about splitting what was left fairly between their citizens and the sectors. "If we start soon, we can probably get a lot of garden setups into place before spring."

"You keep saying *we*," Jas observed.

Finn stilled. The word had come without thought, slipping into his vocabulary at some point during the afternoon. It should have felt awkward, especially since the last time he'd felt a part of something...

This is how we go down. Riding Fleming's hate into our graves.

We can probably get a lot of garden setups into place before spring.

Death and life. No, not just life. Hope. "Is that a problem?"

"No." Jas downed his whiskey. "I was thinking it sounded kind of good."

Finn couldn't help it. He grinned. "Does that mean you're not gonna kick my ass in the cage next week?"

Jas laughed. "Don't get crazy, now."

Jas might still punch him in the face a few times, but then he'd slap him on the back and get him a drink, because part of belonging would always be a willingness to bleed for and with your brothers. And that's what Jas and Bren would be, if he stayed. The brothers Finn had never had, the family he'd barely realized he wanted.

Hawk was still staring at the liquor. "Are there many empty buildings in Three?"

"There's a lot of rubble in the old manufacturing district," Bren told him. "But Eden's strikes were focused there. Plenty of tenements and residential buildings survived."

"Dallas should talk to Shipp. We could use a second base of operations, and most of the guys have been working the farm for a decade or more." Hawk glanced up, and sympathy stirred at the haunted look in his eyes.

Finn owed Shipp and Alya. For the life they'd given up, for the risks they'd taken to get him and Trix home. Demanding so much had been the act of a desperate man. Now that Finn had his feet under him, the right thing to do was give back. "They could be useful as more than farmers. These bastards have the fastest fucking cars in all eight sectors. And they can build an engine out of toothpicks and gum wrappers, if you give them enough time."

"Maybe," Jas agreed as the music changed to something older, with blaring horns and a suggestive jazz line. He almost choked on his drink and looked at Finn. "When you said Trix was working tonight, I thought you meant behind the bar."

He'd thought that too, so he opened his mouth to ask what the fuck Jas meant.

And Trix appeared on the stage. Her breasts nearly spilled out over the top of her tiny green corset, and she carried a spray of peacock feathers at the small of her back. They brushed the backs of her endless bare legs as she crossed the stage, smiling at the audience.

Sweet holy hell.

Her skin sparkled under the lights—that damn glitter the soap lady had sold her, no doubt—and she shimmied as the music sped then kicked into some kind of drum roll. She flicked her wrists, and the feathers spread out into two giant fans.

The crowd whistled its excitement, and Finn wavered between appreciation for how easily she'd captivated every person in the room and the wild, homicidal urge to smash every cheering face into the nearest flat surface until he was the only one gaping at her.

Hawk's voice cut through his confusion. "You might wanna put that bottle down before you do something stupid with it."

Finn blinked at his hand, which had closed around the whiskey in a white-knuckled grip. In lieu of smashing it into someone's head, he took a long gulp and then another, shuddering as it burned down his throat to meet the fire raging in his gut.

She was fucking spectacular. And she was just getting started.

Trix dipped and swayed, the fans flashing around her as she twirled. Every moment of the dance had been orchestrated to tease. The fans obscured what was already covered by the corset and her ruffled panties, but something about the glimpses behind the feathers seemed illicit.

She danced behind a thin screen set up on the corner of the stage. It was directly backlit, clearly showing her silhouette as she moved behind it.

"Here we go," Bren murmured.

A green satin glove sailed through the air to land on the stage, and the crowd went wild.

For a *glove.*

Trix had them in the palm of her newly bared hand, and they couldn't even see it. Because she'd made an art form out of the slow tease, out of letting a man's lecherous imagination fill in all the details she hinted at.

She wasn't giving them a damn thing, and they were eating it up and begging for more. "Fucking hell."

The second glove joined the first, and Finn watched the clear outline of her shadow on the screen as she ran her hands down the luscious curves of her body and back up again.

He didn't realize she was unhooking the corset until it fell away in her hands, and she reached one long, bare arm over the top of the screen and dropped it to the stage.

She emerged with a flourish, both fans spread over the front of her body. It left her back bare when she spun around, presenting the audience with the one part of her still covered—her full, beautiful, mouthwatering ass.

She moved her hips in time with the music, bumping left and then right before circling in a slow grind. The whistles and cheers swelled again, and Trix's hair spilled over her back as she craned her head to look at them.

At *him.*

She winked, then slowly licked her shoulder.

She might as well have licked his cock.

Arousal in public wasn't a new thing. He'd had Trix crawling in his lap during Sector Five parties. He'd had her hands and her mouth on his dick. Usually while he was bombed out of his skull, high enough for the world to be numb even if his body never was. Not numb enough. Not while she was around.

This was different. Hotter, and flat-out wrong. Every man in the crowd was picturing what was beneath those fans, imagining that her saucy winks and the flirtatious swing of her hips was for him alone.

But it wasn't. This wasn't for them, or even for him. Trix was in her element, reveling in every scrap of freedom she'd won, showing off the body she'd reclaimed from the faded wraith she'd been.

She was a goddess, and not a man in this room was worthy of her little piece of heaven.

She resumed her dance. The fans spun in careful time, revealing no more than flashes of pale skin as she twirled. Then the music slowed to a careful, sensuous rhythm, and she slowed with it, sliding the fans over her body.

He couldn't hear it, so he almost missed her hitching gasp. But when she arched her back, one nipple peeked through the green feathers—hard, a shade darker than usual. The way they got when she was turned on.

Oh yeah, this dance was all for her, and she was getting off on it.

Hawk tried to pull the bottle out of his hand, and Finn bared his teeth. "Don't even think about it."

"Let him keep the whiskey. There's more where that came from." Jas chuckled and motioned to the bar. "Besides, he looks like he needs it."

Finn felt secure enough to mutter, "Fuck off," as a brunette approached the table with another bottle. She was wearing a corset, too, and though her rack wasn't as impressive as Trix's, it was on enough display that *someone* should have tried to catch an eyeful on her way past.

When the girl thumped the bottle to the table and leaned over to kiss Jasper, Finn understood why no one was risking it. Up close, the decorative ink wrapped around her throat proved to be more than simple lace. Jasper's name was woven into it, the J resting in the hollow of her throat.

Noelle Cunningham, then. Eden's most infamous refugee. Finn had been vaguely aware of her during her life as a councilman's daughter, mostly because her father had been bitter enemies with Gareth Woods, Fleming's pet council member. Her fall from grace had been spectacular, though, and it had altered the course of Finn's life in ways she'd never know.

It all came back to Woods. Fleming's ally. Cunningham's enemy. Jade's patron, the man who'd demanded her drugged into helpless addiction to ensure her obedience. Every two weeks, Finn had made the miserable trek to Fleming's private love nest. He'd delivered the drugs that kept Jade weak and docile. He'd hated himself, hated Fleming, hated Woods...

That hell might have gone on forever if Woods hadn't tried to kill Noelle. It had been like watching dominoes fall after that, the O'Kanes sweeping through Woods' life on the path of vengeance. They'd rescued Jade, left a dead councilman in their wake—and given Finn the opportunity to sever the relationship between Five and Two for good.

All because one girl had walked into the sectors and fallen in love with an O'Kane.

She didn't look much like a councilman's daughter anymore. She perched next to Jas and gave Finn a look of pure, gleeful mischief. "Has anyone warned you that the glitter gets everywhere? And you can't wash it off."

Finn glanced at the stage, at the elegant line of Trix's spine, her pale skin iridescent as each tiny flake caught the light. Yeah, when this show came to an end, he was going to get that shit all over himself. "A real man can handle a little glitter."

Bren snorted. "She's just busting your balls."

"You say that because Six doesn't wear glitter." Noelle rose, running her fingertips over Jas's shoulder in an absent caress that seemed second nature. The O'Kanes were always touching each other, hugs and slaps on the back and friendly kisses, but this was more. Her fingers found him the way Finn's lingered on Trix, because being around her without touching her just felt wrong.

"You can watch the show from out here if you want," she continued. "Or you can go through the door on the other end of the VIP section and get the backstage view." She grinned and sank her hand into Jas's hair. "You're a fan of it, aren't you, baby?"

His hand landed on her hip. He squeezed tight, his fingers digging into her skin. "You know it."

Finn glanced at Bren, who shrugged one shoulder. "Better move fast, or she'll be done before you get there."

From the sleepy, aroused look in Trix's eyes and the languid, sensual pivot of her hips, it might be true in more ways than one. So Finn abandoned his new friends, abandoned his liquor, and went for the door.

15

TRIX WAS ALWAYS high after a performance. The adrenaline that rushed through her veins was powerful, undeniable, jacking her up in ways her body only knew how to associate with drugs or sex.

These days, it was sex. As the harsh lights heated the sweat sheening her skin, Trix took her last bow and looked out at the booth where Finn had been sitting.

He was gone.

Fuck.

She folded her fans with a groan as soon as she stepped into the cool darkness backstage. So much for grabbing Finn for a quick, hard ride in the kitchen storeroom.

"Hey, baby doll."

The rough voice shivered up her spine like a caress, and she turned. Finn was leaning against the brick wall in the back hallway, watching her.

"There you are." She dropped her fans on a chair by the back curtain and walked toward him. "Did you like the show?"

"Oh, yeah." He pushed off the wall but didn't step closer. He was waiting for her, the sexual hunger burning in his gaze leashed—for the moment.

She stopped just out of arm's reach, her skin heating even further. She was naked except for her shoes and her panties, the only parts of her costume she hadn't left on the stage floor—and she loved it. Loved the way he looked at her, drinking in every inch of bare skin.

"You liked it." She let her own gaze travel down his body to the erection straining the front of his pants. "How much?"

Finn smiled and held out a hand. "Find out."

Her fingertips touched his, and electric awareness ran through her like a shock. Then he caught her hand and dragged her to him. By the time their bodies collided, he already had his hands under her ass, lifting her until his mouth found hers.

It was heaven, the kind of contact she'd imagined on the stage as the feathers had tickled over her skin—but better. He parted his lips, his tongue searching for hers. She met it eagerly, licking in a slow mimicry of her hips rocking against his.

Her back hit smooth wood, and Finn groaned. "Where does this door go?"

"Door?"

He nipped his way along her jaw, wrecking any hope of concentration as he paused to suck the spot just below her ear. "The door, baby. Is it a closet? Should we just fuck up against it?"

"Prop—" The word broke with her shiver, and she wrapped her arms around his neck. "Prop closet."

He braced her weight with one arm and groped for the doorknob, so impatient he had them through the door and her back up against the inside of it before she could stop the world from spinning.

It was dark in the closet, the thin line of illumination beneath the door too faint to give shapes more than the vaguest of outlines. But Finn was pressed all along her body, his hands on her ass, his mouth on her throat. "Tell me what you were thinking out there."

Thinking wasn't part of the process when she danced. It was the one time she could shut off her brain and just *be*, without worrying about anything but how it felt to move her body beneath the lights. "I wasn't. I did what felt good."

He hoisted her higher, pinning her to the door with her thighs spread wide. "You were touching your tits behind that screen. Playing with your nipples. Do it again."

Her hands trembled as she slid them from his shoulders and cupped her breasts. "You could see me?"

Instead of answering, he licked her fingers.

The caress burned through her, wet and rough. She arched off the door, trying to get closer, and the scratch of the wood sparked a realization. This was passion—pure and unrestrained, the kind she'd longed for in those early years with Finn. The kind he wouldn't allow himself.

They had it now.

His tongue snuck between her parted fingers, found her nipple. He circled and teased, and when she spread her fingers wider, he sucked the tip into his mouth.

She held her breath, waiting. Then the edge of his teeth grazed her nipple, and she cried out. She slid her hands into his hair, tugging, pulling, with no idea whether she was trying to drag him away or clutch him closer.

It didn't matter. He was immovable. He took his time, working her to the edge of insanity before switching to the other breast, and she was writhing in his arms before he lifted his head. "Are you with me?"

A tiny shaft of light fell across his face, and she traced its path with her fingertips, from high on his left cheek to the right corner of his mouth. “I love you.”

Finn stilled, his body tense against hers. Silence spun out, heavy until he broke it with a rough noise. “Say it again.”

He’d heard it before. She vaguely remembered whispering the words over and over, high as a kite and spinning away on a kaleidoscope of colors. This was different, not only because she was stone sober, but because she finally understood why she’d never contacted him, even after she was safe with the O’Kanes.

She’d been afraid.

Once upon a time, she’d seen those same emotions echoed in his eyes. Nothing about her feelings had changed with her sobriety, but if she saw him again, she’d have to face the possibility that it had all been an illusion. That he’d never cared about her the way she’d cared about him. That he was still everything, and she was a girl he used to know.

None of that mattered now. He was watching her so intently she could see the truth of the words he hadn’t spoken, and she touched his lips. “I love you, Finn.”

He closed his eyes. “I’m gonna work every fucking day until I deserve you.”

“Shh.” She leaned her forehead to his and shook her head. “Just...show me.”

She didn’t know how he got his pants open and didn’t care when he tore her flimsy costume panties in his rush. All that mattered was his fingers curling under her thighs, hauling them wide as his shaft slicked between her pussy lips.

She rocked, rubbing her clit against him. A pulse of pleasure raced through her, so quick and intense she almost came right then.

“Not yet,” he rasped. “Not until I’m in you.”

Release beckoned, but Trix gritted her teeth with a

groan. "*Hurry.*"

But he didn't. He took forever. Gripping her legs, tilting her hips. Positioning his cock so that the broad head pressed to her entrance, so that all he'd have to do was loosen his hold and let her sink onto him.

His lips brushed hers. His words were barely a whisper. "This is everything."

She hovered there, so close to being filled, for what seemed like an eternity. Finally, she reached down and pried his fingers from her thighs. She held herself up for one more heartbeat, braced on his tense arms, then lurched against him.

He drove into her, and stars exploded in her vision, tiny specks of dancing light that lingered as he slapped one hand to the door with a groan. "Jesus *fuck*, woman."

"Yes," she hissed, beyond caring about anything but the hard thrust of his cock as she locked her legs around his hips. "I need you."

She almost whimpered when he pulled back, but the waiting was over. He drove into her, quick and deep and rough enough to curl her toes. "Take me."

She flexed her hands on his shoulders and arched off the door. "Don't hold back. I want all of you."

His next advance crashed her into the polished wood. "You're tough enough to take it."

"Everything." Every rough, raw part of him, head to toe. Body and soul.

"Hold on." It was her only warning before he dropped his hands to her ass, fingertips digging into her flesh as he braced her for his quickened pace. Steady, hard, thrust after thrust punctuated by his low, rough noises. Satisfied as he came into her and snarling in frustration as he retreated, as if he couldn't stand pulling back but couldn't resist driving her higher.

One of her shoes fell to the floor with a thump. She kicked off the other as well, then braced her feet on the backs of his thighs. The faded denim he wore was warm, but the rest of him burned—where his skin touched hers, where his eyes lingered on her, and especially where he held her captive for his pounding thrusts.

His breath heated her jaw. Her cheek. Her ear. "Touch yourself. Get off on me. Take what you want from me."

It was too much like the old days, when she'd had to beg him to touch her, and then every bit of his guilty attention had been focused on making her come, as if the pleasure could make up for the fact that he hadn't meant to touch her at all.

She wasn't that girl anymore.

"No." She stretched her arms above her head, resting her wrists against the door. "Get off on *me*."

He shuddered.

And then he buried his face against her throat, muffling his groan of surrender, and rode her until his entire body stiffened in release.

The pulsing of his cock made her clench around him. A little harder and she could have sent herself tripping after him—but she couldn't bring herself to give up the moment of quiet abandon. So she held him close, pressed her lips to his ear, and relished the way his heart beat so hard she could feel it through the wall of his chest.

After a moment, he freed one hand from her body and groped at the wall next to them. Light sparked to life over their heads, near-blinding after the darkness, but Finn didn't let her hide from it. He tilted her chin up, his gaze sweeping over her face. "Is that what you wanted?"

He was staring at her like she couldn't be real, like she'd vanish into smoke at any moment—and like he wasn't done with her, not even close. "Yes."

"Good." He was still seated deep, every flex of his hips shivering through her as he pulled away from the door and turned. His gaze swept past her, taking in the full size of the room and the contents of the cluttered shelves. One of his eyebrows edged up. "The prop room, huh? Any of this yours?"

"Some. Why, you want to see another dance?"

He lowered her carefully to the floor and spun her to face the room. "Show me."

There was the sequined red corset she'd commissioned for her very first act, and the dozen diaphanous scarves she'd used for her second. Shoes, jewelry, even an antique rhinestone-studded headpiece from Las Vegas that she'd tried and judged too heavy.

But she knew what he'd really want to see, so she walked to the open wardrobe in the corner and pulled out the hanger with her long strings of faux pearls. "These are mine."

He caught one strand and let them slide through his fingers. "And what do you do with these, baby?"

"I dance in them." The strands clicked as she wiggled the hanger. "Nothing but heels and pearls. You'd be surprised how well that goes over."

His hand closed, dragging the pearls closer and leaving her with the choice to either release them or get drawn into the circle of sudden intensity. "Not anymore. These are for me."

She held on. "Why?"

He frowned, and she could see him struggling for the words, frustration mounting in his eyes.

It made her chest ache. "Because you want it," she whispered, releasing the hanger, and the pearls dropped to hang from his clenched hand. "That's all you have to say."

He curled his free hand around the back of her neck and stepped close, backing her against the wardrobe door. "I'm trying to learn to share you. Maybe it'll be easier if some stuff's just mine."

She stilled his words with one finger over his lips. "Put them on me, Finn."

He smiled and looped the first one over her head. It settled across her shoulders, trapping her hair against her skin, and swung down between her breasts to hang just shy of her belly button. The next one was longer, the cool edges of the fake pearls tickling low on her abdomen.

"Hold out your arms," he murmured, fingering the next strand.

Her breath hitched in her throat as she realized what he meant, and she stretched out both arms in front of her, crossing them at the wrists.

He was so gentle, teasing the pearls over her skin and around her wrists without pulling them tight. Not at first, not until he'd rubbed the silky-smooth edges up and down her arms. This strand was the second longest, looping around and around until she was trapped in a cage that clicked with every movement.

Then he left her to watch as he wrapped the last strand around his hand a few times, those wide, blunt fingers caressing it suggestively while his gaze drifted down her body. "You haven't come yet, have you, baby?"

Oh, God. "No."

"Do you want to?"

"Christ, yes."

"Do you need to?"

She swayed toward him. "I need *you.*"

"Good." He lowered his head, letting his lips almost, *almost* brush hers. But when she reached to kiss him, he smiled and stayed just out of reach. "Lift your arms."

Trix obeyed with a moan. "Tease."

"Maybe." With the last strand still looped around his hand, he ran the backs of his fingers down the center of her chest. "What are the chances someone's gonna walk into this closet and find you riding my fingers?"

Pretty damn good, actually—and, judging from the arousal in his eyes, exactly what he wanted to hear. So she told him, enunciating every word carefully. "They might just stay and watch."

"Yeah?" His meandering caress slipped along the curve of her breast. When he reached the tip, he took his time, working the tight rows of pearls back and forth across her nipple until it was pinched between them. He snagged the long trailing edge with his other hand and rubbed it over her hip. "Do you miss that?"

The words barely penetrated the haze of pleasure. "What, being watched?"

"Being with them." Lower, lower... She shuddered as he worked his fingers over her pussy, worked her open, those damn pearls still trapped between his skin and her body and rubbing against her in caresses as intoxicating as his words. "You can ride me anywhere you want. In a closet, at a party, on the damn stage."

She swallowed a shocked noise, but she couldn't stop her hips from bucking into his touch. "You'd—you'd do that?"

He caught her gaze as his fingertips ghosted so close to her clit—and froze. "I'd do anything."

She couldn't move, and she couldn't look away from his eyes—dark, intent. Serious. He meant every word.

No holding back. No limits.

He didn't relinquish her gaze, not even as he sank to his knees and coaxed her thighs wider. Not even as he stroked that final, taunting strand of pearls lower, gathering plenty of her own slick arousal before slowly working them into her.

The cool beads massaged her inner walls, moving in different directions all at once, and the shock of it dragged another moan from her throat.

His fingers retreated. Returned, pushing still more sensation before them. Not enough to stretch her the way his cock had, but it was a different sort of fullness, one that drove her closer to the edge of release without letting her fall.

"I could do this all night," he rumbled, his breath teasingly close to her pussy as he worked the next few inches of the strand into her. "Play with you. Watch you get high on me."

It sounded like torture—and it sounded like heaven. "*Finn.*"

His fingers thrust into her again. She was so full now, her legs trembling as he crooked his fingers, just a little, and set off a brief jolt of fire. "I went by that shop, you know. The one with the leather...and all the other things. I could get used to some of this high-class, kinky fucking."

The very thought was enough to make her fidget, but shifting her hips even the slightest bit set off another jolt strong enough to make her shudder. "What did you like there? I'll fucking buy it tomorrow, I swear."

"Shh." One more rocking thrust of his fingers and his gaze finally dropped from hers. She'd never been this exposed before, laid bare as he parted her and stared as if her swollen, aroused flesh was the most beautiful thing he'd ever seen in his life.

Then he met her eyes again, and she knew his last filter had been stripped away. He licked one thumb and settled it over her clit, rubbing in slow, deadly circles. "I want you to wear these with that blue dress next time. The one with all those damn lacy layers."

Her blue dress with the polka dots. Her mind filed it away with surreal serenity, considering her trembling limbs and galloping pulse.

"No panties," he added with a sudden, wicked grin. "Nothing underneath it but you, so when I bend you over my lap, it's just all those ruffles and your perfect damn ass."

She had to drop her bound hands to his head to steady herself. "Say it."

The wariness was in his eyes. The fear of scaring her, of hurting her. But he said it anyway, letting the words fall between them with the hoarseness of a man letting go. "I want to spank you. And I want it to get you wet."

The one thing he needed above all others—her

pleasure. "It will."

His eyelids drooped. He lifted his thumb, licked her taste from it, and returned with a firmer touch. "I want to work these pearls into you again, until you're on the edge, just like this."

The knot of pleasure wound tighter, dangerously close to an ache now. But she held back, because she needed to hear more. Every delicious detail.

He rose slowly, catching her wrists and pressing them up above her head. His other hand cupped her pussy, his palm firmly possessive and torturous against her slick, swollen flesh. Holding her gaze, he curled two fingers inside her, setting off a dangerous wobble in her knees.

The pearls shifted. His fingers crooked, rubbing them inside her with slow precision until he found the spot that stole her breath and arched her spine.

Smiling, Finn pressed the heel of his hand against her clit. His voice dropped to a whisper, as if he'd saved the most illicit part for last. "And then I'll take the one thing I missed the most after I lost you. The thing I regretted not doing all the damn time."

He didn't give her a chance to ask. He showed her by capturing her lips in a kiss so painfully gentle, her brain stuttered. For a moment, she couldn't process the dichotomy of that sweet, hungry kiss versus the firm, demanding movements of his fingers inside her.

Then his tongue touched hers, and everything snapped into place. She fell into his kiss as the first waves of orgasm broke through her, and he swallowed her rough, helpless cry as it continued to build.

He was so sweet. So gentle. So *brutal.* After so long on edge, her entire body shuddered under the force of release, and he kept pace with it, pushing her higher so that the first wild rush of release broke open into a second, rougher climax.

Her knees buckled, and he braced her weight with

one arm around her body. He dragged her side against his chest, his renewed erection grinding against her hip, but even that didn't buy her mercy. He thrust his fingers harder, and he groaned in her ear. "You can take more, can't you?"

"Fuck—" Her breath caught on a sob. She couldn't, she just *couldn't.* "Don't stop—"

He bit her jaw and somehow pushed a third finger inside her. Along with the pearls, it should have been uncomfortable, even painful, but all Trix knew was pleasure—blazing, blinding. Transcendent.

Vaguely, she realized they were moving, sinking. When she opened her eyes, she was on the floor, on Finn's lap. He made a soothing noise against her cheek as he eased the pearls from her body. "Next time, we do this on a bed."

"If we can get to one." The words came out sounding slurred and far away as blood rushed in her ears.

"No shit." He tossed the strand of beads aside and slid a gentle hand between her thighs. "You so much as twitch your finger at me, and my self-control goes to hell."

"Good." She was oversensitized, like one giant nerve laid bare to his touch, but she didn't jerk away. He would always be more careful with her than he would with himself. "I like you that way."

"You better, because my dick hasn't recovered this fast in years." But even though she could feel the hard heat of him against her ass, he didn't make any move to get in her. Just kept up his slow, soothing caress.

Trix fought a smile. "Finn?"

"Mmm?"

"We're not done yet."

His fingertip grazed her clit with the softest pressure. "We can be, if you're wrung out."

Sated, exhausted, but none of that mattered when he touched her. Arousal unfurled in her belly again, licking through her like flames.

She shifted on his lap, easing up until she could wrap her legs around his hips. She settled with her bound arms around his neck, her breasts pressed against his chest.

Finn curled his hands around her waist and lifted. So slow. So careful. He pushed into her one agonizing inch at a time, his muscles tense with the effort.

It felt like coming home.

Trix buried her face in the hollow of his shoulder and held on as he rocked her slow and steady, guiding her to roll her hips at a pace that had to be torturous when he was so hard inside her. But he didn't hurry her, just spread both hands wide on her back and groaned. "We'll never be done."

Four years and a world of distance hadn't stopped them from winding up right here at this very moment. He'd thought she was *dead*, and that hadn't stopped him from picking her up when she'd stumbled back into his life.

Nothing would stop him, and she needed to hear it so badly that her throat ached. "Say it," she whispered against his skin. "Just once."

"I'm not going anywhere," he promised, low and rough. "I'll never leave you."

She moaned and turned her head to find his mouth, open and searching. He kissed her as their gentle rocking sped, as his hands slipped down to grip her hips. He lifted her a little quicker each time, brought her down a little harder—but it was still careful. Still *loving*.

Finn used words to distract or deflect, but he used his body when it mattered. He wasn't making love to her. He was declaring it, swearing it, showing it with every kiss and lick and bite and thrust.

A slower climb, but just as high, just as fierce. She clenched her hands in his hair and pulled as her shivers of pleasure turned into a full-body tremble.

He kissed her throat. Buried his face against it and groaned. "Come with me. I need to feel you this time."

Her skin burned and her heart pounded. She was tense, so tense, everything drawn tight. Then Finn shifted her hips, dragged her down into a thrust harder than the others, and she shattered.

He clamped a hand over her mouth, letting her scream her release against his palm as he shuddered and groaned his own. His forehead fell to hers, his hand caught between their lips, muffling their panted breaths.

The door slammed open, and Jeni walked in. "Oh, shit." She squeezed her eyes shut and backed up, only to run into the doorframe. "Fuck, sorry. Shit, I'm sorry—"

Finn let his hand fall away with a choked laugh. "Dammit."

"*Fuck*," Jeni said again.

She sounded so mortified, almost scandalized. Trix couldn't help but laugh. "No, we're finished, thanks."

"You could still close the door, though," Finn grumbled.

The door swung shut, and Jeni's voice drifted through it. "Sorry."

Trix swallowed another round of giggles. "Think she apologized enough?"

"She didn't pull a gun on me." Finn rubbed his thumb along her jaw. "I'd call it a win."

She closed her eyes and leaned in to his touch, letting the quiet peace of the moment steal through her. "The pearls are yours, and so am I."

"Fuck the pearls. I only need you."

I'll never leave you. For the first time, she believed it.

16

FINN HEARD THE voices from inside the garage. Not one or two people having a too-loud conversation or a party that had spilled out of the Broken Circle, but the distinct murmur of an anxious crowd—one that was growing larger.

Abandoning his current project, he stepped out into the courtyard and surveyed the tight knot of O'Kanes hovering just outside the barracks. Dallas and Lex stood to one side, looking grim enough to twist worry through Finn's gut. He scanned the crowd quickly, that worry ramping up when he couldn't find a flash of familiar red hair.

He found Bren instead. Finn stopped next to where the man stood on the edge of the crowd. "Is something wrong?"

"Maybe," he answered cryptically. "Doc's been in there with Flash and Amira."

The bouncer and the waitress weren't the sort of power players Finn had needed to know about for his duties in Sector Five, but on the O'Kane compound one thing set them apart from everyone else—their daughter.

Before Finn could ask about her, a strangled sob came from inside the building. Muffled but audible, more so when the crowd fell silent.

"Shit," Bren muttered under his breath.

The door opened, and the doctor stepped out. He was a mess, his jaw stubbled, his eyes bloodshot. But he looked sober, at least, even if it seemed like he hated being that way.

That discomfort just got worse when he faced the crowd, and Finn got the feeling the man hadn't been coming out to explain what was going on. He was flat-out fucking fleeing whatever had set off those heartbreaking sobs.

Dallas lifted a hand and crooked two fingers in summons. Doc obeyed, but with a snarl. "Fuck off, O'Kane. You want to know, you talk to Flash. Doesn't matter, anyway."

Dallas's stern expression didn't waver. "Tell me. Now."

"Or what? You'll beat the shit out of me?"

"Dylan." Lex's voice cut through the silence, but not in command. She stood there, both arms wrapped around her midsection, as if shielding herself. "Please."

"Oh, fucking hell." The man grimaced. "Hana's sick."

Dallas didn't ask how sick. He didn't need to, with the sound of Amira's grief ripping through all of them. "How do I fix it?"

The doctor's answer was final. Damning. "You can't."

"Bullshit. I can find a regen tech—"

"And it won't do any good, O'Kane."

Dallas balled his hand into a fist, looking seconds short of driving it through the doctor's face. "Stop telling me what I can't do and *explain* it."

"Amira noticed some muscle weakness in the baby, and she told me something was wrong. I thought she was being paranoid—until I did the blood work." Doc sighed heavily. "It's a metabolic enzyme deficiency. The prognosis is—" He cut off with a vicious curse. "The prognosis is shit, that's what."

"There has to be something we can do. Medicine." Dallas shoved his hand through his hair and looked at Finn. Just for a second, but long enough for Finn to read the conflict there.

Even if there was medicine that would help, Beckett wouldn't hand it over. Not without getting something—or someone—in return.

"Gene therapy in utero," Doc whispered. "That's how they'd fix it in Eden. But it's too late for that now."

Not necessarily. In Eden, registration for reproduction involved genetic counseling meant to avoid situations like this. But rich people broke the rules, and there was always a demand for experimental drugs on the Base.

Getting them would be dangerous. Dallas would have to beg for them or steal them, and, in either scenario, Finn was likely to be front and center. He'd promised Trix that he'd stay with her.

He'd promised himself he'd deserve her.

He stepped forward, drawing Doc's attention. "What if I could get my hands on a programmable retrovirus?"

"Excuse me?" Doc stared at Finn like *he* was the crazy, tripping, suicidal bastard.

For once in Finn's damn life, he actually wasn't. "The Base does gene therapy all the time. Experimental and dangerous as fuck...but it happens."

Dallas raised an eyebrow. "Well, Doc?"

"Could you make that work?" Lex took a step toward him. "If this is as bad as you say, anything you can give Flash and Amira... They'll take it."

"I stored some of Hana's umbilical cord blood when

she was born," he admitted. "I don't know, maybe. But it'd take a fucking miracle, even if Beckett's boy here is telling the truth."

"I'm not Beckett's boy," Finn replied, meeting Dallas's eyes. "Though I'm sure he's dying to get me back."

"It might have come up," Dallas said, way too casually. Beckett was making demands, then, which made it a good time for Finn to prove he was useful for more than fixing cars and building gardens.

He turned and gestured to Bren. "When Trix and I were in the tunnels beneath Five, she said something about Noah. That he can hack his way through all those damn security doors?"

Bren nodded. "You got a plan?"

"There's a storage drop on the edge of Five. Fleming was required to keep a stockpile there of everything the Base uses."

It was information, not a plan—but Bren only nodded again. "When do we leave?"

Dallas pointed at Doc. "You stay right here. We're gonna go find Cruz and see what he knows about the Base's experiments. Lexie, love?"

"I'll take care of them." She slipped through the door and closed it quietly behind her.

"Bren?" Dallas jerked his head toward the Broken Circle. "Round up Noah and map out a route. Figure out who you need."

"Yes, sir."

"And you." O'Kane folded his arms across his chest and stared at Finn for long enough to prickle wariness down his spine. He was used to assholes and sociopaths leading sectors, but Dallas O'Kane knew how to level a look that made a man feel bared to his soul, judged for his sins and found sincerely wanting.

Since there wasn't much to say in his defense, Finn stayed silent.

"You," Dallas repeated. "If you fuck us over, Finn,

I'm gonna find you. No matter how the fuck far you run or who you think could hide you. I will find you, and I will turn you inside out. And then I'll bring you back here and let Lex at you."

A threat only an O'Kane could make—saving the scariest for last. Dallas O'Kane could break your body. Finn didn't want to see what kind of vengeance Lex could be stirred to when properly motivated—especially when she knew his most vulnerable spots. "My loyalties are pretty damn simple."

"Trix?"

"From start to finish."

After a moment, Dallas nodded. "Good enough for now. Go with Bren. Get this shit figured out. And, Finn?"

"Yeah?"

"Don't do anything stupid," Dallas said quietly. "Don't break her heart. Come the hell back."

It was the promise he'd already made, the one he had to keep. "I'm planning on it."

Trix stumbled out of the back door, her eyes wide and her chest heaving with shallow breaths. "Lex said..." She trailed off as she caught sight of Finn.

"Hana needs medicine," he said, meeting her eyes. No pain, not yet. Because she hadn't figured out what came next. "I'm going to help Bren and Noah get it."

She wasn't moving, but she seemed to still anyway as realization dawned. "Get it...because it's in Five."

Finn tugged her away from the milling people—and away from Dallas, though his gaze followed them. "Nobody else knows where the place is. It's the kid's only chance."

She opened her mouth, but the argument she obviously wanted to make died on her tongue. "For Hana," she said finally.

He slipped his fingers into her hair and pulled her close, until he could lean down to press his forehead to hers. "For you," he corrected. "This is your family. I get it. I still don't know shit about having one, but let me protect yours."

Trix wrapped her hands around his wrists. "Be careful?"

"I'll be back before you know it." He smiled and stroked his thumb across her cheek. "Donnelly's crazy, but I bet he's real useful in a pinch."

"I mean it, Finn."

He kissed her. Short and abrupt, because it wasn't the place and there wasn't time, but even that brief taste of her made his blood pound. "You think I'm taking any fucking chances with you waiting for me on the other end?"

"Hell, no." Her voice shook the tiniest bit. "I'll be here."

And he'd be one step closer to belonging. "Give me a good-luck kiss, doll."

She brushed her lips over his, softly at first. Then she sank her teeth into his lower lip with a moan. "Remember what you promised me."

Finn caught her hand and pressed his lips to her palm. "This is home. Nothing will change that."

She curled her fingers to stroke his beard. "Then hurry back."

Noah Lennox was a little scary.

Finn had known him for years, since the days when he was a newly recruited enforcer and Noah was still a surly teenager, the brilliant son of Sector Five's bitter, angry tech specialist. Fleming had always gone easy on the kid, too afraid of spooking a valuable resource—especially after the elder Lennox opted to overdose his way out of life.

Then Noah had fallen for a girl. Emma Cibulski, the little sister of one of Finn's least reliable dealers. Finn didn't know when the idiot had started rolling on his own stash, but he'd bet every credit to his name that Fleming had helped Cib along the path to destruction.

And Emma had been slated for a fate like Trix's—addicted to the dangerous shit, held hostage to ensure Noah's good behavior. Scaring the two of them out of the sector had been the first decent thing Finn had done in a while, but fresh off the latest attempt to wean Trix from her addiction, it had been the only choice he could stand to make.

If he'd had a clue just how dangerous Noah could be, he might have chosen a different route.

With a datapad in one hand and a lock override device in the other, Noah led Finn and Bren through doors Finn had never realized were even there and down tunnels he would have sworn on his life didn't exist. "This is fucking insane," Finn muttered to Bren as they watched Noah hack the control panel on a huge steel blast door. "Is there anywhere he can't get with that thing?"

"Through a solid wall, maybe." Bren patted the backpack slung over his shoulder. "But that's where I come in."

Finn raised an eyebrow. "I always heard you were a sniper, not an explosives nut."

"*Nut* is such a strong word. I prefer *enthusiast.*"

"You're a crazy motherfucker, is what you are." But Finn grinned. "Was that your work on the factory? Trust an O'Kane to burn shit to the ground with zero casualties."

Bren's vague smile vanished.

Shit. Maybe there had been casualties—or injuries—and Finn hadn't known. Mac had already shut him out of the inner circle by the time the O'Kanes had blown the factory, after all.

The door whispered open ahead of them, and Noah turned to pin Bren with a serious look. "You're not brooding, are you? We all made it out of there alive. Mistakes happen."

"No, I'm not brooding," Bren muttered. "And fuck you."

Noah waved his arm, and Bren stepped through the door. "All right, big guy. You wanted access to this quadrant of Five, and now you've got it. Where do we go?"

Noah held out the tablet with its map, but Finn didn't need it. He'd studied the tunnel schematics back in Sector Four, memorizing the route from this door to familiar territory. "This way."

The tunnels in this part of Five were in decent repair, lit from above by long fluorescent lights that washed out color and cast creepy shadows. Few people in Five knew this section of the tunnels existed, but they were kept in excellent repair on orders from the military installation known simply as the Base.

Knowing that, Finn kept his hand close to his gun. "The guys from the Base were pretty regular with their pickups, but who knows what the hell Beckett's done to the schedule? If we run into trouble, it could be your kind of scene, Donnelly."

Bren swung a small flashlight from one side of the tunnel to the other as they walked. "If it's all the same to you, I'd rather not run into anyone from the Base."

"No shit." Finn had only had to oversee a handful of the monthly meetings, but the men who usually showed up to collect the experimental medication redefined cold-blooded. Even at his lowest, Finn didn't think he'd looked at the world with that level of disconnected calm.

Hell, even Beckett showed emotions sometimes. Usually greed and sadistic satisfaction, but that was *something*.

A loud clang echoed dully above them, and Bren cursed. "How close are we to the surface, Noah?"

Noah held his hands about four feet apart. "Don't

talk too loud."

Finn snorted as they reached a familiar intersection and swung a right. "Not many people have the passcodes for the doors down here. There should be three guards on duty, but most of the time Mac only spared the manpower when the Base was due for a pick-up." The rest of the time, guarding the stockpile was considered a sweet gig. Plenty of men had spent their shifts blissed out and jerking off to porn on their monitors.

"Nice to know." Bren shifted his pack, revealing a gun in his hand. "Watch your back anyway. Better yet, watch mine."

"Everyone watch everyone's back," Noah muttered, his gaze on his tablet. "I don't want any of your women coming after me for not bringing you home."

It was Bren's turn to snort. "Tell me about the security in the vault. Not the guards—the setup."

"It's got a keypad. A passcode they haven't changed in years." Finn snorted. "Some brilliant jackass bypassed the alarm at one point so it doesn't even trigger if you enter the wrong one. The vault's steel, maybe twelve inches." The hard part, the part that could stop them in their tracks, was the door.

"So if the code's changed, I just hack it?" Noah asked.

If only. "It's got an old-school door. Four inches thick, iron frame, with locking bolts the size of my fucking wrist. It has relockers on top of relockers, so if you make a wrong move with the code panel..." He glanced at Bren. "I guess you get to work that enthusiasm."

"Great." Noah stopped at the next intersection and gestured to the left. "Is this it?"

Finn stopped next to him and stared down the short hallway. The door at the end had the usual access panel. The basement beyond was reinforced, even though the building above was nondescript. Most people in the Sector thought the house upstairs was just another Fleming office. There was no reason for strangers to visit, no chance of having to deal with more than one or two guards at the most.

If everything went well, Finn could get them in and out and back to Four with no one the wiser.

Striding to the control panel on the door, Finn lifted his hand and then hesitated. "If you hack the door, will it leave any trace in the entry logs?"

"I can make sure it doesn't," Noah said, easing up next to him. When Finn stepped aside, Noah held up his tablet and typed something. The lights on the panel blinked twice and turned green, and the door slid silently open.

Yeah, the clever fucker was useful. No wonder Mac had chased him so relentlessly for four damn years.

Inside, the basement was lit with the same low lights as the tunnels. The far wall surrounding the vault was solid concrete. Finn could still remember standing guard, smoking cigarette after cigarette while he watched the workers put in the framework for it.

In the center was the vault door. Bren made his way to it and immediately began running his fingers along its edges. "Just in case," he muttered, almost as if he was explaining himself. "How many bolts?"

"Fourteen."

He nodded slowly, touching the top of the door and then the sides at regularly spaced intervals. "So...two on the top, five on each side, and two on the bottom?"

"Yep." Finn couldn't stop one brow from going up. "You break into a lot of safes as one of Eden's MPs, Donnelly?"

"You have no idea. Noah?"

The hacker had already located the vault controls and was frowning at his tablet. "Fuck, this shit really is old-school. I don't think it's capable of wireless broadcast. I need a knife."

Wordlessly, Finn pulled his from his boot and handed it over, hilt first.

Noah balanced his tablet above the controls and pried the panel free to reveal a mess of wires. "Even if the alarm on the code panel has been bypassed, there's a fifty-fifty chance I could still trigger it manually if I try this."

Finn glanced at Bren, who was still caressing the safe like he planned to seduce his way into it. "Blowing it won't be any quieter. So I guess I'll handle whoever comes down the stairs."

"Mmm." Bren knelt, unzipped his bag, and began to pull out tiny black boxes, no bigger than two inches on all sides. He laid them out by the wall, one by one. "Directed charges. If we can't get in the easy way, I'll blow the bolts."

He sounded almost pleased at the idea, and Finn gave in to the moment with a laugh. "I'm glad we're friends now, because you have got some scary hobbies."

Bren started organizing the charges into neat stacks. "Sure, *now* I'm cool."

"Hey, who doesn't love a good explos—"

"*Fuck*," Noah growled, a heartbeat before the screech of the alarm tore through the room. Finn raised his gun and took cover with a good view of the stairs, while Bren snatched up his carefully ordered stacks of explosives. He deployed them fast, his hands moving in a blur as he slammed them against the frame of the door, fixing them over the spots where the bolts should be.

He'd just dropped to put the last few in place when the door at the top of the stairs crashed open.

For a tense moment, Finn stood frozen, staring up into a familiar face. JC, one of Beckett's favorite guards. Not one of the lazy, strung-out pet bullies Mac always stuck on the cushy gigs, but a cold, smart, ruthless enforcer.

Recognition widened JC's eyes. Finn braced himself, knowing he could show no mercy. They couldn't risk leaving behind witnesses to blab about O'Kanes in their most secret vault, not with relations between the two sectors balanced on a tower of polite threats and less polite lies.

It should have been easy. JC was a mean bastard. He'd undermined Finn more than once, hungry for the power Finn had grown sick of using. A few weeks ago, Finn would have already pulled the trigger. The death wouldn't have bothered him, but it wouldn't have pleased him, either. It would have been one more drop in a bucket of regrets that had been overflowing for years.

So much had changed in so little time, but one thing most of all.

Finn had someone to live for. Someone to fight for.

JC went for his gun, and Finn shot him twice in the chest before climbing the stairs to put one in his head.

No regrets, not this time. Maybe this was what being on the right side felt like.

A series of beeps sounded in the room below, growing faster with each passing heartbeat. Then a dull thud shook the stairs, followed by the sound of solid steel hitting the floor.

Finn raced down the stairs, jumping the last four, and snatched up the empty bag Noah held out. "Everything you can grab off this shelf," he directed to Bren, pointing to a collection of high-quality analgesics and stimulants. If they were gonna knock the place over, they might as well make it good.

The experimental drugs were at the back, along with a stack of sturdy plastic cases. Finn shuffled through them until he found the right label and popped the case open. A dozen vials of the retrovirus sat nestled in foam padding. God only knew what they did with them on the Base.

Finn only cared what Doc could do with them now.

He tucked them into the bag before grabbing everything else Doc could possibly use, along with a few things Finn hoped he never had to. A fortune's worth of the latest medical advances, and Finn was almost sorry he wouldn't be around to see the look on Beckett's face when he realized he'd lost something the Base didn't consider his in the first place.

"Out. *Now*," Bren barked shortly, and the three of them turned for the exit to the tunnels just as more footsteps thundered down the basement stairs. Finn skidded through on Bren's heels with Noah stopping long enough to trigger the door.

"I scrambled the code," he said as he caught up to them. "But that won't hold them for long. You can override that shit from inside the building."

Finn nodded and picked up the pace, but they'd only made it two turns before shouts and heavy footsteps echoed behind them.

A *lot* of footsteps.

The final blast door marking the edge of the quadrant lay before them. They stumbled through, and Noah hauled the door shut behind them as the first shot ricocheted off it. His fingers flew as he tried to secure it, only to bite off a curse. "I'm not set up to reprogram a quadrant door. I need time."

Bren hesitated for only a moment before snatching something out of his bag. "Fuck it," he said, then edged Noah out of the way and slammed a charge against the control panel. "Grab the transmitter."

Finn swept it up and seized Noah's arm. "Move."

The hacker did. Finn followed him, shifting his bag to one shoulder so he could flip the switch on the transmitter. Disabling the door would mean the end of their easy access, but the chances were good that this sort of stunt would only have worked once anyway. So Finn shoved Noah around the corner and glanced back to make sure Bren was clear of the door.

Then he jammed his thumb down. The charge exploded, and the access panel disintegrated. The heavy clang of metal bolts sliding firmly into place echoed deep within the core of the door, followed by frustrated shouts on the other side.

Bren plucked the transmitter out of Finn's hand and grinned at Noah. "More than one way to lock a door."

"As long as you're okay never unlocking it again," Noah grumbled, but he grinned as he tucked his datapad into a pocket on his vest. "Just the same, let's get the hell out of here before they figure out a way around."

True fucking words. Finn wanted out of these damn tunnels, out of the whole fucking sector. He wanted to be back in Trix's room with her wrapped tight in his arms, feeling every slow, even breath against his chest because she was alive, and that would never stop being magical.

He hefted the bag holding the retrovirus and met Bren's eyes. The words didn't come easy. They didn't feel natural. But he tried them on for size and didn't hate them. "Let's go home."

17

THERE WAS ONLY so much tension you could burn off with liquor and cage fighting.

When the going got tough—*really* tough, like waiting to see if Doc's cure for little baby Hana would work—the O'Kanes turned to poker.

Rachel tossed in her cards with a disgusted sigh. "Fold. My luck is for shit tonight."

"Maybe that's your concentration," Jade said lightly as she slid a stack of painted red chips into the middle of the table. "I've noticed Ace only has one hand above the table."

"One hand's all I need," Ace drawled, his flirtation a brittle layer of charm over obvious worry.

Trix slid her own chips into the center of the table. A week ago, the unbearable tension would have been the result of her friends sitting down with Finn. Now, they seemed to accept him as part of the group—and Trix would have traded it in a heartbeat.

The cloud of worry hung over all of them, including Jade. Trix eased her hand over hers for a quick squeeze as the other players called Jade's bet.

Zan leaned back in his chair, his arm still bound up into a sling. "Maybe we should make it a thing—everyone plays with one hand tonight. Just to be fair."

"In the interest of fairness," Cruz agreed, no smile ruining his perfectly serious expression as he dealt the fourth card face up into the center of the table...and then dropped his hand casually under the table.

Next to him, Ace let out a soft groan. "Fucking hell, Zan. Brilliant idea."

It was desperation, pure and simple, a way to forget. Even so, Trix's cheeks heated, and she glanced at Finn. He was studying the three community cards with a look of concentration so intense, she might have suspected he'd missed the groping.

Then he winked at her.

He was trying, too. For her sake, and maybe for his own. Trix answered with a wink of her own, then slid her hand into his.

Zan snorted. "This isn't working. We should have more booze. Or maybe get rid of these chips and go straight for strip poker." He leered at Ace. "Show me your new scars, and I'll show you mine."

Ace made a rude gesture with his free hand. "Don't even whine. So you got shot a couple times. Someone twirled my guts around like pasta on a fork."

"*Ace.*" Jade's complexion took on an unhealthy tinge. "Have mercy on us and bet."

"Nah, my cards are shit, too." He tossed them on top of Rachel's and turned to Finn. "What about you, new guy? How many bullets did Doc dig out of you that first day?"

"A few," Finn replied. "I didn't ask."

A single bullet was all it took, and it was one too

many. The image of Finn falling out of Hawk's car flashed in Trix's mind, and she shook her head to clear it. "This is one fucking morbid pissing contest. Can't you just compare dick sizes?"

Ace leaned across the table and whispered loudly enough to be heard in the hallway. "Only if we want Cruz to win." When Cruz flushed, Ace straightened and gestured. "Come on, new guy. Bet or fold."

Finn rubbed his thumb along the inside of her wrist, a casual caress that seemed absentminded until he caught her gaze again. Smiling, he dropped his other hand to his stack of chips and shoved them toward the center of the table. "All in."

Oh, she recognized that look. He traced a slow circle against her skin, and Trix swallowed—hard. "I can't call that bet. I'll have to fold."

"There's always Zan's suggestion," Rachel said mildly. "I'm sure your panties are worth at least five hundred."

"Not unless she's in them," Ace scoffed. "For five hundred, angel, I'd bend you over my knee and—"

"Ace." Cruz sighed and shot Trix an apologetic look. "You know how he gets when he's worried."

"It's okay," Finn rumbled, his thumb still making those shivery circles across her skin. "Good to know what the going rates are."

Jade propped her chin on one hand and studied Zan. "I hope you can cover the bet. I doubt Finn wants *your* underwear."

"Hey." Zan pointed at her, then Finn. "You never fucking know, okay?" But he called the bet anyway, tossing in a stack of chips.

Trix watched Finn. He hadn't looked at his cards again, which meant they weren't fabulous. He only reassured himself of good things, checking and rechecking, as if he didn't quite believe they wouldn't vanish the moment he turned his back.

The betting made its way back to Cruz. "I'll have to live on Rachel's wealth," he said, tossing his hand away before flipping over the final card.

Finn's hand tightened on hers, and she knew he'd won. On the last lousy card, because his betting hadn't been the result of strategy, but a reflection of the way he lived—full-bore, straight ahead, no slowing down and no regrets.

Well, maybe a few.

Jade grinned at Zan across the table. "No more bets from me, unless Zan really wants to add something to my winnings."

"Nope," Zan said immediately. "I don't like that gleam in your beautiful eyes."

Trix turned over her cards. "Two pair."

"A straight for me, and—oh, damn." Jade made a face as Zan flipped over his cards. "A full house. Finn?"

Silently, Finn revealed his cards—a two and a seven.

Ace let out a whoop of laughter. "You crazy, lucky bastard. You went all in on *crap* and ended up with a straight flush. Now we know your balls are bigger than your brain."

"Good thing we weren't measuring those instead of dicks," Finn replied, cracking the closest thing to a real smile that Trix had seen cross his face since the game had started.

She felt an answering smile tugging at her lips. "Crazy and lucky. Ace calls it like he sees it."

"Thank God he's both." Mad stood at the open door, his conflicted gaze fixed on Finn.

Trix's breath caught in her throat. "What is it?"

"Doc says it's working. It'll be a few days before he can take her off the enzyme replacement therapy, but..." Mad's mouth curved suddenly. A relieved, joyous smile. "Hana's going to be okay."

Rachel raised her arms with a *whoop*, and Zan dropped his face into his hand. Jade pushed back her chair, but she didn't circle the table to Mad. She moved past Trix instead, reaching down to clasp Finn's free hand. "Thank you."

Finn looked awkward. Uncomfortable. "It wasn't really me," he started. "Noah and Bren did the hard—"

"Shut up," Ace interrupted. "You're this week's big fucking hero. Enjoy it."

If anything, the words only seemed to fluster him more.

"Trix." Mad met her gaze across the table, and she could see the hesitation in his eyes. And maybe a hint of apology. "Flash and Amira want to see him."

She tossed her cards on the table and rose. "Alone?"

"You should come too."

Finn eased from his chair but caught Jade's hand when she started to step aside. "Are you okay with me helping out? With your garden, I mean."

Jade smiled, with no hint of turmoil in her expression. If the pain Trix had seen earlier was still there, her friend had either made peace with it or moved beyond it. "You made bad choices when you were trapped in a bad place. I've made my share of those, too. Most of us have."

It wasn't quite an answer, but it was something more. Forgiveness and an understanding that Finn hadn't even bothered to ask for, because he would have assumed he didn't deserve it.

He'd have to get used to it. You couldn't play the hero card in Sector Four without the balls to back it up, and if you had those, you had respect. You had affection.

You had brotherhood.

Amira answered the door to their apartment, her face streaked with tears. "Come in."

Trix kept a tight hold on Finn's hand as she crossed the threshold and wrapped her other arm around Amira's neck. "I'm so glad, sweetheart."

Amira choked out a laugh and whispered, "Me, too."

Flash sat on the couch with Hana in his arms. The

sleepy infant had her mother's dark hair sticking up in all directions and her fingers in her mouth. She looked tiny cradled against Flash's massive chest, but Flash himself looked even more ragged than Amira.

He stood slowly, passed his daughter to Amira, and grabbed Finn in a back-pounding hug. "The next time someone tries to fuck with you in the cage, they can have fun trying to grow back their teeth."

Amira stood there, staring down at her daughter, one hand clenched in the blanket wrapped around her. "You didn't have to do it," she said softly. "No one would have known to ask if you hadn't said anything."

Finn shrugged, trying to dismiss the words. "You're Trix's family. I had to do it."

Flash smacked him on the back again. "Fuck that. You're *our* family now."

From the way Finn's eyes widened, he didn't know what to do *or* say. So Trix wound her arm around his and tugged him closer to her side. "It's new," she explained.

Amira and Flash would understand. So many of them had never had families before coming to Sector Four and being welcomed by the O'Kanes. Trix herself had had moments of disbelief, times where she'd felt she didn't deserve it.

But family was family, full stop.

Amira finally looked up at Finn. "You didn't have to," she repeated. "But you did. There's not—" Her voice broke on a sob. "There aren't any words, okay? Anything you need. *Anything*."

"Okay." Finn freed one arm and slid it around Amira's shoulders. It was an awkward hug, tentative and sideways and over fast.

But it was the first time Trix had seen him reach out to anyone but her. Ever.

A bright smile broke through Amira's tears. "Lex says as soon as we're up to it, they're going to throw a party. O'Kanes only."

"I'm not sure—"

Flash cut Finn off. "Family," he said firmly. "Ink makes it official. But you put your life on the line for Trix, and for us. That's all that matters."

Finn didn't protest again. He slipped his hand into Trix's and grinned. "An O'Kane party, huh? Are they everything the rumors say?"

He'd only heard stories, and Trix knew he wouldn't believe the truth. "You'll have to see for yourself."

18

FLASH AND AMIRA made an appearance at Dallas's party, but they cut out early. Trix wasn't surprised—babies and O'Kane festivities didn't exactly mix, even when the good health of the baby in question was the reason for the celebration.

Especially when the party started winding down—or up, depending on your point of view.

Finn had both arms wrapped around her waist, holding her firmly in his lap as he settled his chin on her shoulder. "It's not like Five at all, is it?"

"I told you it wasn't." Trix reached up and stroked her fingers through his hair as she watched Dallas and Lex sway together at the edge of the makeshift dance floor.

He pressed his cheek to hers, tickling her jaw with his newly trimmed beard. "How long did it take you to believe it?"

Months. Years. She turned her face to his. "You've got time."

"I've got an advantage." His fingers ghosted up, skating over her breasts to trace the plunging neckline of her white button-up shirt. "I get to see it through your eyes."

And through her words. She went around the room, one at a time. "Dallas and Lex are feeling quiet tonight. Private. If they get up to anything, it'll probably be a gift from him to her. Noelle's another story." She nodded to where the woman sat on Jasper's lap, whispering in his ear. "A hundred credits says she's telling him all his bedtime stories early."

He laughed softly against *her* ear. "And what kind of bedtime stories does a girl from Eden tell?"

Trix watched her for a moment, then smiled when she intercepted Noelle's telling gaze. "Mmm, see how she keeps looking at Rachel?"

Finn followed Noelle's gaze. Rachel was dancing in the middle of the room, swaying to her own silent, sensual rhythm. Cruz and Ace were watching her from another couch, Ace sprawled across the cushions with his head resting on Cruz's thigh. "Yes."

"That's the bedtime story," Trix murmured. "All the things she's going to do to Rachel."

"Really?" His fingers caught the top button on her shirt. Toyed with it. "What about Rachel? What's she thinking?"

Cruz had one protective hand resting on Ace's chest, and they were both watching Rachel's movements with something deeper than appreciation. "That tonight's her lucky night, maybe."

"Are the three of them really...?" He trailed off, as if not sure what to call it.

"Together?" she asked softly. "In love?"

"A thing." He smiled against her cheek. "Like us."

That made her laugh. "Yes, really."

"Huh." He finally worried the button free and coaxed

her shirt open far enough to show off her lace-edged plunge bra. "What about Bren and his snarly girlfriend?"

"Her name is Six."

"Six," he echoed, then seemed to get distracted as his fingertips found the top edge of the lace. He traced it, his touch warm against her skin. "Christ, I think Emma already has Noah out of his pants."

Emma liked to show him off every chance she got. "A hero's reward, all right." Trix eased her hand back to tug at Finn's belt buckle.

He exhaled roughly and turned his face into her hair. "Is that what you want to do? Claim me in front of everyone?"

"Yes. And no." She closed her eyes. "I don't need to claim you. But I always, *always* want you."

She had his belt open by the time he stilled her hand with his own. "You're right. You don't have to claim me. Everyone already knows what I am."

Trix shifted on his lap until she was sitting across it and could look down at him. "And what's that?"

"Your personal enforcer." He tugged at the next button, popping it free. "Your own private army." Another button, and her shirt was undone past her breasts, making it easy for him to run his knuckles between them. "Yours."

Goose bumps rose in response to his touch, and she shivered. "I want a lover," she teased lightly, "not an army."

"I'm both." He traced the curve of her breast with the backs of his fingers, slow and warm. "I've been thinking, you know. About all those dirty fantasies I have."

"Yeah? Tell me more."

He parted two fingers and brought them back together around her nipple, pinching until she arched her back. "They're all the same, really."

She swallowed a whimper. "*Tell me.*"

"I wanna make you feel, baby doll." He dragged her

forehead to his, dropping his voice to a rough, seductive whisper against her lips. "I did it all the wrong ways last time. I still can't believe you trust me, but I'm too damn greedy to care. I wanna see how high you can fly when the only thing we're hooked on is each other."

Trix froze as longing twisted in her belly, at once familiar and brand new. So many things she'd always wanted, but this was the first time she could *have* them. Him. The thought alone was more seductive than his whisper, and the possibilities...

Endless.

"Finn." His name escaped her a half-second before her lips met his.

He slid both hands into her hair, disrupting her careful curls and dislodging hairpins. She didn't care, not when he tilted his head and pulled her into a deep, reckless kiss.

The room dissolved as his tongue rasped over hers and his teeth scored her lip. Even the low, throbbing music seemed to melt into an echo of their kiss, another sense wrapped up in the contact.

He ended the kiss with a soft nip to her lower lip and licked away the sting. "Is that a *yes*?"

"Always." With every breath, every heartbeat.

"Good. Because I think Dallas just summoned us."

She looked over her shoulder. Dallas was sprawled out on his couch on the dais with Lex curled up at his side, absently stroking the edge of his vest. He beckoned them with a lazy gesture, and her hand tightened around the leather.

Dallas smiled—a smile Trix had seen a hundred times before. A smile that sent a shiver racing up her spine, a promise of pure, delicious trouble.

Oh, God. She turned back to Finn. "Ever wanted to see Lex naked?"

He choked on a noise—something caught between a laugh and a groan. "Is that what's about to happen?"

"She likes you, you know." And Emma wasn't the only one with the urge to show off her man. Trix slid off Finn's lap and held out her hand. "Can't keep the king and queen waiting."

As they approached the dais, Dallas hauled Lex into his lap. He slapped a hand on the cushion beside them and smiled lazily. "Have a seat, Finn. You should have the best view for your first party, eh?"

Finn stepped up and offered Trix his hand to steady her. "I don't think there's a bad view in here."

"Because you like to watch?" Lex asked innocently.

"Starting to think it's not so bad."

"Good news." She grinned as she leaned over and rubbed a smudge of lipstick from the corner of his mouth. "You should keep him, honey."

Trix propped her hands on her hips and kept her tone light, flirtatious. Just shy of a challenge. "I plan on it."

Lex's grin softened into a warm smile as she peered at the lipstick left behind on her thumb. "Can I borrow this sometime? I bet it'd look good on Dallas."

Not on his lips, either. "Anytime, sweetheart."

Dallas hauled Lex back against him with a laugh. "Be gentle, love. It's his first time."

Some of Fleming's parties in Five had been wilder, but in a different way. They were all about taking—drugs, alcohol, sex, all without a thought spared for anyone else's desires. This was about giving, a distinction Finn had noticed the moment they'd walked in the door.

And she was about to show him how right he'd been.

Trix kicked off her shoes and knelt on the couch in the space between Dallas and Finn. "They have something in common," she told Lex.

Lex sat up straight, curiosity sparking in her dark eyes. "Yeah? What's that?"

She leaned closer, close enough to whisper in Lex's ear. "They both want to know how high we can fly."

Dallas must have heard her, because he reached past Lex to stroke Trix's cheek. "Higher than you know, Trix. Higher than he knows."

Finn's fingertips snuck under the hem of Trix's shirt, warm and rough against the small of her back. "Show us."

It wasn't a command, and it wasn't permission. It was a *plea*, and she shuddered when Lex covered Dallas's hand with hers, holding it in place on Trix's face as she swooped in for a kiss.

It was hungry, a little rough, a far cry from the slow, seductive caress Trix had anticipated. She whimpered, and Lex swallowed her shocked noise.

And then Dallas spoke, low and soft, every word heavy with confidence and control as he twisted his free hand in Lex's hair and pulled her back. "She's so hungry for you, Trix, that she forgot to lay down the rules first. But I think we only need one." He nodded to Finn without releasing Trix's gaze. "Do you trust him to draw the lines for you tonight?"

She couldn't remember a time when he hadn't drawn her lines, good or bad. Every boundary she had was so intimately connected with Finn that he could redraw them in a split second. Her pleasure and his, intertwined so completely that his desire was all she needed to crave something, too.

Back in Five, it would have been dangerous. She could have lost herself. But she knew who she was here, and that she was surrounded by love.

"I trust him." The words came out husky, breathless. "With everything."

Finn splayed his fingers protectively on the small of her back. "You trust all three of us," he corrected, and he didn't sound jealous. He sounded relieved, as if he recognized the safety net for what it was—the chance to let go and know no one would be hurt.

And Dallas knew it. He smiled and brushed his

thumb over Trix's lip, undoubtedly smearing her lipstick again. "That's right. All three of us, doing our damnedest to send you flying straight to the moon. Is that what you want, darling? Be sure."

Trix waited for the uncertainty to break over her in a chilling wave, but it never came. She felt only the lingering warmth of touch, sparked even hotter by anticipation. "I'm sure."

"Good." Dallas released Lex's hair but gave her a stern look. "Next time you want to lick her..."

"I'll ask," she breathed, shifting closer to Trix. "Slowly, with as many dirty fucking words as possible."

Finn remained silent, but the couch creaked behind her as he gathered her hair and pressed a kiss to her nape.

She leaned back against him, but Lex held her tight with both hands wound in the front of her shirt. She yanked it open with one quick jerk, popping the few remaining buttons.

Dallas let out a groaning laugh, full of exasperation. "*Lex.*"

"That's okay," Finn murmured against the back of her neck. He caught Lex's wrist and dragged her hand down to the fastening on Trix's pants. "Don't rip this button off. She comes so much harder if you go slow at first."

"Really?" Lex toyed with the button and slid her other hand up to the front clasp of Trix's bra. "We could test that."

"Slow and fast and then slow again?" Finn asked, teasing his fingers down Trix's throat. "You like that idea, doll? Do you want us to play with you?"

She felt like she could barely breathe, even though her chest was heaving. Every desperate inhalation pushed her breasts against their hands, and it was all she could do to gasp an answer. "Please."

Finn tilted her head up with a hand under her chin.

His gaze was so dark, so gently dangerous. He'd have no qualms at all about commanding the leaders of Sector Four to fulfill every whispered or half-voiced fantasy, because when it came to her pleasure, Finn would always be relentless.

He pressed his thumb to her lips and then parted them, pressing the tip inside. "Help me undress her."

Lex flicked the clasp open in one practiced motion, but the mesh and lace clung to Trix's nipples, rasping over the hard tips. Squirming only made it worse, until Lex peeled away the fabric with a soothing noise.

The hand that slipped across her bare stomach and popped open her pants was larger. Rougher. Finn didn't let her turn her head back as Dallas dragged the zipper down, holding her with his gaze as he withdrew his thumb and rubbed the slick pad across her lower lip. "Two people who want to see you come almost as badly as I do? I never realized how hot that could be."

Holy Christ.

"Beautiful," Lex declared, tracing her finger in a slow circle around one of Trix's nipples. "I promised to ask, didn't I? Before putting my tongue on her gorgeous skin?"

"Soon," Finn promised, exchanging a look with Dallas. Before Trix's scrambled wits could catch up, Finn had hoisted her up and Dallas had his fingers hooked in her pants. As if they'd done it a hundred times, Finn twisted and Dallas pulled, dragging the fabric off her hips and down her legs. Finn stripped her shirt and bra away, leaving her sprawled in his lap in nothing but her panties.

And then he wrapped his arms around her. He cupped her breasts, lifting them, setting off wild shivers as he rubbed his fingertip around one nipple. "Well, Lex? Where do you want to lick her first?"

"Hard choice, love," Dallas rumbled, tracing his fingers along the lacy edge of Trix's panties, her only remaining clothing. "She's so pretty all over, isn't she?"

"Mmm." Lex dragged her own tank top over her head. Bare to the waist, she leaned over Trix until their bodies almost touched. "I've watched you touch yourself while you dance, honey. I know what gets you cranked up." She smoothed her hands up Trix's stomach to her breasts, her fingers bumping into Finn's.

Finn's hands were big, his skin rough. Lex's were nimble, soft, and the difference in sensation was heady. Trix arched into their caresses—and choked on a moan when they pinched her nipple between their fingers.

"Do you suck her tits while you fuck her?" Lex asked intently.

Finn groaned. "Sometimes."

Dallas skated one hand up Lex's back to wind in her hair. "Is that what you want to do, Lexie? Put your mouth on her nipples while he fucks her?"

"Hell, yes." She licked her lips and teased her fingertips under the top edge of Trix's panties. "How wet and tight does she get? Or should I just see for myself?"

"Not yet." Finn caught Trix's wrists and guided her arms up until her fingers met behind his neck. He touched her all over on his way back down, smoothing gentle hands over her skin. Soothing her. Warning her. This was Finn at his most patient, determined to spin out her torment until she was trembling and wrecked by need.

She couldn't wait, not tonight. She twisted in his arms, trying to ease the ache. "Finn."

"Shh." His lips brushed her ear, but his words weren't a whisper. They were for Lex and Dallas, and they were deliciously commanding. "They're both going to suck your tits," he promised, sliding his fingers across her mouth to muffle her moan. His other hand settled over her linked fingers, holding her trapped. "All you have to do is feel it. And trust me."

It was ridiculously arousing. She'd never been into bondage, but here, like this—held down and offered up—

she was free. With every bit of control stripped away, even her voice, she could only focus on sensation.

On pleasure. Blood roared in her ears as Dallas swatted Lex's hip, urging her to move. Then she was surrounded, with Finn at her back, and Dallas on one side, stroking his fingers along the curve of her breast.

Lex stretched out on top of her, all soft skin and supple leather, and breathed a sigh. "Fuck, honey. You look so good like this." She licked Finn's fingers where they covered Trix's mouth, then leaned past her to nip at Finn's lower lip.

Trix turned her head just a little, far enough to see the flash of tongue. They were close, so close that the slick sound of their kiss tickled her ear, and her pussy clenched. They'd fuck her like this, fuck *each other* like this, and she'd drink in every goddamn moment of ecstasy.

Because it was all for her.

Dallas touched her chin, tilted her face to his. "He's ours now, sweetheart. Yours, first and always. But ours, too."

Yes.

Lex's mouth drifted from Finn's, over to Trix's ear, and down to the line of her jaw. "Sweet," she whispered. "So fucking sweet."

"I know." Finn circled one fingertip at the corner of her mouth. "Taste her."

Dallas slipped his fingers into Lex's hair again, dragging her mouth to his for a quick, raw kiss. Tongues and teeth and groans, the way Finn kissed her when his control slipped, when he dared be a little rough. His fingers tightened around Trix's hands, as if he found the sight as arousing as she did. He was already so hard beneath her, his dick straining his jeans as she squirmed in his lap.

And then Dallas and Lex bent lower. Heat streaked through Trix as Lex's lips brushed her breast, then again, hotter, when Dallas's tongue grazed her nipple.

She had only a moment to process the sensation before Lex joined him. Trix cried out against Finn's hand as their tongues circled the hard peak of her nipple, teasing and flicking.

She needed to pull them closer. She needed to push them away. She could do neither, so she arched her hips helplessly, and Lex rewarded her by pressing one firm thigh to her pussy.

Trix bit Finn's hand as Lex rocked, rubbing warm leather against her soaked panties. She was wet and so, so ready, but they held her back, not giving her quite enough pressure on her clit to make her come.

Finn shifted his hand, freeing her mouth but wrapping his fingers gently around her throat. "What do you feel?"

"Please. Oh God, please." She was babbling. She couldn't stop. "It feels so good, please—"

"Oh, fuck me." Lex shuddered. "Is this what you like, honey? His big, strong hand on your throat while he makes you beg?"

"I always give in." Finn kissed her temple. "She knows I'll give in. She knows I'll do anything."

"I can see why." Lex stroked her hand across the top of Trix's chest, just under Finn's hand. "You're so pretty, honey. Flushed and turned on and pleading. I'd give in, too."

"Liar," Dallas chided, voice full of fond approval. His fingers pinched tight around Trix's nipple, the perfect bite of pain to slice through the aching longing. He tugged, toying with her until Trix whimpered. "Don't let Lex fool you, sweetheart. She's more sadistic than I am. Ask her how long she made Rachel wait before she came the first time."

"I've heard." Everyone talked about the night Rachel had shed the last of her good-girl shell with Dallas and Lex.

"I haven't," Finn murmured. He shifted his legs, widening his stance, forcing Trix's knees apart to give Lex more room between them. "Dallas?"

Trix thought he was asking for the story until Dallas nodded and caught her wrists, freeing Finn's hands while keeping her trapped. And Finn didn't waste any time before laying his hand on the back of Lex's head and urging her down. "Show me. Make her beg."

Lex groaned. "You filthy bastard." She jerked her head, not to get away, but to pull against Finn's grip. When he held tight, she groaned again.

Then she reached back, blindly fumbling for Dallas's pocket. Her hand brushed the erection straining his fly, and he hissed and ground up against her, his laugh strained. "You looking for something, love?"

"Found it." She tugged a switchblade out of his pocket and held it up, skating her thumb over the little silver button.

Trix must have shivered, because Finn stroked a soothing hand along her jaw. "Too much?"

"No, it's—" She'd fucking die if they stopped. "I'm good. I promise."

"Then watch her cut those panties off you." He returned his hand to her throat, tighter this time. A hint of darkness under all that careful gentleness, the same wildness that edged his words. "She could hurt you, too. But she never would. You're safe with us."

There was nothing safe about the weight of his hand, or Dallas's steely grip on her wrists, or the look in Lex's eyes as she pressed the button that sent the sharp, shining blade sliding free of the hilt.

They could destroy her, and she'd love every second of it.

Lex trailed the flat part of the blade lightly over Trix's skin, down between her breasts and past her navel. It slipped beneath the lace, cold against her bare, heated flesh.

Then Lex twisted the knife, and it sliced through the fabric like hot metal through ice.

Dallas made an approving noise and caught the satin, dragging it away from Trix's body. "Look at this sweet, neglected pussy. You're aching for it, aren't you, darling?"

"*Yes*," she and Lex answered at the same time, then laughed together.

Finn released Lex, only to slide his hand down Trix's abdomen. His fingertips stroked her pussy lips lightly. "Dallas?"

"Yeah?"

His fingers stilled. Parted her. The cool air shivered over her, enhancing the sudden feeling of exposure. "Do you guys keep your fancy fucking lube in here?"

Trix's heart stuttered. "Finn..."

It was Dallas's turn to laugh as he rose from the couch. "I have something better than that."

Torment was too mild a word for it. Trix was aroused and aching, desperate for deeper contact. Defiance rose in a rough swell, and she bucked up against Finn's hand. He accidentally grazed her clit, and she shuddered through the sharp, sudden flash of pleasure.

His chest rumbled against her back in a low growl, the only warning before the world tilted. He folded his huge hands under her thighs and dragged them up, spreading her wide. Then he hooked his arms under her knees and pulled them toward her chest, leaving her trapped in a different way, bared to Lex and anyone else who glanced at the stage.

"Cut them the rest of the way off," he ordered.

"Bossy son of a bitch," Lex muttered. But she obeyed, then retracted the blade and dropped the knife beside the couch. "You're damn lucky you're hot."

"I'm damn lucky," Finn agreed, pulling Trix's legs higher. She was cradled now, floating, cut off from any touchstone but his body. He nuzzled her temple. "And so are you. Because you get to touch her."

"Mmm." Lex stroked both thumbs lightly up the insides of Trix's thighs, eliciting another shiver. "He really does want you out of your head, doesn't he?"

"You don't even know." Her voice came out strangled, urgent, and Trix took a deep breath. "He'd do this all night."

"That's lovely." Lex reached the tops of her thighs, and she continued on by tracing over the swells of Trix's outer lips. "And so are you."

"She's perfect." Finn smiled, and she felt the curve of his lips against her ear. "Make her come, Lex. Just once. Because we're going to push her so much higher when Dallas gets back."

"My pleasure." Lex was close enough for her breath to feather over skin, and she lingered there for a heartbeat before dropping her open mouth to Trix's pussy. She licked and sucked, teased her tongue over swollen flesh until Trix was shaking in Finn's steely grip.

Then she lifted her head, licked her lips, smiled wickedly—and brought her hand down on Trix's exposed clit in a single stinging slap.

Trix shattered—there was no other word for the shock of it. If she'd had the breath, she might have screamed, but instead she tensed and shook as the shock gave way to pulsing bliss, to a heat that rolled out from her core in heavy waves.

Finn held her through it, murmuring encouragement as she shuddered. When she managed to open her eyes, Dallas was back, kneeling behind Lex with one hand holding her head back at a brutal angle.

"Just for that," he rumbled, "I might not *let* you taste her again."

"You know I'm a greedy bitch." She held Trix's gaze as she lifted her wet fingers to Dallas's mouth. "It's why you love me."

Dallas licked her finger and grinned. "You were

right, love. So sweet." He guided her hand back to Trix's body, slicking their twined fingers against her, and spoke over her gasp. "I bet Finn wants to taste."

"Fuck, yeah," Finn growled, his fingers flexing on her legs.

She was still drifting down, but her hunger had grown claws in the hollow emptiness. It dug in, clinging to the most hidden parts of her, and nothing but deeper contact could sate it.

She was trapped against Finn, could barely move, but she needed to be filled. She rocked her hips and bit off a frustrated noise when they kept their touches light.

"Do you want more?" Finn asked after another moment of teasing.

"Christ, yes. More—" The word broke on a sob. "I don't need to come again. I need to get *fucked*."

"All right," he whispered, lowering her legs. "Turn around."

Her limbs were wobbly, uncoordinated, both from being held and from the dizzying aftermath of her orgasm. Finn had to catch her when she almost tipped over, and she collapsed against his chest, her hands braced on his shoulders.

Smiling, he tilted her head up and brushed a kiss to her lips. "I don't think you need to get fucked. I think you need something else."

His smile, his words. His hands on her face, and that *look* in his eyes—as if he'd never seen anything more precious in his life, and he'd stopped looking, because he knew he never would. "What do I need?"

"To believe." His words were a whispered promise. "That I'll never leave you hanging again."

It had never seemed easy before. Their history was full of missteps, a tangled mess of good intentions gone from bad to worse. But here, now, the way forward was so painfully clear.

She told him so. "You and me, baby. There isn't anything else."

"Yeah, there is," he replied, closing one hand over her wrist. Over her ink. "You and me, and *everything* else."

Her family. She slid her arms around his neck and pressed her lips to his cheek, breathing her own promise. "And everything else."

With Trix trembling in his arms, Finn had never felt the responsibility of her trust more heavily. And he'd never relished it more.

It was trust, not habit or helplessness. Pure, heady faith, giving up control and the things she craved because she trusted him to give her back everything, hotter and deeper and *more* because no one could want her to feel pleasure the way he did.

Almost no one. Lex was gazing at them with a softness in her eyes, one that translated to her touch as she stroked Trix's disheveled hair. "I love the way you look at her."

Finn loved the way she looked at Trix, too. The way they all looked at her. Dallas, who was patient and indulgent, as if he'd sit there all fucking night if that was what Trix—and Lex—needed. Bren and Six, who sat nestled together on one of the couches, watching as if being allowed to was a fucking honor. Even Ace, who had a hand around Cruz's cock, holding it as Rachel bobbed up and down, still found a lewd, approving smile for Finn.

They were all filthy in their own ways. Without shame and without judgment, and it was the most intoxicating fucking thing he'd ever seen. You couldn't bottle the high that came with loving acceptance. You couldn't buy it.

You had to earn it.

Finn raised his hand to Lex's, tangling their fingers in Trix's disheveled hair. "I love the way you touch her. You like to tease."

She hummed. "Any idiot can get someone off. It takes skill to make it a singular fucking experience."

Trix lifted her head and nodded, her expression solemn. "The gospel according to Lex."

It earned her a swat on the ass. "Cheeky bitch."

"You're one to talk," Dallas retorted. With Trix's attention diverted, he held up the objects he'd retrieved—a sleek silver plug and some of that fancy lubricant—and raised an eyebrow.

Maybe Finn was selfish after all. He could already imagine the noises Trix would make, how tight she'd be as he slid into her and her ass clenched around the damn thing. "Have Lex do it," he said, tightening his grip on Trix's hair when she would have turned to look. "Trust us."

She swallowed hard, but nodded. "I do, I trust—" She cut off with a low noise as Lex drizzled some of the lube on her ass.

"Cold?" Lex rubbed it into Trix's skin, squeezing her ass as she caressed wide, slow circles on her skin. "It'll get hot, I promise."

Dallas's hands joined Lex's, stroking, spreading. They moved in concert, a lewd, glorious dance that had Trix whimpering as Lex teased her with the shining steel.

With the grip in her hair, Finn forced Trix's gaze back to his. "I think you like to be full, don't you?"

She bit her lower lip, then licked it. "Is that what she has? A plug to stretch my ass before you fuck me?"

His cock ached at the image that conjured—Trix bent before him, her hips under his hands, her body shaking as he took forever to rock his way into that tight, hot space. "Not before," he rasped. "While."

Her blue eyes widened—at first, he thought, at the

words, but then he saw Lex pressing the glistening plug home. Trix shivered as the tapered tip penetrated her asshole, but tensed as it drove deeper.

Lex kissed the curve of her hip. "Relax, honey. Take it."

Finn slipped a hand between them, down the trembling flesh of her abdomen. Her pussy was so damn wet, slick, and hot. He cupped her, gave in and stroked her, just to watch those eyes widen farther. Every emotion that played across her face was a quiet victory, proof of some truth that defied words.

She was his. Not because she had to be, but because she wanted to be.

She hissed in another breath, and he felt broad fingers bump his. Dallas's hand, and it was Finn's choice to keep her for himself or to push past greedy possessiveness and let her have everything this moment could be.

Spreading his fingers, he parted her outer lips. Then he caught her gaze, held it as she panted and squirmed, the realization of what was coming bright in her eyes even before he spoke. "How many of his fingers do you want, baby?"

"I want everything." Whispered words, words she'd given him before, and undeniable now in their truth.

Everything.

He could give her that.

"Slow," he told Dallas, not looking away from Trix. "But no more teasing. Let's make her fly."

She hissed and rocked back as Dallas's arm flexed, and Finn wrapped his hand more firmly in her hair to hold her in place. "How many fingers do you feel, Trix?"

"One, just—" Her voice cracked, dissolved. "Two."

Her cheeks were flushed, her eyes glazed. Every raspy little noise that fell from those parted lips twisted him up, and no. He would never stop being greedy and possessive. But it was her pleasure he wanted, the thrill of being the one she stared at in wild-eyed arousal as her body tensed.

"Are you ready?" he whispered, grazing the pad of his middle finger over her swollen clit.

She jerked in his arms. "Ready?"

Stupid question. She'd been ready forever. So he gave her what she needed, slow, firm strokes, just rough enough to push her over the edge. She came with a cry, her fingernails digging in to his skin as she shuddered and clung to him.

Then she made a lower sound, harsh and husky. "Fuck. *Fuck*—"

Lex smiled against Trix's hip. Then her thumb brushed Finn's hand, her wrist turned so that she could only be fucking her fingers in along with Dallas's.

The man's words confirmed it, low and approving as Trix whimpered. "You're squeezing us so tight, darling. Taking everything, so sweet and needy."

"Harder," she pleaded. "Fuck me harder."

Lex's black-and-white nails scratched up Finn's arm, then clicked against his belt buckle. "Open his pants, honey."

Trix fumbled with the buttons, her hands shaking. Her fingers landed on his dick, and he bit back a growl as the last hint of his self-control fractured. "Help her, Lex, for fuck's sake."

"Patience," she admonished, but tugged at his pants with both hands—then wrapped her wet fingers around his shaft.

Jesus *Christ*, these fuckers were filthy.

He thrust up into her fist, savoring the slick glide as he framed Trix's flushed face with both hands. "How do you want me to fuck you, baby? Because once I'm inside you, I'm not stopping."

"Take me." The words were thick with feeling, full of every emotion flashing across her beautiful face. "I'm yours, so take me."

Finn shifted his grip to her hips, and he didn't have

to say a word. Lex taunted them all by sliding the head of Finn's cock against Trix's pussy, and when she shuddered at the sensation, Dallas steadied her. All of them, moving in perfect, silent harmony, all of them focused on easing Trix lower—

And thank fucking God, because Finn's ability to think shattered as she took his dick, squeezing hot and tight around him from the first inch. Pleasure almost drove his eyes shut, but he forced them open so he could watch as he pulled her lower.

She was wrecked already, her head lolling back, and Dallas gathered her hair, wrapping it loosely around his hand. "Such a sweet girl, taking him when you're already so full."

"She's not taking it," Lex corrected softly as she cupped Trix's breasts. "He's giving it to her."

The difference between the two could balance on the blade of Dallas's knife, but the truth of the words resonated straight down to Finn's damn bones. He didn't need her to push her boundaries for him. Oh, he got off on it, but he didn't need it. She was the one craving this, the danger of being utterly possessed with the comfort of being completely safe. The mind-bending sensation of dancing along the edge of endurance, and the security of knowing he'd take care of her.

And the one thing he'd never given her—the one thing she'd asked for again and again—was the rough, raw sensation of being taken. Not teased, not pleasured.

Taken.

Tightening his fingers, he dragged her down into a sharp thrust that arched her back and drove a hoarse cry from her throat. She clenched around him, her pussy gripping his cock.

Anchoring with one hand, he wrapped the other around the side of her neck, his thumb resting under her chin. "Look at me," he demanded. "Watch me take you."

She blinked, her eyes dreamy and hot. "Love me,

Finn."

It had always gone without saying, because loving her had been effortless—and useless. A woman in Sector Five needed a man to fight for her, kill for her, bleed for her, *die* for her. He'd done most of them, and would still do any of them.

All of them.

But he could do this, too. Thrust up into the heat of her body, so fucking perfect his whole body ached, and give her the words that mattered here, in her home. In *their* home. "I love you, baby."

She locked her arms around his neck and kissed him—wildly, savagely, her mouth every bit as hungry as the rest of her. Taking him in return, and there was nothing sweet left in the way they came together, flesh slapping against flesh, her teeth closing on his lower lip as he pulled her hair and dug bruises into her hips.

He fucked up into her, sinking deep and trusting her to take him. She growled and moved, tilting her hips so that the weight and pressure of the plug buried in her ass rubbed the underside of his dick with every thrust.

Too much. Too hot, too tight, too slick, too *good.* He closed his teeth on her throat, muffling his groan as he fought a quick, vicious battle with his body. She'd dragged him over the edge the last time, but this time—

This time they were coming together.

Trix shuddered and screamed his name. Lex took over her movements, grasping her hips and slamming her down onto Finn's cock. Once, twice, with Trix's pussy clenching hard around him in primal, undeniable proof.

She was coming, coming apart. So he drove up into her and gave her everything.

Trix pressed her face against the hollow of his shoulder as the last of the spasms wracking her subsided into soft shivers. Her breath blew hot on his skin with every helpless pant, and she stroked the back of his neck in a quiet, possessive caress.

Finn pried open his eyes in time to watch Dallas rest a hand on Trix's back. "Catch your breath," he said, meeting Finn's gaze. There was a question behind the leader's easy smile, an invitation Finn had never expected to see.

Neither of them would give it voice, not until everything with Sector Five had been settled. But soon enough, he'd be sitting in Ace's studio, watching the O'Kane logo take shape on his wrists. The second chance Bren had promised him.

A whole damn life of bliss and hope and tripping over rainbows.

He answered the silent question with a nod before turning his lips to Trix's cheek. He could stand turning into some crazy-eyed hero if it bought him another fifty years of Trix snuggled up to his chest, soft and warm and utterly sated. "You with me?"

"Mmm." She stretched languorously, rubbing against him. "I'm here. I'm..." Her eyes fluttered open, and she met his gaze. "I love you."

He wrapped a lock of hair around one finger, savoring the silky slide and the vivid color. "I'm never gonna get tired of hearing that."

"Good, because I'll never get tired of saying it."

"Really?" He closed his eyes and pulled her closer. "Say it again?"

"I love you." She brushed a kiss over his lips. "I have always loved you."

"Tracy cared about some asshole who never did right by her," he corrected, voicing the guilt one last time before letting it go. "As long as Trix loves me, the rest doesn't matter."

She smiled against his mouth. "Count on it."

ryder

IF YOU LOOKED closely, if you paid attention, Sector Two was falling apart.

Ryder stood on a balcony overlooking the street, smoking a cigarette. All the signs were there, if you knew what to look for. Less traffic, even at this relatively early hour. Darkened townhomes surrounding the square, as if they'd been closed down and locked up while their owners were away. The banquet their hostess had offered was somewhat less than sumptuous, and he'd heard murmurs from some of the sector leaders that they'd never seen so few girls offered to the guests.

Then there was the tension. Cerys's eyes had been tight with it, brittle, every stare alight with challenge. She'd been getting shit, all right, from Eden and the other leaders. She had the look of someone whose empire was slipping away, bit by bit, even as she tried desperately to cling to it.

Yeah, Finn had fucked her over but good by framing her for that councilman's murder on Mac's watch. No question she'd come down on Beckett's side tonight.

He lit another cigarette and waited for his boss.

The door behind him slid open before his second drag. "It's done."

Ryder swallowed a vicious curse and took a deep breath. "There's been a vote?"

"O'Kane will have to hand Finn over. He never really had a chance, with Gideon as his only firm ally and Cerys so determined to punish him."

And with no vote of his own. It was a nasty business, meetings held in secret. The thin veneer of democracy amongst the sector leaders was an illusion, after all, and it quickly broke down when they started running around behind each other's backs. None of the others would like having it done to them, not a single goddamn bit, but the hypocrisy of it got lost in the shuffle.

Now Finn would have to come back to Five, and there was no question what would happen to him. He'd be dead as soon as he crossed the border, because Beckett couldn't afford to take chances.

Ryder dropped his cigarette and crushed it beneath his boot. "Can we stop it?"

"No." Jim Jernigan stepped forward to lean against the balcony railing. "Gideon tried like hell, but O'Kane's made too many enemies. The only concession is that Beckett will have to send Dominic back to Four in exchange. One traitor for another."

"Dammit." Ryder scrubbed his hands over his face. "Beckett's crazy, Jim. Nuts."

"I know. That's why we can't risk your place on the inside." Jim turned to study him, his expression coldly impassive. "The bigger picture, Ryder. One man, even a friend, can't be allowed to endanger that."

"It's too much," he argued. "You give enough and, pretty soon, you've lost everything that counts."

"Perhaps." Jim looked back out over the sector, the moonlight catching the silver strands in his hair. There were more every time Ryder saw him. "Keeping a sector safe requires personal sacrifices. Even Dallas O'Kane understands that. You'll see."

Jim's personal sacrifices were legendary—and as mysterious as the man himself. Everyone knew he'd suffered loss on his way up, but he never spoke of it.

Ever.

"O'Kane should have had a vote." Ryder wrapped both hands around the wrought-iron railing. "Hell, he should have had two—one for Four and one for Three."

"Even two votes might not have helped. Colby and Scott both sided with Beckett." Jim shook his head. "Do you understand what that means? Six and Seven *never* agree on anything. If Beckett has secured their loyalty and Cerys's... I need you focused. I need you close to him."

Ryder's pistol felt heavy in the holster at his side. "I could take care of it. Now. Before we even leave the sector."

"None of us can afford the scrutiny," Jim replied. "I can ease the way for a change of leadership, but I need time and information."

Time. Time for Beckett to rampage across Five, doing all the damage he could. Ending lives, addicting more people to his designer drugs.

Killing.

Only the knowledge that Jim didn't like it any more than he did calmed Ryder. "Yes, sir."

"Good." Jim squeezed his shoulder briefly before turning back to the door. "You're saving lives in the long run. If Eden decides we're not worth the trouble, they'll do more damage than a hundred Becketts."

"Yeah." He could play along—for now. As long as the end was in sight, and Beckett would be out of the picture for good.

As for Finn... He could give the man the clean death he deserved, instead of whatever Sector Five's new leader had in mind for him. It was the least he could do.

19

THREE DAYS AFTER the party, the other shoe dropped.

Finn had almost stopped bracing for it, which made stepping into Dallas's office that much worse. Dallas looked like he hadn't slept, his eyes bloodshot and his chin stubbled. But Lex...

Lex was *furious.*

"No," she gritted through clenched teeth. "Fuck 'em all, Declan. I mean it."

"Lex," he chided, but there was no heart in it. Fuck, there was no heart in *him.* O'Kane looked like a man staring at two impossible choices, and Finn could guess what they were.

Without being prompted, he dragged out a chair and sat, meeting Dallas's gaze squarely. "What's the demand?"

"You for Dom," Dallas replied flatly. "Beckett talked

the rest of those assholes into a secret fucking meeting, and they had some sham of a vote."

"You're not going," Lex said immediately. She turned a chair around, dropped into it, and folded her arms on the back. "We wouldn't do that."

"Not to Trix, and not to you." Dallas shoved his fingers through his hair with a rough sigh. "Beckett bought them off somehow. Gideon said Colby and Scott agreed, though Christ knows what could have made that happen."

Finn knew. "Stims. I made good money pushing them into Six through Hawk and his friends. The farms use them to increase production. Beckett can open his medicine chest and find a way to buy damn near anyone." It was an advantage Mac had never been clever enough to appreciate, but one Beckett was clearly all too willing to use.

Dallas laughed roughly. "So much for our pretensions. If this is how we're defining democracy now, I'm ready for a little anarchy."

"Agreed." Lex shook her head. "If Beckett wants a fight, he's got one."

Except for the fact that, sham or not, the other leaders had attended this secret meeting. They would back Beckett in a fight for all the reasons they'd agreed with him at the meeting. To punish Dallas, to please Beckett, or simply to maintain order. If Dallas was allowed to ignore their decree, the sectors really would descend into anarchy.

Until Eden wiped them all out.

And O'Kanes would die. Trix's family would die. Men like Bren and Jas, who had believed in Finn enough to hold him to a higher standard. Women like Lex and Six, who were too viciously protective to stay behind in a fight.

Sector Four might survive a war, but the heart of what made it so damn special wouldn't. And Finn could save all of them with one simple choice.

Trix would never forgive him.

Dallas's brow furrowed as he leaned forward. "You better not be thinking anything stupid, Finn."

He was the only one in the room who was thinking smart, because he was the only one with undivided loyalties. "I'm thinking you two haven't gotten this far by being soft-hearted."

Lex bit off a harsh curse. "You made her a promise. The kind you can't take back."

"So did you," Finn retorted. "You promised to keep them all safe, didn't you? What does one man's life weigh balanced against war with every damn sector?"

"It depends on the man," she shot back. "And the reason for the war. It depends on what's *right*."

Dallas was still watching him, an odd look on his face. Like he was seeing Finn clearly for the first time—and regretted it. Finn had seen that look before, but never mixed with such sad approval. "Lay off, Lex. He wouldn't deserve her if he wasn't thinking it."

"*Declan.*"

"I didn't say I was going to let him do it."

As if they could stop him. "You should," Finn told him bluntly. "You're stretched thin for manpower across two sectors. You aren't well positioned for a sector war. I'm not worth the risk."

"Not if you keep talking like that," Dallas agreed. "I thought you were starting to understand how things work here."

It was one thing to rule a sector on hugs and doing what was *right* when things were going well. In his gut, Finn had never believed it could hold true when everything went to shit. Or maybe he did, and that was what made it worth protecting. "The rest of the world doesn't give a shit. You're not ready for a war, but I can buy you time."

"Time." Lex scoffed, then pinned him with a hard,

glittering gaze. "Do you know what this will do to Trix? I want to hear you say it."

"It will hurt her." Even admitting it ached, because it was the worst fucking feeling in the world. Almost. "But she'll be safe. She'll have her family." And maybe, someday, she'd understand. She had wanted so badly for him to feel the support and affection that came with belonging, so she couldn't hate him for caring about the people she loved.

"Hurt her," Lex echoed. "You son of a bitch."

Finn stiffened. "Do you think I want to do this? I spent four damn years not giving a shit if I lived or died because she was gone. Trust me, lady. I want to live. But not if it means Trix has to watch her friends die."

Lex dove out of her chair, knocking it to the floor, and leaned over him, her eyes blazing as if she was seconds from pulling a knife and saving Beckett the trouble. "Then fight it. Help *us* fight it."

"How, by shooting a few guys? Nothing I could do would help as much as stopping the damn war before it starts."

"You can't stop the war," Dallas said quietly. "You could give us time to prepare, true enough, but Beckett's a bully. If I hand you over, what will he ask for next week? *Who* will he ask for?"

"No one," Finn promised. "If you hand me over, I'll find a way to kill the bastard."

Dallas hesitated. Frowned. And Finn knew he had him.

Lex threw up her hands. "This is bullshit. I'm done trying to reason with either one of you."

Dallas watched him for a long, tense moment. "I'm going to try to stall," he said finally. "Because Sector Four doesn't act until its leaders are in agreement. And you have a very uncomfortable conversation with Trix ahead of you. Why don't you see if that changes your mind?"

Finn rose and looked at Lex. "You matter to her, more than you know. The gang comes first, right?"

"Of course it does." She exhaled, and her shoulders slumped a little. "Why the fuck do you think I'm fighting you on this?"

"For Trix, I know."

"And for you," she corrected. "Whether you buy it or not."

He did. Which was why Lex and Dallas and every last one of these crazy, beautiful, hopeful motherfuckers were worth fighting and dying for. They'd seen the good in him before it was even there to see.

But not before Trix. And talking to her was going to hurt.

The Broken Circle was slammed, though the night was still young. The booths and tables were full, and customers who couldn't find room to belly up to the bar lined the walls.

Jeni's shows were getting popular, all right. Popular enough to fill *all* their pockets.

Trix was well on her way to pulling a double shift when Rachel took her tray and jerked her head toward the back door. "Finn was looking for you. Lex asked me to cover."

"Yeah?" Trix swallowed past the sudden, anxious lump in her throat and wiped her hands on a towel. "Something up?"

"I don't know." Rachel patted her on the hip. "Why don't you go and see, huh?"

He wasn't waiting backstage, and no one was in the courtyard or the garage. Trix climbed the stairs to her room, willing herself not to overreact to what was probably nothing.

One look at Finn's face blew that to hell and back.

He was too serious, that blank, careful look from his earliest days in Four back on his face.

He rose from the couch. "Trix."

"Rachel said…" She let the words trail off. They didn't matter, anyway. "What happened?"

"Beckett." He rubbed his hands on his jeans with a sigh. "Come sit down."

She did, but only because her knees felt wobbly already. Weak. "What about Beckett?"

"The sector leaders met." He sat close to her—but not too close. Not touching, as if he wasn't sure he had the right. "They demanded Dallas hand me over to Sector Five. If he doesn't…"

Dallas would never do that, not in a million years. "You don't— That's not anything to worry about," she reassured him. "You may not have your ink yet, but you're here. You're one of us."

"Trix…" His hands curled into fists. "Do you know what it will cost Dallas and Lex to protect me? What it will cost this sector?"

Her mind spun in dizzy circles. He was saying something important, vital. Something so terrible she couldn't quite grasp it. "They wouldn't send you back there, Finn. They wouldn't."

"They wouldn't send me," he agreed. "But they need to."

A chill swept over her, a stark counterpoint to the acid heat twisting her gut. No, Dallas and Lex would never send him back to Five. It was tantamount to marching him off to certain death.

They'd never do that to him. But Finn would do it to himself.

Maybe the universe had a sense of humor, after all, some sort of lopsided version of karmic retribution. Four years ago, she'd walked out on him. Now, he was about to do the same to her.

"You'll never leave me, huh?" She stared at him, everything going numb and still except for the wild, frantic rhythm of her heart.

He flinched. "I don't want to. I swear to God, Trix. But fuck, you're the one who wanted me to like these bastards, and now I do. Would you want to be the reason half of them end up dead?"

Never, not in a million years. "Then we'll split. They can't demand Dallas turn you over if you're not here. We can pack up and go tonight—head west and drive until we hit the ocean."

His words, thrown back at him. And he remembered it, because something wistful flared in his eyes before he shook his head. "This is your home. And if we cut out, they sure as hell will come down hard on Dallas for letting me go."

"Finn—" Her hands had started to shake, and she squeezed them still between her knees. "They'll kill you."

"Maybe not." He half-smiled. "I'm pretty tough to kill. But if I manage to take Beckett down once we're back in Five, no one can pin it on the O'Kanes."

Is that what he was telling himself? That he was gonna play the hero, fix all their problems with one more bullet, one slice of a blade? "Beckett will be ready. He won't give you the chance. If you can't own that that's true, you have no business even thinking about this."

"So what do you want me to do?"

"I don't *know*." She sprang up off the sofa. "Anything but sacrifice yourself."

"So sacrifice everyone else?"

"No. Give us time to think of something." The words tumbled out, and she didn't try to stop them, just threw them recklessly in his lap. "I'll go with you."

"*No*." Finn lunged to his feet, lunged at *her*, his fingers closing around her shoulders. "Don't fucking say that."

"Why the hell not?" She struggled against his grip. "Does it scare you, Finn? Make you want to throw up?

Because now you know how I feel."

For the first time, he didn't release her. He held her tighter, clenching hard enough to bruise. "If I go to Five, they might kill me. If you go—" He choked on a snarl. "Do you know how long they can string out dying over there? Or maybe Beckett wouldn't get fancy. Maybe he'd just addict you again and see how many times you can survive the withdrawal."

Her tears spilled over, burning her cheeks. "Can't hurt worse than staying behind."

"Yes, it can," Finn whispered roughly. "You were happy without me for four fucking years, Trix. You'll be happy again, as long as you're here, with the people who matter."

He may as well have slapped her. The words hit her like a blow, stinging and nauseating. "You bastard. You don't deserve to know how miserable I was without you. You think I wanted to leave?" She wrenched away. "Since we're laying everything out, I almost didn't. I almost gave up. But knowing what you'd do—what Mac would do to you—I couldn't."

"Beckett would do things to you that Mac never dreamed of," Finn replied, flat and harsh. "And you know what? Not even because he's a sick fucker. He'd do it to hurt me. And he'd do the same shit to me to hurt you. I would put a bullet in my own damn head before taking you back there."

"Right. Because I'm a victim, and you're a hero." She couldn't look at him anymore, so she turned away. "It would be different, you know, if you just admitted it. That you don't believe losing you would hurt me. That you don't *believe*."

"Your friends had to fight themselves to accept me at all. How long can that last after they start dying for me? Because of me? When some bastard hits Six with a lucky shot, how long before Bren wants me gone? Don't tell me I'd still belong here. Some dreams are too perfect."

"So you want to let it go before it gets snatched away." The hell of it was, she could understand that. Some part of her screamed for her to do it now, to shove him away before he could leave her.

"I want to keep it whole. For you."

"And to hell with how I feel about it." Her stomach ached, and she pressed one hand over the throbbing pain, as if that could ease it. "Mac was right. I'm a weakness, and it's never going to stop. I'll have to live the rest of my life knowing that it was all because of me. That I'm the one who got you killed."

"Trix, no." He touched her arm. "You're the one who gave me something worth dying for."

It was so horrifying she almost laughed. "I'm sure I'll find that very comforting when Beckett sends me your head in a box."

"Fucking hell, I thought—" His voice caught, so rough he sounded like he was broken on the inside. "I thought you'd understand. I've never been a part of something good before. I ruin things. I ruin *people*. Don't make me ruin this place. It's like a pre-Flare fairy tale, and we need the hope. The whole damn world needs it."

She couldn't do this. She wasn't strong enough to give him what he needed—acceptance even in the absence of understanding, reassurance without breaking down. Her throat ached, and her hands itched. She could beg him with her words and her touch, but that was the coward's way, just like the anger was.

She had to love him, and let him go anyway.

Trix swallowed her tears and faced him. "You're determined to do this?"

"If Dallas can't figure out a different way, yes."

"No," she told him firmly. "We both grew up in Five, Finn. We don't have the luxury of lying to ourselves." She reached for him, laid her hand on his cheek. "I need to know your head's on straight. That you understand what you're doing."

He stilled, staring down into her eyes forever before laying his hand over hers. "I will do everything I can to come back to you. But I know what the odds are, baby. I know—" He swallowed. "Maybe I can take him down with me."

"You're not coming back."

"I'm not coming back."

The ache grew, digging deeper into her soul, but there would be time for that later. Forever, even. As long as she lived. "You'll always be the best thing that ever happened to me," she whispered, knowing he wouldn't believe it.

He touched her lower lip. "Coming here is the best thing that ever happened to you. I'm glad I got to see you like this. I'm glad I got to meet Trix."

She cracked, just a little, and she had to close her eyes to hide a fresh wave of tears. "When?"

"I don't know. It could be soon."

It could be tonight. Trix clenched her hands in his shirt. "Not yet."

He exhaled roughly and cupped her face. "I'm yours for as long as I can be."

It could never be enough, but she'd take what she could get. She tugged at his shirt as he slid his hands toward her hips, and they tumbled back to the bed.

Finn had no patience this time. No finesse. Maybe he heard the same invisible clock ticking down the last seconds of their happy ending as loudly as she did. He rolled her beneath him, coming down with his hips between her thighs, and claimed her mouth in a hard, starving kiss.

The ticking never wavered, not as his tongue slicked over hers, and not as she dragged her shirt over her head. It didn't quiet until his bare skin was pressed against hers, generating a heat and tension that had nothing to do with pain or loss.

He kissed her everywhere. Her lips, her chin, all

along the bare skin of her throat, skin that would never carry the ink that marked her as *his*. Skin that would never carry any ink at all.

His mouth paused at her collarbone as he fumbled with her pants. "I love you."

Don't. She bit her tongue and slipped her fingers into his hair, holding his lips to her skin. "I know."

He got her pants open before his mouth found hers again, kissing her as he tore at her jeans and then his own. She kicked hers to the floor and helped him, shoving at the rest of their clothes until they were naked.

More kisses. Frantic and fevered, his mouth touching everywhere and lingering nowhere, not an exploration but a prolonged, yearning farewell. Every touch was a brand, seared into her body as surely as her ink.

So she marked him in return, the only way she could. She scratched her fingernails down his back, up his sides, along the back of his neck, leaving red welts that would take days to heal.

Days he might not have.

He slid down her body, pushing her thighs wide, and even this was different. His fingers, quick and demanding, two and then three working into her as his tongue found her clit. No time for teasing.

And no need. She responded as surely as she ever had, her body attuned to the inalienable truth that she belonged to him. That it would never stop, this need, this *craving*, even when he was gone.

Trix gave in to it, embraced it. Let go and came apart as he groaned his encouragement against her skin. One swift, hard orgasm, clenching tight around his fingers as pleasure smashed through her, and her fingers and toes were still tingling when he crawled back up her body and thrust home.

"Finn!" His name tore free of her on a harsh cry.

"Feel me," he rasped, tangling both hands in her hair to pin her in place. "Feel me tonight. Feel me—"

He didn't say the words, but she heard them, felt them. *One last time.*

"I do," she promised, locking her legs around him. "I will."

He kissed her and drove deeper, making her feel the stretch, the need. His muscles flexed under her hands, every part of him focused on fucking her, fast and hard. Trix met every thrust hungrily, their hips slamming together again and again.

It was everything she'd wanted all along, raw and messy and real, and she reveled in it, even knowing it would hurt more later. Especially when he pressed his cheek to hers, his breath falling hot with every panted word. "Love you, baby. Forever."

Then don't leave me. She held back the words because they were selfish, horrible. She couldn't stop them from existing, but she could keep them from hurting Finn.

He raised his head and met her eyes, and she knew that even her silence hurt him. But then he was kissing her again, muffling anything she might say. Taking away the chance that she might not say anything.

Then she couldn't, because the frantic pressure was building once more. She tried to stave it off this time, but Finn slipped one hand beneath her ass and lifted her hips, tilting them so that his next plunging thrust tipped her over the edge. She came hard, insensible to everything—her own cries, the room, the world. Everything but Finn and the way he rode her release, prolonging it as long as he could before his restraint cracked.

He came with her name on his lips, on *her* lips, whispered against them so bittersweet she couldn't hold back the tears. They streamed from her eyes, soaking into the hair at her temples as he dropped kisses to her lips and cheeks until his mouth tasted like salt.

He didn't speak as he rolled them over, cradling her to his chest. The tears gave way to sobs, just as her pleasure had yielded to sadness, and she cried. She cried until the muscles between her ribs were sore, until her throat was raw. Until she was exhausted, and the world drifted away into dreamless sleep.

20

THE BUZZING STING of the needles had faded into a surreal sort of aching pleasure by the time Noah held up a tablet in front of Finn's face. "I've mapped out every tunnel in Five on here. Coming this way, going toward Six, and even the ones headed into Eden."

Not something he could take with him, but he and Bren had spent hours poring over the maps, figuring out the best places to hide supplies, along with the most likely route of Finn's impossible escape. "Thanks."

Bren reached out and tapped the edge of the tablet. "Memorize it, hot shot."

Finn had a good memory, but he couldn't fix the ridiculous labyrinth under the city and sectors into his head in a few hours. But he'd promised Trix he'd try to come back, even if she didn't believe it. If there was a scrap of a chance—

He grabbed the tablet with his free hand.

"Quit moving, new guy," Ace grumbled. "Don't make me strap your ass in."

"Sorry." Finn looked to where the artist bent over his right wrist, filling in the last lines of his second cuff.

O'Kane ink, because Dallas wasn't going to let him die for the O'Kanes without the highest honor the sector had to offer. It should have been an empty, stupid gesture, but Finn couldn't look at them without feeling a weird jolt in his chest.

"Don't be such a perfectionist, Ace," Jas said from where he leaned against the wall, his arms crossed over his chest. "Those maps are at least as important as your line work right now."

"Fine, if you're going to be practical about it." Ace grinned up at Finn. "Since you're getting wobbly lines now, I'll give you a free tattoo when you get back."

"Deal. Now I'm gonna come back just to collect," Finn replied, appreciating the chance to step back from the weight of the moment. Not that it lasted for long. His brain kept circling back to Trix, sobbing herself out on his chest…

It shook his resolve. Her pain always did. In his gut, Finn knew she could have made him stay. Even if it felt like turning his back on everything she'd taught him, even if it meant dooming everyone she loved to a brutal, bloody war.

Trix could have forced him to sacrifice everything else before himself. And she hadn't.

God, he *had* to come back. He glanced down at the tablet, trying to focus on the first section of the map. "I went to Six last time. If I get away, they'll expect that."

Zan glowered at the tablet. "You're gonna be armed, right?"

"No." Pulling a weapon would defeat the damn point. Dallas had to play by the sector leaders' rules to avoid blowback, and handing over an obvious assassin instead of a prisoner would bring shit down on Sector Four as fast as not handing Finn over at all.

Bren shrugged. "We'll take care of that when we plant your supplies."

"Thanks." He met Bren's gaze. Even though they weren't saying goodbyes, weren't saying anything at all that acknowledged the probability Finn would never reach those weapons, he couldn't leave it at that. "I mean it, Bren. For everything."

"You're welcome. And I mean *that*."

Finn gripped the tablet until the edges dug painfully into his palm. "You'll look out for her, right? Take care of her. Until I get back."

"Yeah, man. We all will."

Cold comfort. For Trix and for Finn.

"There we go," Ace said, swiping Finn's wrist one last time before straightening. "Too bad we don't have time to drink you in, but you probably don't need to be puking up sixteen shots right now."

"Probably not." Finn lifted his wrist and studied the tattoo. The O'Kane skull insignia sat front and center, but it was surrounded by pistons and gears and edged with lines of what looked like chain-link fencing. "Shit, Ace, you're as good as you think you are."

"I know." Ace rose and slapped him on the shoulder. "You're ours now. You know what that means, right?"

"O'Kane for life," Jas said as the miniature tablet in his hand beeped. He glanced down at it, and his jaw tightened as he shoved it in his back pocket. "Time to roll."

"Let me wrap his damn wrists before you slap cuffs on them," Ace grumbled, coming back with a tube of med-gel and two bandages. Finn suffered through the pointless exercise because he recognized the manic edge to every word out of Ace's mouth. He felt it, too.

Having time to say goodbye didn't make shit easier, it just drew out the suffering. Which was why he didn't ask Jas if Trix would be there, didn't let himself consider going to find her one last time.

They'd had their moment. Anything else he took now would be selfish, more pain for her to sweeten whatever hours he had left. Too high a price.

He just wished he could have heard *I love you* one last time.

Ace finished wrapping his wrists, and Finn rose. "Let's go."

Noah shoved open the door to the studio. Finn followed him through, only to stop abruptly inside the courtyard. People were standing around, faces he'd never even seen interspersed with the ones he knew well. They were silent, grave.

Respectful.

Lex stepped forward with a pair of handcuffs dangling from one hand. "Hang on to these. You can wait and put them on when you get close to the rendezvous point."

Finn took them. "Thanks, Lex."

She hesitated. "Trix is— She said to tell you..." She looked away.

It was better like this. If he repeated that enough times, he'd believe it. "I know. Tell her...fuck. Whatever will help. She knows I love her."

"Yeah." Lex smiled and brushed his hair back out of his eyes. "We all do, honey."

They all loved Trix, or they all knew Finn loved her. Both were probably true. Neither made it easier to squeeze her hand. "She's got you."

Hawk was waiting with Bren beside the open trunk of the car, and Jas was already behind the wheel. Dallas stood next to the passenger door, his gaze utterly unreadable. "No one'll blame you if you turn around, man. Don't do this because you think you won't have a place here if you don't."

Easy words to offer. Finn even believed them...to a point. But damn near every person standing in the courtyard had a line, a person whose loss they couldn't come back from. Dallas had dozens that could cripple him, and one that would completely destroy him.

Finn had told Trix the truth, and had seen the reality of it reflected back from her eyes. Only so many O'Kanes could die before the dream died with them. "I'm good," he said, reaching for the back door of the car. "Let's get this shit over with."

"Wait," Trix called. She hovered in the open door of the garage, the light filtering through her tangled hair like a halo. She stood there for an endless moment, then ran across the space between them and threw her arms around Finn's neck.

He caught her, dragging her to him so tightly his brain clamored that she couldn't breathe, but it *hurt* to loosen his arms. He couldn't remember the last time he'd cried. Maybe the night Tracy had died, when booze had stripped away everything but the idea of forever without her.

His throat hurt now. He swallowed hard and sank his fingers into her hair. "Hey, baby."

She pressed a trembling kiss to the side of his neck. "I love you. I'm sorry I didn't say it before."

"Shh, I know. I know, baby doll." He buried his face in her hair. "I'm going to try. Believe me. Believe that all I want in the world is to come back to you."

Trix nodded and tugged at one of his hands, prying it open. "I brought this for you. You should have it." She placed something warm in his hand.

The chain slithered through his fingers as Finn lifted his palm and stared at the familiar white-gold band made of delicate Celtic knots with tiny, glinting amethysts. He'd seen the ring on his mother's hand every day until she died, and it had been the only thing he'd managed to hang on to.

He'd given it to Trix five months before she disappeared from his life. And she'd *kept* it.

Wrapping the chain around his fingers, he smiled. "This thing must be good luck, if you ended up here."

"I hope so." She took a step back, then another, and Lex slid an arm around her shoulders.

Getting into the car was the hardest fucking thing he'd ever done.

Beckett had arranged the prisoner exchange with all the paranoid finesse of a pre-Flare spy villain. Finn, Hawk, Bren, Jas, and Dallas stood two hundred feet back from the road separating Sectors Four and Five.

It looked different at night. Eden's walls shone in the distance, but not brightly enough to illuminate the surrounding area. It would be hard to hit a target in the dark, and the lack of buildings or structures gave Bren no convenient perches to set up a perfect shot.

The only real illumination came from the headlights on their car, and the ones shining back at them from Five. Just one vehicle—that had been in the rules, too—which meant no more than five or six men on the other side of the line.

If Beckett was playing fair.

"Shipp and Alya are going to kill me for letting you do this," Hawk muttered before pulling Finn into an awkward, one-armed hug. It was as close to affection as he'd ever gotten from the man, which meant Hawk was pretty damn sure this was the end.

"Get them out of Six," Finn replied, slapping Hawk's shoulder. "You'll do good with O'Kane. So will they."

"I know."

Hawk moved aside, and Finn stepped up to where Bren and Jas were talking with Dallas. Well, arguing.

"I don't like it," Bren said, shaking his head. "We all know Beckett's crazy. If you go up there without protection, what's to stop him from trying to take you out?"

"The fact that he's asking the same damn question." Dallas checked his pistol before shoving it into its holster. "And the fact that I'm capable of snapping him in half and dying for the fucking chance?"

"Don't get your panties in a wad," Jas growled. "In a one-on-one fight, you'd take him easy. But nothing about this guy screams *fair play*. It's worth thinking about precautions."

"It's a chance we have to take. If he's smart, he won't do anything to risk losing the backing of the other sectors. If he's not..." Dallas shrugged and glanced at Finn. "The first sign of foul play, you haul your ass right the fuck back over here, because I'm not sacrificing you for nothing."

Finn nodded and snapped the cuffs around his wrists. The chain between them had enough give to be comfortable, but not enough that he could do much more than let his arms hang in front of him. "I'm not in a hurry to die either, it turns out."

Someone whistled from across the way, and Beckett's voice rang out. "Any time tonight, O'Kane."

Finn shared a final look with the other men before turning resolutely toward his fate. Dallas fell in beside him as they took the first steps toward the south road.

They made it halfway there before Finn spoke. "Promise me she'll be okay, O'Kane."

"We'll take care of her," Dallas replied, reaching for Finn's arm. His grip was firm, reassuring—and didn't change the fact that Dallas hadn't answered the question.

There wasn't time to ask another. Beckett and Dom grew closer, backlit by the headlights on Beckett's car, and Finn's gut twisted. Only the fact that Bren had promised to put a bullet in Dom's head before he got within a mile of Trix made it possible to hold himself still as Dom's vicious scowl became clear.

Beckett stopped a few yards away. "Dallas."

"Beckett." Dallas tightened his grip, pulling Finn to a stop on the opposite side of the road. "You gonna play by the rules you made up at your secret meeting?"

The man shrugged one shoulder beneath his impeccable suit. "I'd have had no need for such theatrics if you had responded to my requests. My *repeated* requests."

Dallas was still gripping his arm, silent and angry, and Finn knew he was fighting for the coldness to hand him over, not to mention struggling for a last-minute miracle, when the only hope they had left was Beckett's treachery.

Finn had bet on longer odds.

He tugged his arm free of Dallas's grip and stepped forward. Beckett nudged Dom into a walk, his stare fixed on Finn. He didn't take his eyes off him, not for a second. A heartbeat.

Finn didn't watch Beckett. He watched Dom, because Beckett wasn't the sort of man who did his own dirty work. And Dom was walking too willingly, and it sure as hell wasn't out of some noble impulse or a desire to save someone.

They crossed close enough for their shoulders to brush, and Dom bared his teeth in a feral grin. "Did you keep her warm for me?"

Finn clenched his fists, fighting the urge to knock all those teeth down his fucking throat. "Donnelly's gonna kill you and leave your body in the desert for the vultures."

"You think so?" Dom's grin only grew wider. "Then I'll see you in hell, asshole."

Dom shoved past him, ramming his shoulder hard enough that Finn staggered, had to twist to keep his balance.

If he hadn't, he wouldn't have seen the flash of silver catch the moonlight as Dom started toward Dallas.

His brain scrambled to piece together the meaning while his gut took over. A lifetime of experience with assholes like Beckett, like *Dom*, kicked in, and the math was so fucking simple.

Dallas. Dom. A knife.

His fucking miracle had arrived.

Dom was still easing the blade from his sleeve when Finn pivoted. Beckett shouted behind him, and Finn ignored it, lunging for Dom as the man went for Dallas. The knife flashed again—right there out in the open, right in Dom's fucking hand—and that was proof enough.

Finn looped the chain between his cuffs over Dom's head and jerked back, pulling him off his feet. He dangled there, thrashing and choking for a moment before shifting the knife in his hand and stabbing back blindly.

The blade sliced through Finn's jacket, his shirt, but it didn't slow him down. Finn pulled harder, satisfaction overwhelming the stinging pain—and everything else. "You'll have to keep hell warm for me."

There was shouting behind him, shouting in front of him, but Finn only tightened his grip until the cuffs dug into his wrists and the chain cut into Dom's skin. Hot blood trickled down over his hands, and Dom's thrashing stilled.

Finn let the body thump to the ground. The knife clattered to the road with him, the blade slick with Finn's blood.

And all hell broke loose.

Scowling, Jas stepped forward and pulled his gun on Beckett. "You treacherous bastard!"

Across the way, the men from Five pulled their weapons, too—leaving Dallas and Finn in the line of fire.

Bren waved them back. "Get down!"

Dallas lunged for the cover of the car, and Finn started to follow. Then he saw Beckett scrambling toward the line of buildings, abandoning his men as quickly as Dallas rushed toward his own.

It was everything that mattered about both leaders

distilled to a single moment, and Finn's own instincts made the decision for him. He took off after Beckett, ignoring Dallas's furious shout.

Beckett had little hope of rallying the other sectors after this. But humiliation would burn in his gut, and his capacity for revenge outstripped Mac's the same way his competence had. Beckett would never forgive Dallas. The next time he came for Sector Four, he wouldn't be coming for Finn alone. He'd be after the blood of any O'Kane he could get his hands on.

But only if Finn let him live long enough to try.

A shot rang out, and a bullet chipped a brick inches from his head. Beckett cursed when he missed and turned back to running, and Finn fought a wild grin.

Soft-ass motherfucker wasn't used to doing his own dirty work.

Beckett rounded the end of the street, his fancy shoes skidding on the dirty concrete. He disappeared down a narrow alley, and Finn turned the corner in time to see a garbage can clatter to the pavement, spilling pungent trash everywhere.

Finn barely slowed as he jumped it. He knew these streets better than Beckett ever could, knew them because he'd walked them every day while Beckett sat his fancy ass in an office. There were dead ends everywhere, alleys closed off by new buildings or barricades.

And Beckett was headed straight toward one.

"Fuck. *Fuck!*" Beckett slammed his hand against the chain-link fence at the end of the alley with a clatter, then turned with his gun raised. Finn was already on him, slapping it from his hands with one swipe.

It skittered across the alley, beneath some busted crates, and Finn lunged for it. The splintered wood scratched his hands as he felt for the gun, but the moment his fingertips brushed the barrel, pain exploded through the right side of his head.

He hit the ground, grunting at the impact, and rolled

to the side just in time to avoid taking a second hit to the face. The board bounced next to his ear, and Finn twisted and kicked, driving his boot up into Beckett's hands. The board went flying, and the man staggered and hit the wall behind him with a groan.

He rebounded with a louder groan and drove his foot into Finn's side.

It hurt. It hurt like a bitch, grinding into the lacerated skin over his ribs, but Finn let Beckett take another kick just so he could grab the man's fancy fucking shoe and jerk him off his feet.

Beckett went down swearing, and Finn reached for the gun again.

"You *bastard*." Beckett clawed at his arm and his side, his fingers digging in with surprising strength. "Son of a fucking whore."

Finn drove his elbow back, nailing the man in the chin. His hand closed around the gun, and he rolled back, swinging it up to point at Beckett's face. "You always were predictable, asshole. Selfish people usually are."

Footsteps thundered on the pavement, almost eclipsing the shouts that accompanied them. But nothing could eclipse the sight of the dim light glinting off nickel and steel as Ryder and two of Beckett's other men approached, their weapons drawn and ready.

Finn searched Ryder's face, desperate for any clue, any sign of the man he'd started to think of as a friend. But his expression was unreadable, his dark eyes blank as he stopped a few feet away, his gun pointed directly at Finn.

Beckett heaved a hoarse laugh and wrenched the gun from his hand. "Decent show, Finn. I see why Mac relied on you so heavily in the past. You're tenacious." He waved the gun in the air, then dropped the magazine and cleared the chamber in a few practiced movements. "But you got stupid. Never go soft over a piece of ass, man. *Never*."

Finn rolled to his knees, because he refused to die on his back, staring up at a walking piece of trash. "Yeah, I'm real soft. Even handcuffed and unarmed, you needed reinforcements to take me down."

Beckett tossed the empty gun to the ground with a clatter. "Those are your last words? I expected something a little more profound from Fleming's great thinker."

Finn judged the distance between them. There was no way he could get the chain between his cuffs around Beckett's throat before taking a dozen bullets in the back. His side felt sticky, slick, as if those cuts were bleeding more than he'd realized. It was dripping from his forehead, too, sliding down his aching face.

And Ryder still had that gun trained on him, hands steady enough to be their own reminder—friendship had never meant much in Sector Five.

I'm sorry, Trix. She wouldn't be okay, not for a long time. But she wouldn't be alone, either, and maybe Finn's death would satisfy Beckett's need for revenge. At least long enough for Dallas to rally strength behind him. The other sectors wouldn't stand with Five, not after tonight.

Not the ending Finn had hoped for, but the one he'd suspected was coming from the moment he walked through Fleming's office door and found Trix alive, his own personal miracle. He'd had more time with her than he'd ever hoped for. He'd loved her, held her. He'd said his goodbyes this time.

Exhaling slowly, he lifted his gaze to Beckett's. Then he gave him the only words he had left. "O'Kane for life."

The man's bruised jaw clenched, and he gestured to Ryder. "He's your friend. You do the honors."

Ryder huffed out a breath, and his hands tightened on his gun. "Motherfucker."

If Ryder didn't do it, someone else would. And the two guards were Beckett's men. They'd take delight in blowing holes through Finn—preferably in painful places that would take a while to kill him.

Finn met the man's eyes and hoped their friendship went as far as a clean, swift death. Ryder stared back at him for a moment, his arms taut and trembling, then spat out another curse.

He swung around and fired twice, taking out both of the other guards with neat shots to the head. By the time they dropped, he'd turned the barrel of his pistol to where Beckett stood, shocked and sputtering.

Finn sighed roughly and slumped forward, dizzy under a wave of pure, giddy relief. "Jesus Christ, man. I thought you were gonna do it."

"I almost did, you dumb shit." Ryder grimaced. "Fucking hell. I have a job to do, Finn, and you're fucking it all up."

"That's kind of my specialty." Finn straightened and forced himself to his feet. It only took two steps to reach a guard and pluck a gun from his limp fingers. "If you can't be here when I kill this bastard..."

Ryder snorted. "Be my guest. I'm tired of listening to him run his goddamn mouth, anyway."

Beckett tried to take a step back and hit the wall. "The other sector leaders—"

Finn lifted the pistol and cut him off with a bullet.

Blood splattered back against the wall, and Beckett slumped, mouth still open, eyes already glazing, but Finn wasn't taking any goddamn chances. He emptied the magazine and tossed the empty weapon on top of the body before turning away. "I should have fired faster the first time I had a gun pointed at him."

"Truth." Ryder jerked his head toward the mouth of the alley. "Get gone. I'll clean up here. You got a whole new life waiting for you back in Four."

Finn hesitated. "You could have one, too."

"Like I said..." Ryder holstered his gun. "I've got a job to do."

Finn thought of the bag, the map. All those elegant

routes plotted out, all headed toward Sector Six. But there wasn't a damn person in Six *or* Seven with the brains and resources to send a well-trained man like Ryder undercover in another sector.

So Jim Jernigan had plans for Sector Five. "Is your boss a danger to mine?"

"You ask a lot of questions for a man in handcuffs." Ryder lifted one eyebrow and turned away. "Tell your lady I said hi."

"I will." Finn picked up the second guard's gun on his way by and headed for the street. But he couldn't stop himself from pausing one last time. "If you ever need a favor, you know where to find me."

"Bet on it."

It was good enough. It had to be. Finn turned back to the street, every ache and pain swallowed by the growing realization that he was still alive.

He only made it two blocks before he ran into Hawk and Jasper. Hawk bit off a curse and grabbed Finn's arm. "Shit, we thought you were finished."

"Crazy *and* lucky," Jas muttered. "Beckett?"

"Dead." He waved off Hawk, who was trying to check his side, and thrust out his wrists. "Dallas and Bren?"

"They're securing the car." Jas had to search his pockets, but he finally fished out the key and unlocked the cuffs. "They're good. We're good."

Finn let the metal drop to the ground and stripped off his bandages, too. His wrists hadn't entirely healed, and Ace would probably kick his damn ass for the pressure he'd put on the artist's precious work while choking Dom, but Finn's ink was whole and vivid. A far more promising symbol than his last words.

He was an O'Kane now, baptized in blood, and the words felt right this time. "Then let's get our asses home."

The third time Trix's hand slipped, making a mess of the smooth liner she was applying beneath her eye, she gave in. Instead of wiping it away, she smudged it roughly, then stared at her reflection in the vanity mirror.

She was a mess. No polished, perfect shows tonight, not for her. But she could work with that. Leather and stiletto heels, mesh to rip away. A whole new kind of performance for a whole new Trix.

Lex sighed and leaned over her shoulder, putting her face squarely in the left half of the mirror. "Honey, you can't go out there tonight."

"Why not?" Trix positioned the pencil, rubbed a shaky black line beneath her other eye, then blended it carelessly. "I'm a fucking professional."

"You'll make the men cry, and not in the good way. Shit, you're about to make *me* cry." Lex hesitated, her breathing uneven and ragged. "Take the night off, Trix, and see what shakes out. Maybe—"

It was madness, interrupting the queen of Sector Four, and Trix did it too readily. "I got enough maybes from Finn, thanks."

Lex held her gaze in the mirror for a moment before looking away. "I deserved that."

Instantly, Trix felt like hell. "No, you didn't. I just—I can't do this. I can't be here right now."

"So take the night off," Lex urged.

She hadn't been talking about the club. She'd actually pulled a bag out of her closet and laid it out on the bed. It was still sitting there, empty, clothes stacked beside it, ready to pack. Without Finn, everything seemed so hollow. She'd only just wrapped her head around the idea that he'd be there with her, sharing her home, and now he was gone. And nothing felt the same.

Trix spun around on her stool, ready to tell Lex as much, but stopped short at the veil of anxiety darkening the other woman's eyes. Jesus Christ, she'd been so tangled up in her own loss that she hadn't even thought about anything else. "Lex, I—"

"You're not the only one," Lex confirmed. "I can't sit still, either. Every time Dallas rides out of here, there's a chance that he…" She trailed off.

"That he might not come back?" The fact that she managed to get the words out at all was its own little accomplishment.

"Yeah. Fuck me." Lex straightened and propped her hands on her hips. "Come on. Let's get you some tequila. Lots and lots of—"

"Uh, Lex?" Ace popped his head around the door, his expression tense. "You need to get to the garage."

Lex snapped to attention, her spine straight and tense as she turned for the door. "What is it?"

Ace's gaze swung to Trix, and he cursed. "It's not—they're not back yet. But Logan Beckett's fucking wife is down there in her damn nightgown, demanding your presence."

Lex skidded to a halt and blinked at him. "Excuse me?"

"You heard me," he retorted. "A silk nightie and a fur coat splattered in blood. And cool as can fucking be. If she's not high on something, then I'm a virgin."

Trix rose, a strange numbness washing over her. "What the hell's going on over there?"

"Let's find out." Lex stalked out the door and rushed down the hallway to the back exit.

Trix followed, shivering in her thin T-shirt. The garage was bright but barely warm enough to fend off the chill—especially when she caught sight of Lili Fleming.

Ace hadn't been lying. Lili's virginal silk nightgown peeked out from beneath an expensive coat with a thick fur collar and blood staining the sleeves and front. Her long blonde hair was coiled in a painfully tight knot, and her blue eyes were icy.

That cool gaze swept over Trix without recognition before settling on Lex. "Are you Dallas O'Kane's...?" She hesitated, and Trix knew she had to be searching for a word that wouldn't offend, because in Five there were only three possibilities—wife, mistress, or whore.

"I am." Lex circled her warily. "How'd you get out of Five, and why?"

Lili dipped a perfectly manicured hand into her pocket and pulled out a pistol. Zan reacted immediately, driving her against the nearest wall with iron fingers locked around her wrist.

Not even that altered her blank expression. She let Zan strip the weapon from her grip without protest, her gaze never leaving Lex. "I shot my guard. And then I walked."

"And why's that?"

Her jaw clenched, the first and only glimpse of any emotion before she closed her eyes. "I want to speak to the other sector leaders," she said flatly. "He killed the rest of the Flemings. My family. My mother, my brothers and sisters. The youngest baby. All of them."

Lex was already asking the obvious question, the reasonable one—who?—but Trix barely heard her through the roar of blood in her ears. There was only one answer, and it terrified her.

Beckett. He wasn't just a greedy bastard with a hard-on for vengeance. He was *crazy*.

An arm slid around her. Mad, strong and warm, supporting her even as he looked at Lex. "Should I round up the guys?"

"Take Cruz and Zan," Lex ordered. "Ace, go upstairs and fetch Doc. And for Christ's sake, make sure he's—"

The rumble of an engine cut through her words, and one of the wide garage doors began to roll up. Lex clamped her mouth shut, closed her eyes, and bowed her head.

Dallas ducked under the door before it was more

than a few feet up, coming to an abrupt halt when he caught sight of Lili standing near the wall, rubbing at her wrist. His brow furrowed, but he still pivoted to face Trix and jerked his head toward the door. "He's okay."

It took a moment for his words to sink in. Even when they did, they made no sense. So she stared at him and shook her head.

The doors creaked to a stop. Finn stepped into the light spilling from the garage, looking ragged and bloody. He wore a jacket with no shirt, because he had what was left of his wrapped around his ribs. A split lip and bruises rising on one side of his face made his smile look painful. "Trix."

The dull, burning ache in her gut wrenched and scattered, sweeping over her in a rush. Every bit of pain and grief she'd shoved down surged up, and she bit her lip until it bled, trying to hold back the first sob.

But no one could contain an ocean, and that's exactly what it was—deep, endless, and her relief couldn't counter it. She'd been prepared for his death, for a loss so complete and visceral that even standing there, with him looking back at her, her body refused to accept what she was seeing.

"You..." That was all she managed, because it was too much. Her bereavement had so exhausted her that her joy fell into an empty, hollow place, because she couldn't process it.

It was too much.

She sagged against Mad, then turned in his arms, hiding her face blindly against his shoulder as she began to cry, giant, wracking shudders that *hurt.* Everything just fucking hurt.

Mad's arms tightened. "It's okay, sweetheart. He's okay. Looks a little torn up, but most heroes do from time to time."

"I can't," she whispered. She'd soared so high and crashed so hard that she didn't know if she'd ever recover.

"Trix?" Finn's voice was closer this time. Low and as hesitant as the fingers brushing her shoulder. "Beckett's gone. It's over. For me, for all of us."

"I'm sorry." She said it again, but she couldn't bring herself to turn around.

Mad let go. Finn slipped an arm around her, turning her toward his chest. His bare skin was hot beneath her cheek as he wrapped her in a tight hug and pressed his lips to the top of her head. "*I'm* sorry, baby. I'm sorry."

It was the scent of his skin that finally shattered her incredulity. Beneath the blood and gunpowder, he smelled the way he always had—like smoke, leather, and engine grease.

Like *Finn*.

She sagged and Finn lifted her, dragging her hard against his body as he whispered the same words in her ear, over and over. "I'm here. I'm okay. We're okay."

"You're not dead." The obvious, but it felt like a revelation.

"I'm not dead," he agreed.

"You're not *dead*."

He tilted her head back and met her eyes. "I told you I'd come back if I could."

"But *how*?"

"Does it matter?"

Maybe it didn't, and asking was just borrowing trouble. "You came home." She slipped her arms around his neck and held on tight. "You're home."

"I am now." He kissed her, and she clutched him closer, stroking her fingers through his hair—until they tangled in half-dried blood.

She jerked away. "You're bleeding."

He half-smiled. "I got hit in the face by a board. And sliced up a little. I haven't come out of a fight this uninjured in years."

"Jesus Christ." Trix gripped his shoulders and lifted

her head to search for Lex. "Doc is upstairs?"

"In the empty room beside mine and Dallas's." She nodded. "Go on, get him fixed up. There's plenty of time, baby girl."

Trix helped Finn through the back door of the main building and up the stairs, all the while with Lex's words tickling at the back of her mind. Every now and then, they brushed against something coiled tight, a lingering bit of tension that wouldn't relax even as the rest of her did.

Plenty of time. The tiniest flame of panic flickered to life. She locked it down and spared only a moment of worry at how damn good she was getting at that.

dallas

CERYS'S SQUARE CONFERENCE table was starting to feel a little lonely.

Or maybe that was just for Dallas. The sector leaders met as they always did, arrayed around the massive table by sector number. The seat to Dallas's right had been empty since he'd taken down Wilson Trent all those months ago.

Now the one to his left was empty, too.

The faces around the table were unusually somber. No one had enjoyed listening to Lili Fleming's dull-eyed recitation of her husband's barbaric crimes. No one at the table had tears to waste for Mac Fleming, but his wife had been a quietly suffering martyr, and her children…

Shit. Even the coldest of them didn't sit right with slaughtering babies.

"No more secret meetings," Gideon declared from the head of the table, before the door had swung shut behind

Lili. "You lot took the word of a sociopath as gospel and didn't bother to ask the one man who might *know* Beckett was trouble. If we're going to fracture like this, Eden will snuff us out one at a time."

"We played into the man's hands," Jim agreed, "and the bastard betrayed our trust."

"Supposedly," Cerys interjected. "The fact that he murdered his wife's family doesn't prove he brought an armed man to the prisoner exchange."

"Gee, Cerys. I'm sorry I didn't let him stab me a few times so I could show off the scars." Dallas leaned back in his chair and pinned her with a look. "I don't feel too compelled to prove my honor to a bunch of people who violated their own rules. I made a good-faith effort. Which of you can say the same?"

"Enough." Colby pinched the bridge of his nose and sighed. "That's fair, but what's done is done. The question now is much more important."

Jim steepled his fingers. "You mean what happens to Sector Five."

Scott cast Dallas a suspicious look, so he held up his hands. "Don't look at me. I don't want the place. Eden's already watching my every damn move."

"None of us want it, and O'Kane can't take it," Colby observed.

Jesus, the bastards didn't listen. "Hey, O'Kane doesn't want it, either."

"There's another option," Jim pointed out. "Beckett was a wild card, but I know how Mac ran his operation. There have to be half a dozen men waiting in line, ready to fight it out to see who takes over. We can wait, watch. See who comes out on top, and deal with it then."

Dallas had been waiting for it. He'd been waiting for it since the car ride back from Five, when Finn had related the vague, obviously edited story of how he'd taken down Beckett, told with the awkwardness of a man torn by conflicting loyalties.

Is there anything I need to know, Finn?

Jim has a man in Five.

How high up?

Pretty high.

Yeah, Jim knew how Mac had run his operation. No doubt Jim knew who would end up running it next, too. Dallas could have pressed Finn for a name, but now he didn't have to. In a few months, Jim's inside guy would be calling the shots, and Dallas would have to decide what to do about it.

So would Finn. But the fact that Finn hadn't wanted to reveal his name—the fact that Jim's man might have been the one to save his life—gave Dallas something he hadn't felt much of at this table in a long time.

Hope.

"I'm with Jim," he said, meeting the other man's gaze. "Something had to be done about Three because it was a mess even before it lost a leader. Seems like we can give Five some time to figure this out on their own. That's how we always did it before."

Colby hesitated, tapping his fingers on the polished table. "And if they start to break down?"

"Then someone steps in," Gideon replied. "If any sector can survive a little upset, it's the one that delivers all the fancy medicine to Eden. The city leaders won't do anything permanent before we have time to act."

"That much is true," Scott conceded.

"So we let them fight it out for themselves," Dallas said, resisting the urge to poke at Jim. Knowledge was more powerful when no one realized you had it. "I don't know about the rest of you, but I'm going to keep my head down for a few months. There's been too much excitement."

Jim's gaze lingered on the empty seat next to Dallas. "An understatement, if I ever heard one."

Gideon's smile was downright evil as he glanced at Cerys. "I'm sure we could all stand to stick close to home and clean house for a while."

Cerys flashed him a chillingly cold smile in return. "We don't all have the gods on our sides, Gideon. Some of us have to make it work."

"Not gods. Just the one. One's enough if you can stand before Him with a clean conscience and an open heart."

"That's adorable." Cerys held both hands out to her sides. "Are we finished here?"

Murmurs around the table came in the affirmative. No one was anxious to linger in Two, not with the cracks showing through Cerys's pretty façade. It was depressing here, even more than usual, so Dallas was all too ready to shove off and head for the exit. They hadn't accepted rooms this time—Lex and Lili were waiting in the car with Mad.

Everyone wanted to get the hell out of here.

Jim passed by him on his way out the door. "How did you fare against Beckett's machinations, anyway? No loss of life, I hope?"

"We're more or less in one piece."

The corner of his mouth quirked up in a smile. "More than less?"

Dallas grinned at him. "Someone in particular you're asking about?"

"No," Jim answered, his expression mild. *Too* mild. "I wouldn't expect you to tell me, anyway. A man has to keep his own counsel."

"That he does," Dallas agreed. "Some secrets would be dangerous if they got out too soon."

"It's been known to happen."

Dallas wondered how many more secrets Jim had hiding behind that deceptive face. With his silvering hair and the new wrinkles around his eyes, Jim looked like a pleasant, older businessman. Not the most ruthless leader in all eight sectors—the only one who'd been around from the start.

A man could build up a lot of secrets over that many years. “You should come to the Broken Circle sometime. I’ll crack open one of the special bottles, and we can chat.”

This time, Jim broke out in a full-fledged grin. “You after my secrets, O’Kane?”

“Hell yeah.” Dallas returned the smile. “I’m just a simple bootlegger. I gotta learn somewhere, right?”

“Right. And I’m just a guy who makes toilet paper.” Jim turned down the hall and tossed a wave over his shoulder. “See you when the next crisis hits.”

Dallas bit back a laugh and headed for the front door. But the urge to smile had faded before he hit the street.

When the next crisis hit, not if. Trouble was the only certain thing about life after the Flares but, Gideon’s God willing, maybe they had some breathing room. He sure the hell hoped so, because Dallas could already feel the next storm gathering.

Eden’s greedy waste. The empty warehouses. Special Tasks soldiers defecting. Sector leaders falling one by one.

The luxury of being a simple bootlegger was long gone. From now on, Dallas O’Kane was a man preparing for war—and not the messy-but-confined brutality of a sector war. In his gut, he knew where the real danger lay.

He paused on the sidewalk and twisted to the west. Eden loomed above Two, the walls and skyscrapers climbing high over the two- and three-story structures in Cerys’s sector.

A man prepared to take on paradise could do worse for allies than Jim Jernigan.

21

IT TOOK FINN two days to realize Trix wasn't with him anymore.

She was *present*. In his life, in his bed. She'd held his hand while Doc patched him up, and clung to him all night long. But Finn had touched her now. All of her, not just her body but her heart and soul. He'd felt the weight of that responsibility, the power of her love.

And it was slipping away, even when she sat by his side and smiled and promised everything was all right.

He had shattered something precious inside her. Her trust, maybe, or her belief in a happy ending. She was holding back from him, building walls to protect her heart, and he didn't know how to stop it.

Lex poured him a double and slid the glass across her desk. "Well? What do you need to talk to me about?"

"Trix." He reached for the glass but didn't lift it to his lips. The sweet, comforting burn of liquor was a distraction he couldn't afford and didn't deserve right now. "You were right."

"Yeah? About which part?"

"I hurt her." But hurt was too soft a word. Too gentle. "I broke her."

Lex snorted. "Well, you did walk out on her. Not just that, but on your way to a certain death. I mean, don't get me wrong, the fact that it didn't take is a good thing, but it doesn't change what you did."

Finn gripped the glass until he was surprised it didn't shatter, digging glass shards into his hand. "It was the right thing."

"For a man who tried to sacrifice himself to save us all, you've got some pretty black-and-white ideas about the fallout."

He'd never had black-and-white ideas before. His world had been ugly, soul-crushing shades of gray. "I thought being a good guy would be easier."

She slowly sipped her whiskey. "Well, it's not. It's hard as hell—but worth it."

Nothing was quite as unfair as a world where the right choice was the one that hurt the one person he needed to protect. "I tried to get her to run away with me, you know. When we were out in Six, I would have headed west and never looked back, because she was my damn world. But I was never hers. This place was. I wanted to keep it safe for her."

"Her world, huh?" Lex arched an eyebrow. "Then why did she start packing her shit the night you left?"

"She *what*?"

"I'm not supposed to know, I guess," Lex allowed. "No one is, probably. But yeah. Packing." She glowered down at her glass before draining it. "Maybe you underestimated how big a part of her world you are."

Finn drank, too. The burn in his throat couldn't match the one in his chest. "I'll do anything. Tell me how to help her."

Lex set her glass aside and squinted at him. "Let me guess—she's distant. Says nothing's wrong, but you know that's not true."

His jaw clenched, Finn nodded.

"Maybe she's worried," Lex said softly. "Wondering what you'll do the next time some asshole decides to flex and threaten us all. If she'll lose you again."

He wanted to protest that it would be different, because it had to be. This situation had been personal, pitting Finn's life against the security of the O'Kanes. No one else could have taken that risk. No one else could have saved so much. He hadn't been planning to throw his life away recklessly.

This time.

He'd been stumbling forward blindly since the moment he met her, stumbling toward self-destruction from the second he lost her. And Trix knew it.

Maybe she didn't realize how much that had changed. He'd told her she'd given him something worth dying for. He'd just assumed she'd understood that all the same things were worth *living* for.

Lex was still watching him. He thumped down the glass and shoved it across the desk. "I won't fight for you next time. I'll fight with you."

She refilled it. "Life here is dangerous, Finn. That's the flat truth, and Trix knows it. But she also needs to know that nothing short of another fucking apocalypse is going to drag you out of her arms again."

"All right." He lifted his glass to Lex. "I guess proving that's my new job."

"Not even close," she shot back. "Proving it's what you do because you can't imagine your goddamn life without her in it."

"All due respect, Lex?" He drained the drink and took his life in his hands. "That's the only part no one's ever doubted. If I do this, it's gotta be because I can't imagine her life without me."

Both eyebrows rose, then sank again as a slow smile curved her lips. "Now you're catching on, new guy."

"I try not to make the same mistake more than three or four times."

"An admirable trait."

Finn set the glass on the desk. "Is Lili—?" He hesitated. He knew the girl through scattered moments of her life. The night her father had promised her to Beckett. The night she'd married him. Celebratory dinners. Planning sessions, when she'd ghosted in and out to refill drinks and serve food in silence. She might know his name, but she didn't know him any more than he knew her.

Lex's voice gentled. "She'll be all right. Eventually. She may even stay here. Where the hell else is she gonna go?"

Nowhere. She had no survival skills, no way to earn money short of selling herself. And if she was like most of the wives in Five, she'd been taught to consider a bullet between the eyes preferable to letting a man who wasn't her husband defile her. "If she needs cash or credits or something... Hell, Noah cleaned out my accounts. I've got plenty."

"The world isn't yours to save all by yourself," she reminded him gently.

"Yeah, but I took enough of her father's dirty money. She earned her share, too."

Lex shrugged. "Then take it up with Lili."

Still pushing him to face his past—and already pushing Lili to face her future. Finn shook his head and rose. "You're a hypocrite, Lex."

"Then I'm in good company." She kicked his chair beneath the desk. "You've got shit to take care of, don't you?"

"And you've got a world to save." By the time Lex was done shoving Lili to her feet, the girl would be better off than she'd ever fared in Five. "Don't forget, you owe me a party."

"I owe you a lot more than that." She sat up straight and eyed him soberly. "You stopped Dom from getting what he was after—Dallas's blood."

And Trix's pain. He held up one wrist and flashed his O'Kane ink at her. "You gave me a family. Turns out fighting for something feels a hell of a lot better than fighting against everything."

"Good." She capped the whiskey bottle and winked at him. "Welcome home."

Trix was pushing herself, and she knew it.

She got off an early shift at the Broken Circle and headed straight for one of the warehouses, where the dancers from the club had commandeered an empty corner to choreograph and rehearse their dances.

The idea to do a new routine based more firmly in the guns and leather aesthetic of Sector Four had been a lark at first, a wild idea brought on by her dizzy, spinning grief. But in the days since Finn had come home, it had turned into something else. A driving need to prove to herself that she could do it, perhaps. That she had finally shed the last bits of the woman she had been in Sector Five. That she was an O'Kane.

That she'd survive if he left her again.

She stripped down, despite the chill, and spent a couple of hours testing out new moves. The music was different, odd until she turned off her brain, stopped thinking, and just *let go*. Then it filled her, not only the throbbing beat, but the meaning behind it. Sexuality, strength, and the steel that could only come from both.

She worked until her feet ached, then kicked off her shoes and kept going. When she couldn't dance anymore, she got dressed, curled up behind a crate, and cried.

It was stupid. It was all so fucking *stupid*. She had

everything she wanted, but she couldn't seem to banish the dark cloud that hovered over it all. The bone-deep fear that it was only a matter of time before it slipped through her fingers.

She dried her eyes and gathered her things, threw a tired wave to two of the new girls coming in as she was leaving. She trudged home and held her breath as she took the last few steps down the hall. Finn would be waiting. Once again, he'd ask her, with dull, worried eyes, if everything was okay.

But he didn't. He didn't even look up as she stepped through the door, his gaze fixed on a folded piece of paper in his hands, his shoulders tense.

Guilt lay heavy in her belly. "I'm late," she murmured. "Sorry about that. I was working on a new dance."

"It's okay." He glanced up at her, his expression impossible to read. "I just got here."

Trix dropped her bag beside the couch and leaned over to kiss the top of his head. She lingered, and a little of her unease melted away as she stroked his hair. "What's that?"

He didn't answer right away. Instead, he hooked an arm around her waist and tugged her into his lap. "I screwed up."

Paralyzing fear gripped her, and she had to choke out the question. "What?"

"No, it's not—" He sighed and pressed his lips to her temple. "This is what I mean. I screwed up. I hurt you. You need to tell me that I did."

How could she? "Finn…"

He caught her chin and forced her to meet his eyes. "I promised I'd never leave you. And then I turned right the fuck around and left you."

Her eyes stung. "It wasn't exactly a normal situation. I get that now."

"No, it wasn't." He stroked her cheekbone, his touch

whisper soft, as if he barely dared. "But I did it all fucking wrong. I told you that you were worth dying for, but that's not what I meant."

Trix shot off the couch, because she didn't trust herself that close to him. If he kept looking at her like that, *touching* her like that, she'd say whatever she had to just to make his pain stop. "I never wanted you to die for me."

"I know—"

"No, you don't. You never did. You never understood." Her lungs burned, but she couldn't stop the words, not even long enough to draw a breath. "Women used to say that to me. They'd say it like it was some fucking badge of honor—*Finn would die for you.* And all I could think whenever I heard that was that, someday, Mac would find a way to use it. And he *did*."

Finn stared at her, expression stricken.

"I wanted—no, I needed *one thing* from you. One thing." Christ, she sounded like a crazy woman now, a half-step away from ranting. "I needed you to be strong enough to let me go if that's what had to happen. You couldn't do it when I was trying to get clean, and I knew you wouldn't be able to do it when Mac—when he—" She dragged in a ragged breath. "And then you came here. And you finally did it, Finn. You let me go. But you were still dying for me."

"Not for you," he said softly. "It was more than you this time, more than Dallas and Lex. It was this damn place. It was..." He shook his head. "Fuck, I don't know. Puppies and rainbows and all the stupid shit I made fun of O'Kane for believing in. It was for *me*, because that's what you gave me. If Beckett was coming for me, I deserved to die for the right reason."

Her throat squeezed tight, and she covered her face with her hands. "God, please tell me I've given you better things than that."

"Everything." His voice sounded rough. "A family, a home. Something to live for."

"What good is any of that if you're going to leave it?"

"I used to go into every fight not giving a damn if I walked away from it. Dying didn't mean shit." The paper crumpled in his fingers, and he thrust it toward her. "This is how hard I'd fight to come back now."

She unfolded the paper. It was a drawing—one of Ace's, judging from the vivid color and the flourishing lines. A tattoo of a peacock-feather choker, embellished with silver Celtic knotwork and edged in purple stones.

Just like the ring Finn had given her.

Trix sank to the couch and smoothed the page with trembling hands. "Is this mine? For me, I mean?"

"Ace said that's how an O'Kane says he's serious." Finn dug the ring out of his pocket and held it out. "I want you to have this, too. But the ink is different. It's forever."

A ring could be put away, hidden in a drawer along with memories, to be taken out only when loneliness proved too great to ignore. But ink... Finn would never have done it before, never marked her in a way she couldn't set aside if she lost him.

"Are you ready for this?" she asked hoarsely. "Do you believe it? That I want you on my skin because, even if I lose you, I will never, ever get over you?"

"I know what the ink means." He touched the edge of the paper. "I can never walk away and tell myself you'll forget me. That you'll just move on. And no, baby. I can't believe you want it, but I'm still asking."

"What did you do when Tracy died? Did you move on?"

"No." He closed his eyes. "Fuck, no."

"Neither would I." She caught his hand. "I want this, Finn. I want it because it means you get it now. That you'll be with me, all the way, and that I deserve that. That I deserve *you.*"

"You deserve the moon and stars, baby doll." He pressed a kiss to the inside of her wrist. "If you're willing to settle for me, I'm too damn selfish to give you up. So wear my ink, and you'll always know I'm coming home to you."

The tense little knot between her shoulders unraveled. Trix climbed over onto his lap and hid her face against his neck. "It's not settling. Someday, you'll see that."

Instead of answering, he slipped the ring onto her finger. "This was my mother's. It's the only thing of hers I still have."

"You never told me that." That he'd given it to her so many years ago, that he wanted her to wear it now, brought a fresh wave of tears to her eyes. "If I had known..." She never would have taken it from him.

"It was yours from the day you first put it on," he said gruffly, folding her fingers toward her palm as if to keep her from taking it off. "I'm glad you took care of it when I couldn't."

There was one more thing she needed to say, one more wall left to crumble between them. She met his eyes and swallowed hard. "I'm sorry I left you, too."

He cupped her cheeks and shook his head. "We both needed to get straight. Maybe we couldn't do it together. I wasn't strong enough to let you hurt."

The truth, laid out between them along with everything else. But it was also the past—and this time they both needed to let go.

Trix placed her trembling fingers over his lips. "No more apologies for shit that's already happened. We start clean now."

"With ink?" He shifted one hand to stroke her throat. "Ace made a big deal about doing this tattoo for free."

"Did he?" Finn's hand warmed her skin, and her eyes fluttered shut before she forced them open again. "Ace doesn't work for free. You must have a new admirer."

"That'll come in handy." The pad of his thumb lingered over her pulse, and the soft circles shifted from soothing to sensual. "I'm thinking about another tattoo for myself."

"Yeah?"

"I want you on my skin, too."

No more walls. Relief flooded her along with dizzy joy. The marks were like the ring, a symbol—a way to tell each other *and* the world that they were building a life. That walking away wasn't an option, and they knew they were so much less apart than they were together.

Words couldn't express how she felt, so she kissed him instead.

Finn groaned, spearing his fingers into her hair, tangling them deep as he licked past her lips and into her mouth, as he claimed her more surely with one kiss than he ever had with words.

All the talking, and it always came down to this—they needed each other more than anything else in the world. They'd been torn apart and thrown back together, but underneath all the machinations of Fate, one fact remained.

They belonged in each other's arms.

"You and me," she whispered against his lips. "Forever."

22

TRIX'S NEW ACT was bringing down the damn house.

Watching from the side of the stage didn't give Finn the best view, but it was his favorite. Especially when the dance ended and she hopped into his arms, her eyes full of fire and her body already hungry.

She was winding toward that point now, tugging down the zipper running up the side of her leather pants. She started slow, then almost ripped it away, and another round of cheers rose from the crowd.

No feathers and fans tonight. She was pure O'Kane, leather and steel and an edge of danger that would slice up any man who got too close. It was intoxicating, especially when she tilted back her head and Finn caught sight of his ink wrapped around her throat. Ace was a true fucking artist—from this distance, she could have been wearing the choker he'd tattooed onto her skin.

She reached for the other zipper but lingered with her fingers on the tab. She rolled her head back, those wild red curls spilling over her shoulders, and met his eyes.

Then she licked the corner of her mouth.

Arousal stirred. So did his dick. She knew he was watching, and he knew what that meant. Her performance would be hotter. Wilder. Every grinding thrust, every tease designed to taunt him.

If she pounced on him when she came off that stage, they'd end up in the closet again. Judging from the predatory look in her eyes, *she* wouldn't be the one tied up this time.

There were worse ways to kill an afternoon than letting his lady have her way with him.

Trix stripped off her pants and threw them. The leather landed in a heap at Finn's feet, and he bit back a grin. Yeah, she was coming for him, all right.

She dropped to her knees, rocking her body as the song wound to a close. Crumpled dollar bills hit the lip of the stage, along with more than a few credit sticks. The lights cut out as the music ended with a heavy bass beat, and the noise of the audience's reaction almost drowned out the sound of her heels as she walked off stage.

And straight for him. She wrapped her arms around his neck and pressed her body to his in the darkness. "Did you like it?"

Like was a weak-ass word. It didn't come close to getting the job done. Most words didn't, so he slid his hands under her ass and lifted her so he could nuzzle the ink that said it all. "I think I like you showing off your dangerous side."

"Sometimes." The lights came up again as stagehands began to prep for another show, and she gasped and trailed her fingers down to his upper arm. "Ace finished the color."

He glanced at his right arm and smiled. The new

sleeve had been taking form over the past two weeks, joining up with his—as Ace so bluntly put it—inferior artwork and stretching down to his new cuff. "Yeah," he said, holding it out so she could admire the ink.

So she could admire *herself.* Ace had worked magic, designing a likeness of her posed as a classic pinup, covered by her peacock-feather fan—and nothing else. "I like having you on my skin."

"It's beautiful," she breathed. Then her brow furrowed, and she laughed. "Is it weird to say that? It feels a little vain."

"Better you than some lug in the bar," Finn replied, fighting to keep his voice deadly serious. It was hard, because he wanted to smile. He was smiling all the damn time now, like he was strung out on Sector Five's finest happy pills. "They get too complimentary, I'll just have to punch them in the teeth."

"Liar. You love it." She nipped at his lower lip. "You love *me.*"

"Damn right I do." With her ear so close to his mouth, it was too easy. He gave it a little tug with his teeth, just to get her squirming, and laughed. "Wanna go sully the storage closet again?"

"Christ, yes." She wiggled against him, sliding her hands beneath his shirt. "I can't wait to get you naked. Or half naked. Or shove your clothes out of the way. Whatever works."

"Hit the brakes, Red." Bren snagged her silky green robe from the hook by the dressing room door and held it up. "Your boy's got work to do."

Finn groaned. "Are you kidding me, Bren?"

"Nope." Mad leaned against the wall and grinned with a friendly ease Finn wouldn't have expected a few weeks ago. Mad's warmness seemed to grow in proportion to Jade's delight in his latest updates to her roof garden. If it would keep the peace, Finn would help her grow a jungle. "Welcome to life as an O'Kane," Mad continued. “Sometimes we play, and sometimes we bust heads.”

Sighing, Finn looked back to Trix. “Sorry, baby. I guess I’m busting heads.”

“It’s okay. I’ll get a drink with the girls.” She leaned in to whisper against his ear. “I’ll keep the pearls handy, though.”

The mental image that conjured threatened to weaken his knees. But beneath it was something so much more precious—her confidence and trust. She could let him walk away, even if a job might earn him a few bruises, because she believed he was coming back to her.

He still wasn’t sure he deserved it. After all, it was more than a second chance. It was a woman putting her heart into his hands, though he’d dropped it the last time. It was Trix giving him more than a family or a home or her love.

She believed in him. So he’d spend the rest of his life not letting her down.

Her body dragged against his in a hundred delicious ways as he lowered her to the floor, and he swallowed another groan. Tonight would be a good lesson in the frustrations and rewards of delayed gratification. Hopefully, she’d have mercy on him.

But if she didn’t, that was okay, too. Even if she didn’t let him come fast, he’d always come home.

Kit Rocha is the pseudonym for co-writing team Donna Herren and Bree Bridges. After penning dozens of paranormal novels, novellas and stories as Moira Rogers, they branched out into gritty, sexy dystopian romance.

The Beyond series has appeared on the New York Times and USA Today bestseller lists, and was honored with a 2013 RT Reviewer's Choice award.

ACKNOWLEDGMENTS & THANKS

The list of people we need to thank grows with every book, because keeping up with a series is tough. We owe eternal thanks to our editor, Sasha Knight, our eagle-eyed proofer, Sharon Muha, and to Lillie Applegarth, official Keeper of the O'Kane Bible. We owe bunches to our early readers, especially Tracy and Jay, who always keep the peace at the Broken Circle while we're finishing a book or starting a book or crying over how we just broke a book. Speaking of crying, a million thanks to the people who hug, pet, slap and kick us through and out of our panic attacks--The Loop That Shall Not Be Named and the Awesome Indies especially.

Last, but never least, our readers. Whether you're a regular at the Broken Circle or on your first trip to Sector Four, thank you for buying, reading, sharing and celebrating. O'Kane for life!

Beyond Shame

Beyond Control

Beyond Pain

Beyond Temptation
(novella — first published in the MARKED anthology)

Beyond Jealousy

Beyond Solitude
(novella — first published in ALPHAS AFTER DARK)

Beyond Addiction

Beyond Possession
(novella — coming November 2014)

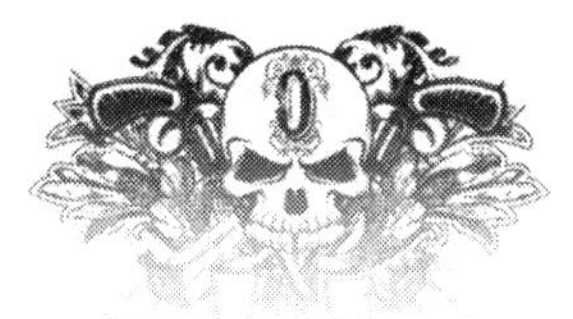